I0746991

Dead by Morning

Rituals of the Night Series

Book One

Kayla Frederick

This is a work of fiction. All of the characters and events portrayed in this novel are either products of the author's imagination or are used fictitiously.

Dead by Morning

Copyright © 2025 Kayla Frederick

Cover by Warren Design

Edited by Danielle Yeager, Hack & Slash Editing

ISBN: 978-1950530403
Library of Congress Control Number: 2024920377
First Edition May 2025
Nacogdoches, Texas
https://authorkaylafrederick.com

Other Books by the Author

Voices
Flirting with Death
After the Devil
What I Did
Runners (The Core #1)
The Residency
Memento Mori

To anyone harboring a secret of their own.

Rituals of the Night Series

Book One: Dead by Morning

Prologue

THE CORRIDOR WAS long and bleak. Seemingly endless in the low light of the late-night hour. A figure slunk around the corner, sticking to the shadows. He didn't need light to navigate this place. He'd walked these paths enough to travel them blindfolded if he needed to.

A stream of blood caressed the side of his face, and he wiped it away before it could reach his lips. The taste of blood was one he was far too familiar with. The cut above his temple was fresh, the entire side of his skull sore from the impact of the weapon that had hit him. Ignoring it, he took two more steps down the passageway and paused, waiting for signs of life, for an alarm to go off and announce that he'd been caught.

With any luck, the others were asleep. With *more* luck, they would stay asleep.

He hurried the last few feet into his room, a cramped little space that was smaller than a prison cell. It was all he had to call his own. Once upon a time, it had been his haven. That seemed like eons ago. Creeping to the dresser, he eased the drawer open. It had a tendency to screech when it caught on the track, but he'd practiced getting it to move without making a sound.

In one quick motion, he gathered an armful of his clothes and threw them on the bed. A small duffel bag had been hidden beneath his mattress, and he yanked it out, stuffing it with as much as he could get to fit.

He pulled the zipper shut and grabbed his last possession from his end table. Arguably, his most important one—a snake-handled dagger. He put it in his pocket and slung the strap of the bag over his shoulder before he hurried back down the corridor and out into the night.

Chapter One

LUNA KETZ WOKE so early in the morning that the sun hadn't crested the horizon yet. Was it necessary to be up this early? No. Had she done it on purpose? Yes.

She dug an outfit out of her closet, nothing flashy, just some track pants and a black T-shirt, and pulled them on. The house was quiet as she crept down the hall, passing framed photos of her, her father, and her mother as she gathered her bag and books for school. She reveled in it. When her father, Abrahim, was awake, silence was not a thing she could enjoy. Luna grabbed an orange out of the fridge and slid her boots on. She thrust her bag over her shoulder and gently, *quietly,* eased the front door open and went outside, closing it behind her.

With a sigh of relief, she slumped onto the porch and started to peel the orange, careful to tuck the bits into her pockets, leaving no evidence behind. If her father caught on to her routine, he would ruin it. Waking before dawn gave her a chance to decompress before any of her normal stressors could rear their ugly head. Every other time of day, the fights with her dad were nearly constant.

She was almost eighteen, and the "growing pains," as her mom called them, were a strain on their relationship. Luna didn't think she was entirely to blame. She and her dad had never gotten along well. Not the way her friends did with their parents. There had always been a *distance* between them.

If everything went according to plan, Luna wouldn't have to deal with it much longer. In five weeks, high school would end, and she had her sights on college. She'd already been accepted to her dream school. All she had left to do was secure the financial aspect and choose a major. Then, when the time came, she would leave this town and simply never come back. Yesterday, her father had been at her throat about the fact that she hadn't decided what she wanted to study yet. Luna didn't know what she wanted to do with her life, only that she wanted to do something. Her father had very specific ideas on what she *should* do.

When I graduate, none of it matters. I can become my own person, she told herself. It had become her mantra, the one thing she could hold on to for hope, but it didn't make her situation any easier. If anything, the pressure cooker that was her life felt as if it had been turned all the way up.

Luna finished her orange and walked two blocks, watching the slight pink line grow larger above the horizon line. It was almost time to meet up with her friend, Violet, who lived a few streets over. When Luna's family made the move from Egypt to America, she'd been three years old. Luna's mother, Rose, had met Abrahim while traveling abroad, and they'd fallen in love. Rose had been ready to settle down with him until he suffered a series of illnesses, and she had to take over as breadwinner. Rose had made the decision to move back home so Abrahim would have help while she was working. Luna wouldn't say as much out loud, but she suspected part of her father's hostility toward her came from some part of him blaming her for the direction his life had gone.

Violet was Luna's first friend. Her *only* friend for her first few years in the country. All these years later, their friendship persisted. She understood Luna in ways no one else did.

Luna slipped a pack of cigarettes from her jacket pocket and looked at the crinkly white box. Supposedly, smoking could help with stress. She'd never smoked before, but all the other methods of stress relief she'd tried had all been ineffective. So she'd coerced a random man at the gas station to buy her a pack, figuring it couldn't hurt to see what all the fuss was about.

Hesitantly, she held one to her lips and lit it. She took a deep breath, inhaled the smoke, and coughed when it agitated the lining in her throat. Spluttering on a mouthful of smoke, she tossed the cigarette to the ground, crushing it beneath her boot. She didn't feel better, not at all. Disappointed, she spat, trying to rid her mouth of the awful taste. *What a waste of five bucks,* she thought and shoved the nearly full pack into her pocket, making a note to herself to throw it away later.

Luna rounded the block, spotting her friend at their meeting place. Violet was both taller than her and bulkier, with a round face and blue eyes. She had a habit of wearing a green headband to keep her blonde hair from her face. She fidgeted with it as she waited.

Luna struggled to hold in her coughs as she approached her. "Morning!"

"What's wrong with you?" Violet asked as they started to walk.

When she regained her composure, Luna said, "Ugh, don't ask." The lingering traces of smoke burned her throat, and she couldn't wait to get to school and drink from the fountain until she was blue in the face.

"Long night?" Violet guessed.

"That's *every* night."

"What made you think getting into an Ivy League school would be easy?" Violet asked and laughed.

"I already *got* in, remember? That's not really the issue," Luna reminded her. When the envelope had come, she'd been so excited that she showed it off the next day. Violet had tried to match her excitement, but it was clear her feelings were torn.

"Yeah, I remember," Violet said flatly, all teasing gone from her voice.

Not for the first time, Luna felt a sense of pity for her friend. *Family* was a loose term to describe Violet's homelife. She took care of her brother the best she could while her father disappeared whenever he wanted, sometimes for days on end. She wouldn't be going to college. She couldn't afford it. Her life after graduation would be the same as it was now. Except she wouldn't have her best friend anymore to help her through it.

Luna decided to drop the conversation and studied the houses around them. Lima, Ohio, was a quaint town. There was a busy side, some gorgeous neighborhoods, and a more rural side. When she was little, Luna used to love looking at the houses. That hadn't changed, but to her, their beauty was dulled by familiarity, and she longed for new sights and sounds.

They made it to the high school a few minutes later. It was

a single-story brick building with a big field of grass. The front door was marked with a big staircase that led up to the double doors.

As they ascended the steps, Violet said, "Enjoy the time you have left in high school. These are the golden weeks—the time that people remember for the rest of their lives."

"That's kind of sad," Luna remarked. She didn't want to remember the constant fights with her dad, the headaches, the late nights filling out scholarship paperwork, and the extracurricular tasks around town to bulk up her applications.

"I disagree," Violet said. "I don't know any of our classmates who aren't looking forward to prom and graduation."

Graduation, Luna could get on board with, but prom was an entirely separate issue. Violet had dreamily mentioned the dance since the beginning of February when posters had been hung all over school. Now the date was approaching, and Luna had done her best to pretend she hadn't seen them. "Clearly you've never met me then."

"I don't think I've heard of such a thing as a girl *not* wanting to go to prom," a new voice said.

A chill ran down Luna's spine, and she glanced over her shoulder to see a boy with shaggy blond hair, a thin face, and piercing sapphire eyes. He wore baggy black clothes—a black T-shirt and cargo pants. Chance Welfrey. Perhaps one of the most popular kids in the school. Not popular like the jocks, but in a different way. Some people found allure in his bad boy persona. To Luna, he was a pest, a bully, and another reason she couldn't wait to graduate. On instinct, she grimaced and looked away. He was perhaps the only person who possessed the ability to get under her skin more than her dad.

"You don't think you'd have a good time?" Violet asked.

Luna side-eyed her friend. She'd never been interested in social events at this school or middle school. Year after year, she'd skipped the dances, the games, the pep rallies, the parties. None of it sounded like fun. Plus, what would her dad say? "You already know my situation," Luna said, instead of giving details when she realized that Chance was keeping pace with them.

"If you've never gone to a dance, why do you think you wouldn't have a good time?" he asked, raising one thin blond eyebrow.

"Call it a hunch," she said stiffly. "Crowds aren't for me. I'd rather study."

"That's lame. Work's good, but it's nothing without some fun," Chance told her, then winked before he turned to head down a branching hallway.

"Good riddance," Luna muttered after him.

"What's your damage?" Violet asked. "He's just trying to talk to you. I think he's cute."

Luna didn't repress her shudder. It didn't surprise her that Violet thought that, a lot of their class did. But Luna couldn't bring herself to feel the same. There were a lot of rumors about him. His string of girlfriends and the supposed stint he'd had in juvie a year or so prior being the most popular of them. "I think he's trouble. Besides, making friends at this stage is pointless since we're most likely not going to see any of these people once we graduate anyway."

"Yeah, how could I forget? Miss Ivy League here is gonna up and leave us all behind," Violet said, chuckling bitterly.

Luna winced. It sounded harsh when she worded it like that, but it wasn't wrong.

Violet readjusted her headband over her blonde bangs. "I've gotta get to class."

"Right," Luna said, admittedly glad to end the conversation. "See you." There were only a few things she would miss about this town; Violet was one of them. She hoped her friend didn't take it personally. It wasn't as if she *wanted* to leave her behind, but what else could she do? She couldn't bring her with her.

Maybe we could figure out how to get an apartment together, she mused but shot it down. Violet would never leave her little brother behind.

Luna stared at the floor as she continued through the hallway, pushing away everything but the test she had in first period. With the scholarship application she'd worked on the night before, she hadn't had time to study. She plopped down at the bottom of the staircase and pulled out her notes, determined to give them a quick read-through before class. Almost as soon as she was settled, someone cleared their throat beside her.

Luna jumped and peered up at the girl. She had a fox-like face and blonde hair. One of the senior cheerleaders. Kate something.

"Stop blocking the stairs, you freak," she said and laughed as if she were amused by her own joke.

Luna blinked, unfazed. "Plenty of room to go around me,

bimbo. Or can you not see that?"

Kate scoffed as Luna turned her attention back to her notes but left without another word. After years of dealing with abuse at the hands of the popular kids, the taunts didn't bother Luna anymore. Real life gave her too many other things to worry about.

Chapter Two

IOLET WALKED THROUGH the halls with a huff. She never wanted Luna to know how jealous she was of her, but sometimes, she couldn't keep it from seeping out. A good family, a nice home, and a solid future? Violet would kill for any of that. But the real icing on the cake was the attention she got from boys, which she didn't even notice. It was obvious that Chance had hinted at wanting to take Luna to prom, but she'd shrugged him off as if he were a pesky fly.

How can one person be so lucky? Violet lamented, thinking of the way her life seemed to only be going downhill. She'd had to get a job recently because her father had been gone for a solid week now and resources were sparse.

Violet had no plans for when high school ended. Every time someone talked about graduation, it took her all not to tear up. She could save enough money to move out but feared leaving her brother behind. Until he was old enough to fend for himself, she was stuck. The more she pondered her future, the bleaker she felt.

"Hey," someone said, startling her back to reality.

She jumped and held a hand over her chest, turning to glare at the voice. A whiff of cologne hit her, and she locked onto a pair of blue eyes.

Chance Welfrey.

The anger dissipated, and her knees went weak. He was cuter up close, and she found it hard to focus. "H-hi," she stuttered, her brain turning to mush. What had she been so concerned with a minute ago?

He fell into step beside her as if this was something they did on a regular basis. Tilting his head, he said, "Forgive me if this is none of my business, but what was all that prom talk with you and the Ketz girl a few minutes ago?"

"Luna?" she asked, barely able to remember her own name, let alone her friend's.

"Yeah. I mean, surely you guys aren't planning on going together," he said and laughed. A short burst of sound that made Violet's heart pound harder.

"Oh, no, nothing like that," Violet said, but she didn't know who else she'd go with. She didn't have a date, and it seemed better to go with friends than to go alone. With Luna being her only friend, she didn't have many options.

"So she doesn't have a date?"

"She hasn't told me about one," Violet said.

"Oh."

The conversation fizzled, and she racked her brain trying to think of ways to keep it going. "I think that's why she doesn't want to go," she added, though that couldn't be further from the truth.

"Far out," he said. "She shouldn't have any issue going with me then."

It wasn't a question, but Violet agreed to it anyway. Maybe

if she got Luna to go with him, he would set one of his friends up with Violet, and they could double-date.

"Thank you for the information. It'll be put to good use," he said.

"Y-you're welcome." Violet managed.

"Gotta get to class. See you later."

"Bye," Violet said and watched him go, giddy from the interaction. As soon as he disappeared into a classroom, her senses came back, and she wilted.

Luna would be furious if she found out what Violet had done.

Why did I do that?

***

CHANCE RESTED AGAINST the brick wall, staring up at the sky, and waited for the end of the day to come. He'd managed to slip out of class a few minutes early with the lie that he had to use the bathroom. Instead, he'd used it to get ahead of the crowds. Luna was usually one of the first out of the building, and he didn't want to miss her.

When the final bell rang and the sea of teenagers emerged, it was easy to spot her among them. Her head was bowed, eyes focused on the ground rather than anyone around her. He stepped into her path, smiling when she crashed directly into him. She looked up, startled, but her eyes darkened the instant she realized who he was. Though her eyes were filled with loathing, she had a haunting type of beauty to her. Big green eyes and a heart-shaped face framed by shoulder-length black hair.

"Where are you off to in such a rush?" he asked, doing his best to dial up the charm.

"None of your business," she muttered and tried to move around him, but Chance grabbed her shoulder, stopping her in place. Her eyes traced his hand up to his face without a change in expression. "What do you want?"

"We should hang out sometime," he said. "We can go see a movie. Or maybe you'd be willing to go to prom with me? I'd love to take you."

Luna gawked at him. He raised his eyebrows, waiting for her answer. It didn't come. She broke into a cackle, knocking his hand away before resuming her journey through the crowd without glancing back.

Chance was too stunned to move. Had she really rejected him? Laughed in his face in front of everyone? That had never happened before.

Violet lied to me, he thought. What was the purpose?

His chest hurt, an odd mix of humiliation, anger, and shock. He didn't want it to, but *that* mind was starting to take over. The one no one knew about. The one he kept to himself. Somebody bumped into him, bringing him back to reality. Chance breathed in and composed himself the best he could, brushing the front of his shirt to hide the ache inside.

"It was a joke," he said to the cheerleader eyeing him strangely, then went to move away when his foot crunched on something.

He lifted his boot to see a smashed pack of cigarettes. Had

Luna dropped them? He scooped them up and put them in his pocket, descending the staircase in time to catch a glimpse of her raven hair as she ran from the school and presumably from Chance himself. He put his hand in the pocket, caressing the plastic with his thumb.

In spite of the rejection, he smiled.

Chapter Three

LUNA EXHALED AND set her drink on the counter. She could stay in the smoothie shop all day, grateful for the excuse to delay going home.

Got to enjoy it while I can, she thought.

As a freelance contractor, her father sometimes left the house in the afternoons to help people with various projects around the neighborhood. Recently, though, with his health on the decline, it had happened less and less often. Battling chronic illnesses meant he had good days and bad days. More time at home had only led to them butting heads more frequently. Sometimes, it almost felt as if he waited for her to come home to ambush her.

The soft Muzak playing from the speakers overhead was the perfect background noise as she pulled her worn copy of *Hamlet* out of her red-and-black checkered backpack. She'd read it a dozen times before, loving the way it made her think. How hard could it be to piece together a crime if there were no witnesses to see it?

Engrossed in her reading, she didn't hear the stool beside her pull out. A pale hand slid under her book and closed it. "*Hamlet,* huh?" Chance asked after he read the cover.

With a side-eye, she flipped it back open and said, "Yep.

Miss Kessler's class."

"I must be cruel if only to be kind," Chance recited in a mock soliloquy. Then seriously, he said, "I always found that to be a particularly powerful line."

Huffing through her nose, she closed her book and asked, "Did you need something?"

"Actually, yes, while we're on the subject," he said, lacing his fingers together on the counter. "I believe *someone* owes me an apology."

Luna scoffed. "For what?"

"I think that was a rather rude rejection to my proposal earlier, don't you?"

"No, because a date is *not* happening." She tucked her book into her backpack and hopped down from the stool, taking one last sip of the smoothie before tossing it. She went out the door, Chance behind her. "Why are you following me?"

"I'm curious. Humor me a little," he said. "I mean, what's your deal? I heard through the grapevine that you don't have a date for prom. Why not accept my invitation?"

"Because I don't care about prom and have no intention of going. A *date* is not the issue."

"Is that right?" Chance asked.

Luna kept her gaze on the road, expecting him to go his separate way, but he continued at her side. "What is it now?" she asked, irritated. "I answered your question. Don't most people back off when they're rejected?"

"Yeah, but I'm determined," he said.

Luna was about to ask *what* he was so determined for

when her shoe hit the curb, and she lurched forward, hands held out to catch herself from falling. Her palms and knees screamed at the impact.

"Damn it!" she cursed and held up her hands to see the damage. Some of her skin had torn away, revealing red patches beneath it. When she looked at her knees, they were in a similar condition as her palms, but worse, and now her father would have something new to go after her about when he saw that she had ripped her jeans as well.

"Are you okay?" Chance asked, wide-eyed. He reached out a hand to her. "Let me help you."

Luna sneered and climbed to her feet, brushing herself off. "I don't need your help."

Chance gaped at her, as if he couldn't believe that she would reject him again, and then he stood. When he did, light glinted off a silver object sticking out of the pocket of his black cargo pants.

Luna stopped patting herself down. *What is that?*

Chance followed her gaze, shoving his hand into his pocket to hide whatever had been there. "What?"

Luna noted his body language. It was off. There was a *dark* look in his eyes that she didn't like. *He's nervous.*

"See something you like?" he asked and smirked.

Luna huffed and turned away to resume her journey home. "Ugh. Gag me with a spoon. How about you do me a favor and leave me alone?"

Thankfully, he did.

Luna spent the rest of the walk thinking about what

could've been in his pocket, and why he'd been so eager to hide it. He'd always been a strange one, but that interaction had seemed odd even for him. By the time she reached the front yard of her home, she chastised herself for caring either way.

She had bigger fish to fry.

She took her time crossing through the grass and onto the porch. Inside, the television blared with bits of sounds each time her father changed the channel. She threw down her backpack in the living room and plopped down in the soft armchair in the corner.

He said nothing at her entrance, but when she went to work taking her shoes off, she could feel his gaze burning two holes into the top of her head. "Something happen at school?" he asked.

Luna pulled off the first shoe and started untying the other. "No. Same old day. Why?"

"Your knees are bleeding."

"Yeah," Luna said and used the excuse of putting her shoes next to the door to not look at him. "I fell when I was walking home. Tripped on the curb."

It was a half-truth. As close to the truth as she was willing to go when it came to Chance. She didn't want him to know about the situation, part of her assuming he would blame her for Chance's odd behavior and somehow twist it to be her fault.

"It's *not* fine, young lady. This means you're gonna have to buy new clothes, and they aren't free," he said. "You think you can walk around with holes and tatters?"

Luna pursed her lips and went silent. In her opinion, a few

rips didn't amount to *tatters*, but interrupting her father when he was on a rant would only extend it.

"Absolutely disgraceful," he said to finish up.

"Great," she replied and went to the bathroom, locking herself inside.

In the bright fluorescent light, her bloody knees looked worse than she'd first thought. She grabbed a washcloth off the rack and ran it under the faucet, then scrubbed off the blood. Once that was done, she went to her room and threw herself on the bed, letting her body sink into the mattress.

In the silence, she listened to her father's television playing down the hall and rolled over, snagging a random book off the stack she'd left on her end table. She wanted to finish *Hamlet*, but she'd made the mistake of leaving her backpack in the living room and didn't want to have to duke it out with her father again to get it.

So she settled into her bed and started to read.

"LUNA! COME HERE!" her father called.

Luna tensed. It hadn't been an hour since she'd gotten home. What could he possibly have to tell her? She considered feigning sleep to get out of another argument, but that would only make this drag out, so she set her book on the nightstand and wandered down the hall.

Her father stood in the middle of the kitchen, arms crossed.

"Yeah, Dad?" Luna said, already exhausted by the

expression on his face.

"You have something you want to tell me?" he asked.

Confused, Luna looked left and right, trying to figure out what it was that she was supposed to be admitting to.

"Luna?" her father prompted.

"No, Dad, there's not," she said, baffled.

He reached into his pocket and pulled something out, tossing it onto the table. Luna's mouth went dry. Her cigarettes. Hadn't she thrown those away? *I forgot they were in my jacket. How did he find them?*

"I found this in the mailbox," her father said, holding up a folded piece of paper.

"Let me see that," Luna said, snatching it from his hand with more force than intended.

To whom it may concern,
These came from your daughter. Thought you might like to know.

It wasn't signed at the bottom, and she didn't recognize the handwriting. Who would've done something like this?

Did *Violet* do it?

She wouldn't. She didn't know, Luna thought. Unless she'd smelled the smoke and put two and two together.

How could it be that everything she did to make life more tolerable only made it harder in the end? Luna could've started crying, bawling her eyes out from frustration. "Okay, fine. They're mine. I *fucking* smoked. Is that what you want to hear?"

"Language, young lady." Her father seethed. "Proper

women treat themselves with respect."

"Oh, bite me, Dad. This right here is why I craved a cigarette to begin with."

"I have been patient with you for all these years, but if you're going to start smoking, then I really must insist on finding you a proper living arrangement."

"Mom won't let you send me off," Luna said, but she didn't feel too confident. Her father was her primary caregiver. If he put his mind to it, she didn't know what could happen. "Maybe I shouldn't have smoked, but jeez, Dad, don't throw me away for making a mistake."

Abrahim glared at her, and she prepared for him to tell her off, when his face softened. "I don't want to see you go down a bad path."

"I'm not," Luna insisted. "I tried *one*, and I didn't finish it. I meant to throw them away. I forgot, is all."

His forehead crinkled, thick eyebrows drawing into one unamused line, and she could tell he didn't believe her. He said nothing else as he crossed the room and picked up the phone. Holding it before he said, "Why don't you go sit in your room for a while? I have a phone call to make."

Luna's eyes stung at the dismissal, and she wanted to argue. To try to talk her dad down from a punishment. But he wasn't yelling, and that she counted as a win. He would call her mom, and they'd talk about next steps. Whenever things got out of hand between them, that was his go-to move.

"Okay," Luna murmured and left the kitchen. She went to her room, wondering who had written the note.

Luna tried to go back to reading her book, but she couldn't focus on the words and tossed it down, waiting for her father to burst into her room and tell her why she was a horrible daughter and that her mom felt the same way. When he finally did appear, it was to tell her to answer the phone.

"Is it Mom?" Luna asked as she followed him down the hall.

"Who else would it be?"

Luna could've been annoyed by the sarcasm, but it had been a long time since she'd talked to her mom. She wished they'd have more opportunities to spend time together, but that never seemed to be the case. As a CEO, Rose was often traveling and didn't have much free time for anything else. Whatever time she could allocate to a phone call usually went to her father. With his failing health, Luna couldn't blame her mother for checking on him as often as she could, but it made her sad that she didn't have the same level of dedication to her daughter.

Luna scooped the handset up off the table and held it to her ear. "Hi, Mom," she said, keeping her eyes on her father's.

"Darling, what is going on?" Rose asked, sounding exhausted. She probably was. "Your father has told me some concerning things."

Her father watched her a moment longer before turning away to sit back down on the couch. Luna watched him go before she plopped down in the hard kitchen chair, staring at the utensils hanging on the wall next to the stove. She didn't want to talk to her mom about what happened. It was embarrassing to admit out loud. "He told you about the cigarettes, huh?"

"Yes, young lady. We've discussed this. Your father can be stubborn and has some old-world views that can be hard to deal with, but we have an agreement. You stay on track and keep to your studies, and your father keeps those beliefs to himself."

Luna stared out the kitchen window as she said, "I'm sorry, Mom. I've been so stressed lately, I was just hoping to find a way to cope."

"I understand, but that isn't the answer. You have little more than one month left and then all your effort will be worth it." Rose continued, voice both lecturing and soothing at the same time. "I'd hate to see all your hard work go down the drain now."

Luna pressed her lips together. "So what's my punishment going to be?"

"Your father thinks you need to spend more time in the community," Rose said. "Around people who share our values."

All things considered, that wasn't the worst punishment her father had ever decided on. "Makes sense, I guess." Luna sighed, resigned.

"Good," Rose said. "Look, I have to go, but remember— no matter how hardheaded your father gets, I love you, and you've got this. You're strong."

"I love you, too," Luna murmured before the line went dead.

It buzzed in her ear, but she didn't hang up right away. She bowed her head, barely able to hold back her tears. She missed her mother. Out of her parents, she had always loved her mom far more than she would ever love her father.

With a heavy heart, Luna hung up and went to bed. She

expected Abrahim to say something else, but he left her alone for the rest of the night to think about all the day had brought.

25

Chapter Four

THE NEXT MORNING, Luna woke up and went about her usual routine, starting her walk through the neighborhood. She tried not to think about the strange evening she'd weathered. Violet waited at their usual meetup place, and the weight on Luna's shoulders felt somehow heavier when she imagined trying to share her story with her friend. Then she remembered her suspicion that Violet had been the cause of what had happened.

She must've made a face because Violet asked, "Are you okay?"

Luna considered lying, but she didn't have the energy. "No, I'm not."

"Something . . . happen yesterday?"

Luna side-eyed her. "It was . . . weird, is all," Luna said, wondering if Violet would bring up the note without provocation.

Violet gave her a strange look but ended up saying nothing.

Luna welcomed the silence, enjoying the morning sounds of birds instead. As much as she tried to put the note out of her head, she couldn't shake off the tension. They ascended the stairs in front of the school, and Luna opened her mouth, ready to push the issue, but Violet was already walking away. Luna watched her go and went down a different hallway, keeping an eye out for Chance along the way.

Inside the school library, there were dozens of shelves. Books after books after books. The middle of the room had five maple desks to study at. Near the door was the librarian's counter. She nodded at Luna as she entered. At this time of the morning, the tables were empty so she picked one in the center of the room, pulling out a notebook before setting her bag on the floor next to the table leg. Almost as soon as she started reading, the chair on the other side of the table creaked.

Her friend, Amy, sat down, brown eyes looking almost amber in the yellowish library lights. "Hey."

"Hi," Luna replied, watching Amy rummaging through her backpack.

Amy, being on the smaller side, was often teased for her size. That was how the two girls had met. Luna had saved her from a bully in ninth grade, and they'd become fast friends. At school, at least. She'd never hung out with her the way she did Violet but found comfort in her presence, which was a rarity for her when it came to *anyone*.

***

YAWNING, CHANCE FLEXED his fingers around the steering wheel. There was a pain in his neck, and he'd almost slept in but managed to get himself up at the last minute. The morning sun glared into his eyes, and he pulled the visor down, already ready for the day to be over with.

At school, he parked his truck and looked at his reflection in the mirror on the back of the visor. He was annoyed and tired, but his face reflected none of it. Flashing himself a smile, he paused when he saw someone passing by.

Violet.

Irritation prickled in him when he remembered their conversation the previous day. She hadn't been honest with him, had she? *Only one way to find out.* He hurled himself out of the seat, catching up to her in a few strides. "Why'd you lie to me?" he demanded.

She turned to him and flinched. "I didn't . . . lie."

"You must think I'm a fool," he said, grinding his teeth to hold the worse of his anger at bay. "I asked Luna to prom, and she *laughed* at me. Why did you set me up like that? It was totally bogus."

Violet shifted her weight as if she considered running to get out of the conversation. "I-I—" she stuttered, and he knew he wasn't going to get a solid answer.

Chance shouldered his way past her, biting back all the comments he wanted to make. Nothing he could say would make the situation any better anyway.

"Wait!" she called out behind him.

Chance inhaled a long breath through his nose, debating if he should stop and hear her out or keep walking and shake off the bad mood. His curiosity won out, and he turned back to her. "You better make this good."

Violet twined her hands together, looking at the ground. "Have you ever hung out with her after school? I could get something set up."

Chance drew his eyebrows together, more confused than he'd been before. "Why would you do that?"

Violet shrugged. "I think it could be good for her to get out of her house for a while."

This has gotta be another trick, Chance told himself. There was no way she would throw her friend under the bus like that. *What do I really have to lose if it is?*

Despite his doubts, he was intrigued and found himself saying, "I'm listening."

Chapter Five

WHEN SCHOOL ENDED, Luna prepared herself for the long day ahead. Before the incident with the cigarettes, she had been responsible for helping care for an elderly widow named Sidra one day a week. Others from her mosque would fill in the rest of the days when her grandson, Nazir, was busy at college. Outside of the mosque, Luna was vaguely familiar with Nazir because he'd attended the same high school as her, a senior when she'd been a freshman.

Now, she was expected to watch after Sidra three days a week until she graduated. That was fine by Luna. She got along with both Sidra and Nazir well enough, and it was a welcome respite from going home and bickering with her father.

Time passed easily with Sidra. She was a gentle woman who sat by the window and knitted, recalling stories from her younger days. Luna hadn't met either set of her grandparents, so she considered her to be the grandmother she'd never had.

Luna set a steaming cup of tea on the end table beside Sidra and slipped back onto the couch. She'd been in the process of telling her about the seemingly endless fights with her father.

Sidra listened, waiting to speak until Luna stopped talking. "How old are you now?" she asked and picked up the mug, cradling it in her lap.

"I'm seventeen," Luna said. "I'll be eighteen in a few months. Plenty old enough to make my own decisions but my father insists on treating me like I'm five. He has to say something about *everything* I want to try to do. It's like he can't accept that I'm almost an adult."

"So young." Sidra blew on her tea and took a tiny sip before setting the cup on the table beside her. "He probably doesn't. It's never easy for a parent to let their child go out in the world."

Luna doubted that was the reason for his hostility. It had been tense between them for months. "I think he'll be relieved to have the house to himself."

"Now don't say that. He loves you."

Luna gave her the stink eye.

"In his own way," Sidra added.

Luna wished that was the truth, but it hadn't felt like her father truly cared about her in some time. When she was a kid, they used to be inseparable. Not for the first time, she wondered what had happened. If it was something she had done to cause the rift.

The cost of time.

"Maybe some time apart will do you good," Sidra said, picking up her needles to resume knitting. A colorful throw draped halfway over the chair and onto the floor. Luna wondered how much bigger she would make it. "Who really knows when it comes to men?"

Luna certainly didn't.

"But I'll tell you one thing, you have the choice to make

your future whatever you want," Sidra said. The *click, click* of her needles enunciating each word. "When I was about your age, my *baba* had a suitor picked out for me based solely on dowry. I'd never met him and wouldn't meet him until the wedding, but I was told I would love and honor this man for my entire life. And so I did."

Luna sat in silence, trying to imagine a life like that. Her father had hinted on more than one occasion that he considered Nazir to be a good match for her, but thanks to Luna's mother, he'd never tried to arrange anything.

"How did you do it?" Luna asked.

"I had to," Sidra said. "You are a strong, smart girl. You will do what you need to as well."

Embarrassed by the sentiment, Luna looked at the clock for a distraction, surprised at how much time had already gone by. "Nazir will be by tonight, won't he?"

"Oh yes," Sidra said, pausing her knitting. "You go ahead and get home now. I'm sure your father is worried."

I'm sure he's not. Out loud, Luna said, "Thanks."

"Things will get better, darling." Sidra smiled politely. "Keep your head up."

Sidra's story occupied Luna's mind the entire walk home. Her father had never gone as far as Sidra's had, but she felt cold when she remembered his threats the previous day. *Fathers are supposed to provide love and guidance.* Luna felt none of either from him. When she was younger, she used to blame herself, as if maybe she had failed as a daughter somehow.

Now, she wondered if the coldness came from never

wanting a daughter to begin with. He'd wanted a son, and the fact that he never had any other children meant no one would carry on his family name.

Maybe that's a good thing, Luna thought as she walked up the concrete path to her house. Though she couldn't deny the fact that sometimes, she wished she had a sibling. Someone to share in her upbringing who could understand her better than anyone else in the world.

In the house, her father wasn't occupying his usual place on the couch, and there was no note on the fridge saying he'd gone out, so she guessed he'd gone to sleep early. Nearly as soon as she slipped her shoes off, the phone started to ring in the kitchen. Afraid the sound would wake her father, she hurried to answer it.

"Hello?" she asked in a hushed whisper.

"Luna, what's up?" Violet's cheery voice a contrast to Luna's mood.

It wasn't as if they *never* called one another. When they were younger, they'd spend hours on the phone, but it had been a long time since they'd had a conversation like that. "I just got home from visiting Sidra," Luna told her finally.

"Whatcha got planned for the rest of the evening?"

Luna longingly thought of her copy of *Hamlet.* "Nothing really. Sleep, I guess."

"We should hang out, I'm bored."

Luna's instinct was to tell her that it was too late in the day, but when she looked at the clock, she was surprised to find it was only seven p.m. *I'm getting old.* Fighting back a migraine, Luna said, "I guess. Where do you want to meet?"

"There's a good restaurant over on Fifth. We could eat, then hang out at the park."

"Isn't that place expensive?"

"Don't worry. I got us covered."

"If you insist," Luna said, out of possible excuses.

"Rad. I'll see you around eight."

"Okay," Luna agreed, and the line went dead.

Her gut told her something was wrong, but she couldn't put her finger on what. She didn't think too much of it. Everyone was weird at this point in the year. Sentimental for what would be ending soon and the changes that were coming. *She wants to spend time with me before I leave,* Luna told herself, and when she put it like that, how could she possibly say no?

Luna put her boots back on and slipped out the door. She drew in a lungful of crisp spring air and started to walk. The dusk sky was beautiful in the way the day blended into night. By the time the restaurant came into view, Luna's stomach rumbled with hunger, reminding her that she had yet to eat dinner, and she picked up the pace. Orchestra music played from the speakers as she walked in. The lighting was dimmed, hanging bulbs above each individual table providing highlights throughout the space. A dozen smells assaulted her nose, rich and pungent. The maître d' looked up at her from his podium as she approached.

"Excuse me, I'm looking for someone," Luna said to him. "Girl my age, about yea high, blonde hair, blue eyes, kind of on the heavy side?"

He looked thoughtful before he gestured to a table toward

the back of the room. "Could you mean her, perhaps?"

Luna looked in that direction and caught blonde hair clipped in place by a green headband. It was Violet, all right.

"Yes, thanks." Luna dashed off before he could respond. "Finally found you," Luna said, slipping into the seat across from Violet. "I thought you ditched me."

Violet took a sip from her glass of water. "No, I just figured you'd be more comfortable sitting at the back of the place. It's calmer here."

The waiter approached, taking Luna's drink order. When he left, Violet said, "It's a nice restaurant."

"Seems so," Luna replied, tapping her fingers on the table. And it did. *Way* too nice. "What made you want to hang out here?"

Violet shrugged. "Call it a celebration meal, I guess."

"Celebration?"

"For graduation."

"That's like a month away."

"So? I know you're excited for it."

Luna couldn't argue with that. The waiter delivered her drink and she took a sip before watching him go. Then she noticed a figure with platinum hair and black clothes maneuvering through the restaurant. A *familiar* figure. Her heart dropped.

Chance Welfrey.

Before she could point him out to Violet, he approached the table, grinning. Rather than being flustered, the way Violet usually was when Chance was nearby, she beamed at him. "Glad you made it," she said and stood up so he could slip into the booth across from Luna.

A stunned chuckle fell from Luna's lips. "Forget this, I'm out," she said, slamming her cup on the table with a *thunk*.

"Come on, Luna, don't be like that," Violet begged, looking genuinely hurt. "Just because I invited other friends doesn't mean you have to leave."

Other friends. The words bounced around Luna's head. Since when were Violet and Chance *friends?* Luna stared her down. If it had been anyone else, she would've continued on her way, but because it was Violet, she gave in. "Fine. It's fine."

"Thank you," Violet said, pleased, then slipped into the booth beside her.

Chance gave her what she imagined was supposed to be a heartwarming smile but came across as creepy instead.

Luna stared down at the table, not wanting to make eye contact. It was silent for an entire minute, and her skin crawled with the awkwardness. Finally, she turned to Violet and asked, "So when did this friendship start?"

Chance answered, "We had a project together in chemistry."

"Hmm," Luna said, not believing him. Before today, she'd been under the assumption they'd never said more than two words to each other.

The waiter reappeared to take Chance's drink order and the table's food order. After the change in plans, Luna didn't feel particularly hungry, but she would eat anyway.

Beep, beep. Something chimed in Violet's pocket. She pulled her pager out and looked at it. Dread crawled up Luna's spine a moment before Violet said, "Oh shoot. That's my job. I gotta go."

"I think I should go, too," Luna announced, ready to climb out of the booth after her.

Violet blocked the path. "There's no reason to run off before the food comes."

"I don't have any money on me," Luna said.

"I'll pay the bill on my way out. No worries."

Luna rolled her eyes and sat back down. "Fine."

Violet patted her hand before she pulled her coat on. "I'll see you later, okay?" She smiled and took her leave.

Luna stared after her.

"I don't bite. I promise," Chance said with a grin.

Luna flared her nostrils and looked him in the eyes. She didn't really *know* him. They'd never had a full conversation. All she knew of him came from rumors.

Maybe this won't be so bad, she told herself.

The silence for those first few minutes was unnerving. She tapped the table uncomfortably, trying to figure out something to talk about, but her mind came up blank. She tried to pretend that she didn't notice him staring at her, but the longer she ignored him, the more blatant he was.

"What?" she asked finally.

He kept his gaze on her. "Just looking."

Luna considered leaving again. It wasn't as though he was *making* her stay.

Chance cradled his chin in his hand and shifted in his seat to lean a little bit closer. "I think I should start off by saying I'm sorry if I've come on a little too strong in the past. I like to do things with passion. All or nothing. And I like *you,* so that's kind of how I prove it."

Luna digested the silence before she said, "I guess it's my turn to say something. Why did you and Violet plan this? This is really cheesy, you know." Then the gears turned in her head. If Violet was friends with Chance, then there was probably a lot he knew about her. Could *he* have been the one to write the note? He knew where she lived from walking her home. A flare of anger wiggled in her gut. "And that thing with my Dad? That was lame. Really lame."

Chance widened his eyes with fake shock. "No idea what you're talking about."

"Bullshit," Luna said. "No one else would rat me out like that."

Chance tilted his head from side to side and sat back in his seat. "Maybe you don't know your friends as well as you think you do."

He was lying. The feeling in her gut said as much, but *why?*

He continued. "You need some new friends, like me."

"We're *not* friends."

"Not right now, no, but I want to change that."

Uncertain suspicion came to Luna. She'd made her disinterest in him clear on multiple occasions, but he was stubbornly persistent. Luna would never push so hard to be someone's friend. *It doesn't make sense.* "Why?"

"You're different from the rest of them."

Anger replaced her previous uncertainty when she looked at her dark clothes and brown skin. "Could you be any more vain?"

He rolled his eyes. "I don't mean your *looks*, though you *are* a very pretty girl. No. You . . . are *interesting.* There's something about you that I feel drawn to."

Excess water in the corner of Luna's eye ran down her cheek. She wiped it away with the back of her hand, glad for the distraction because she had no idea how she should respond. She glanced toward the other tables with normal smiling couples and wondered if their table looked like theirs. The waiter approached with a tray and relief settled into her stomach. Not much longer, and she would be able to go home.

"One rare steak and a chowder," he said, setting their plates of food on the table between them.

Chance smiled as he accepted his. "Thank you."

Luna started to eat, watching him cut a piece off his steak. A gush of watery blood flowed onto the plate, and she winced, directing her gaze to her own food. They ate in silence, the time passing painfully slow.

"I . . . haven't changed your mind about me at all, have I?" he asked after they'd finished eating.

"No."

His shoulders slumped. "Okay."

Grateful for the night to be over, Luna led the way out of the restaurant. She started to walk into the night when a loud *chirp* stopped her. "What's that sound?"

Chance didn't answer, but it was clear from his quizzical expression that he'd heard it too. He crept toward the street leading up to the valet stand, and cautiously, Luna followed behind him. In the divot next to the curb, a small bird struggled to climb out of the street. Its wing hung at its side, a mess of blood and ripped feathers.

"Oh no!" Luna said, stomach twisting at the gore. If there was one thing she couldn't stand, it was seeing animals in pain. "What do we do?"

"Only one thing *to* do," he said, then lifted his heavy black boot, bringing it down on the bird's head.

With a sickening *crunch*, its cries stopped. Chance pulled his foot back and went to the valet without a word. Luna couldn't move. She eyed the bloody smear on the pavement, her stomach threatening to expel her dinner.

Chance came back, keys jingling in his hand.

"How could you do this?" she asked.

"It couldn't be saved," he said with a halfhearted shrug. "A bird with a broken wing? It was already dead. I did it a *kindness*."

Luna glanced at the red smear again. "Kindness, my ass."

Chance, who had already started walking toward his truck, called over his shoulder, "Get in. I'll give you a ride!"

"No, thanks. I'm fine walking."

Chance stopped and turned back to her, sullen. The warmth that had been in his eyes a second ago drained away, leaving nothing behind. "That's nonsense. You shouldn't be walking alone at night."

"I don't feel comfortable getting in a car with you," she said.

"And I don't feel comfortable letting you go home alone,"

he said and grabbed her wrist, attempting to drag her to the truck.

"Let go of me!" Luna insisted, trying to pull herself free.

"Yo, man, what's going on?" a familiar voice asked.

Luna turned, nearly wilting with relief as Nazir came to her side.

Chance released Luna's wrist. "Nothing. I'm just trying to give my stubborn date a ride home."

"It sounds like she don't want to go with you," Nazir said to him, then asked Luna, "You want to go home with him?"

"No," she said, rubbing her wrist.

Chance scoffed and held both hands up. "Fine. That's fine. I'm leaving."

When he was gone, Luna sagged in relief and looked up at Nazir. He was a good foot taller than her with short black hair combed out of his eyes. His features were sharp and his smile warm. Five o'clock shadow colored his cheeks and chin.

"What are you doing here?" she asked, not wanting to think about how her night could've gone if he hadn't shown up.

"I didn't feel like cooking so I ordered takeout. What are you doing with that clown? Your father would kill you if he knew you were on a date."

"It wasn't on purpose," Luna said. "I came out here because I expected to meet up with Violet. She invited him, too, then left me alone with him."

"Ah," Nazir said and looked at the Styrofoam container in his hand. "Tell you what. Let me go pull the car around, and I'll drive you home. Wait here."

Rocking on her heels, Luna watched him cross the parking

lot. As soon as he left her side, a black extended cab truck pulled up to the curb, tire stopping over the mess of bird guts beside her. She stiffened, gauging how far away the entrance of the restaurant was in case she needed to make a run for it.

The passenger window rolled down, and Chance leaned over his middle console from the driver's seat to get closer. "You're judging me right now," he said quietly, in a tone Luna couldn't decipher.

Luna folded her arms across her chest. "No. To judge implies I had expectations. You proved me right, is all."

"Sometimes, it takes real darkness to survive."

"I don't understand."

"I know," he said, a dark gleam in his eye. "But in time, you will."

"Is that a threat?" she asked.

"No. It's a promise. Have a good night."

Before she could question him further, he rolled up the window and drove away.

Chapter Six

CHANCE DROVE PEDAL to the metal down the highway, trying to burn off his anger. It didn't work.

"Fuck!" he cursed and punched the steering wheel.

His horn beeped at the car ahead of him, and the driver shot his hand out the window to give him the middle finger. Chance was so angry, he considered pushing harder on the pedal and rear-ending the car.

Don't, he thought and forced himself to do the opposite.

With nostrils flared, he took in some breaths to quell the edges of his rage. All he could think about was the man who had stepped in. *Nazir,* Chance thought his name was. He remembered seeing him around school but couldn't remember seeing him outside of it.

Who is he to Luna? he wondered.

He didn't want to think of her name. Doing so conjured images of her unhappy expression in the restaurant. He thought if she spent some real time with him, that would change how she felt. Instead, he'd fucked it up by killing the bird.

Stupid, he chastised himself and wished he could go back in time to avoid the situation altogether.

Chance threw his turn signal on and pulled off the highway. Normally, he'd go home, but in his current mood, he didn't trust himself to be alone. He never thought he'd need advice about a girl before, but here he was. He had a friend who might be able to help him decode her.

Susan Cross. Like a lot of the other girls in their class, she was infatuated with him, which meant it was easy to bend her will to whatever he needed her to do. A bonus was that he didn't have to worry about anyone interfering with his plans. The Cross sisters were primarily in the care of their mother who traveled a lot for work. That meant Susan and her sister, Sarah, were often left alone for days at a time. He had never asked what happened to their father and didn't care to know. It gave Chance a sense of comfort to be able to come and go as he pleased without the questioning eyes of people he wouldn't be able to get under his influence.

He navigated through the neighborhoods and up to the fancy house that belonged to the Cross family. There were two cars outside. A pink car that belonged to Susan and a white one that belonged to her friend, Kate.

Chance hesitated turning off the truck. He didn't like Kate and didn't want to involve her with his problems.

Ignore her, he told himself and climbed out of the truck. It was rare to catch Susan when she *didn't* have one of her tagalong friends at her side.

He walked up the path and into the house. He didn't bother knocking because Susan always insisted her friends not do that. That they were more than welcome to come in any time of day.

Voices drifted down the stairs, and he followed the sound to Susan's room. Before he announced his presence, he studied the three girls inside. Kate was the first one he saw, leaning against Susan's dresser. On the bed beside the dresser, Susan sat cross-legged. She had wide green eyes and flowing brown hair down to her waist that she usually tied back with a frilly white ribbon. Her sister, Sarah, who often dressed in all black and dyed her hair to match, had haunting ice-blue eyes that were somehow more unsettling than Chance's. She sat in a pink beanbag chair on the other side of the room from Kate. A pair of black headphones sat cocked on her head so that only one ear was covered.

"Knock, knock," Chance said, tapping the doorframe twice.

"Hey!" Susan greeted, beaming at him.

Kate had a similar expression, but Sarah wouldn't look up from her Walkman.

"What's up, girls?" he asked, slipping into the seat in front of Susan's vanity.

"We were talking about prom," Susan said.

"Oh?" Chance asked, perking up.

"Yeah. We're thinking about going without dates this year. Make it a real bonding moment for us."

Chance bobbed his head. "That's different."

Kate batted her eyelashes at him before she asked, "What about you? Do you have a date?"

"Not yet," he said. "But I've got someone in mind."

Susan perked up, and he could guess what that look meant. Part of her was hoping he would ask *her*. She didn't *really* want to go to prom without a date, she just didn't want a date who wasn't *him*.

"Luna Ketz," he added.

The silence in the room could've choked him.

"Are you serious?" Sarah asked.

"I'm sorry. Color me shocked. She's so *weird*." Kate seethed.

"I don't think so. I think she's interesting. I'm trying to figure out if she's seeing anyone. Do you guys know anything about that Nazir dude who graduated a few years ago?"

Susan and Sarah exchanged a glance before Sarah said, "Not really. He's in college now, isn't he? Why?"

"Have you guys heard about him and Luna dating, or have you heard about her dating *anyone*?" he asked.

Susan shrugged uncertainly. "I honestly can't say. She keeps to herself."

"Ask her," Sarah said, pinning him with a disgusted stare before she put the headphones on her other ear.

"Yeah. Why are we even talking about her?" Kate sneered and rolled her eyes.

Out of all the Cross sisters' friends, Kate had to be his least favorite. She was shrill, bossy, and rude. Not to mention the fact that he hated how she inserted herself into every conversation, whether she was welcome in it or not.

"Because I like her. That's why," Chance snapped, rubbing his temples and trying so hard not to let himself slip into *that* mind. "And I want to spend some time with her before we graduate."

"Whatever," Kate murmured and got up to leave the room.

Chance sucked in a deep breath to compose himself and looked at Susan. "Will *you* help me?"

"What can I tell you that I haven't already?"

"You're a girl. She's a girl. Take her shopping or something and find some stuff out for me."

"I don't know," she said, tapping her pen on her notebook. "I doubt she'd appreciate it."

Chance got up and approached her, getting into her personal space until she blushed. "Please. For me?"

She looked up, her eyes hardened green gems as if she was going to argue, then her shoulders slumped. "Fine. I'm going dress shopping tomorrow. I'll bring her along."

"Thank you." Chance beamed. "You're a doll."

"Don't mention it," Susan said and pulled her hand out of his. She was doing her best to hide it, but there was a crestfallen look in her eyes. "But it's getting kind of late. I'd like to get ready for bed now, if you don't mind."

"Of course, I'll see you tomorrow," Chance said and took his leave.

Outside, the cool night air rejuvenated him, and he felt better now that he had a plan in place. He snagged his keys from his pocket and stopped walking when he realized Kate was sitting on his tailgate.

Chance took a deep breath, anger boiling in the pit of his stomach as he approached her. "What the hell are you doing?"

"Waiting for you, silly," she said, batting her eyelashes at him.

"For what ungodly purpose?" he asked, clenching the keys

in his fist until the edges hurt his palm.

"You really into that Ketz girl?"

"What does it matter if I am?"

Kate reached out, setting a hand on his chest, the other resting on his shoulder. "I was thinkin' we could fool around." She leaned toward him, preparing for a kiss.

Chance instantly leaned away, taking two steps backward so that she lost contact with him. "You're out of your fucking mind if you think that's gonna happen."

Her eyes opened, and she looked at him, wounded. "But why not?"

"I am not in the mood for this," he said and started to walk toward the driver's door, fully prepared to drive off with her on his tailgate.

She grabbed his arm, and he slung her off. "Stop it!"

But she didn't. She pawed at him, trying to pull him into a hug. With his full strength, he swung her away. The back of his hand cracked against the side of her face, knocking her to the ground.

On her hands and knees, she sobbed, holding a hand to her cheek. "I'm telling everyone!" she wailed.

Chance didn't look at her as he closed his tailgate.

"*Everyone!*" she screamed, louder and more high-pitched.

His vision swam red with anger. Like it or not, he was slipping into *that* mind, and it couldn't be stopped this time. He lunged, grabbing Kate and heaving her up off the ground before he wrapped an arm around her waist, dragging her toward his truck.

"What the hell are you doing?!" she screeched and swatted at him.

"You wanna fool around? We'll *fool around*." He seethed, holding her tighter as he opened the door. He thrust her inside and climbed in after her, shoving her into the passenger seat before he started to drive.

"What the fuck are you doing?" she demanded, seething with rage.

"Shut up," he said, with no hint of remorse and pressed harder on the gas.

Even if he wanted to stop, he couldn't. Kate must've sensed the shift in him because her angry screams slipped into something desperate. Primal. She clawed at the door, trying everything she could to get it to open, but it wouldn't. He kept driving. Right out of the city and into the surrounding woods.

"Chance, please. Whatever it is you're thinking about doing, don't do it," she said over and over again.

He huffed. Didn't she understand she'd done this to herself? *Stupid girl.* Outside the windshield, the darkness of the night called to him. They were deep in the forest now, but not deep enough for what he had planned.

Another angry snarl from Kate, and he screeched the car to a halt. Immediately, she went for the door, but he was already on her, fingers tangling deep into her hair to wrench her head back. He pulled his knife from his pocket and sank it into her chest. She gurgled, struggling for breath as Chance kicked open the door so she would fall to the ground before any of her blood could hit his interior. She lay in the dirt, bleeding but not moving.

Most likely in shock. Slowly, one hand reached to her chest in a last-ditch attempt to staunch the bleeding.

Good luck. He got out of the truck and crouched beside her, using two fingers to draw a variety of sigils in the dirt.

When he finished, he wiped the muck onto his pants and grabbed Kate by the tops of her arms. She'd stopped moving and didn't protest, her limbs limp. He dropped her onto the sigils, watching the wells fill until they appeared to be weeping blood. He gathered an armful of supplies from the back of his truck and returned to Kate's side.

"Forgive the improper ritual, my lord," he whispered. "But I give you her soul to take."

He repeated the chant and pulled the bloody knife from his pocket, aggravated by his own carelessness. On top of the work he already needed to do, he would have to destroy his clothes as well. He turned the knife toward Kate, ready to finish his work so he could slip back into his phony life before anyone noticed he was gone.

Chapter Seven

THE NEXT MORNING, Susan, Sarah, and Sarah's friend, Maddie, walked up the staircase and through the entrance of Shawnee High School. Susan halted inside the door, looking out the wide window. It was a nice day, hinting at the perfect summer that was to come. She thought longingly of the beach and lazy afternoons in the sun. Then she looked back at her sister and her friend and had to accept that those days would be filled with their company and no one else.

As if she could sense her dip in mood, Sarah side-eyed her sister.

"We should wait for Luna," Susan said, trying to hide her sadness.

The words were laced with her usual optimism, but she didn't feel any of it. Gathering information about another girl to report to the guy she had a crush on was tough. She didn't want to let him down, but this would not be an easy task.

"You're really going through with this?" Sarah asked, black-lined eyes closed to slits.

"Yeah, I am," Susan said. "I promised." She wanted to believe that since Chance had come to her for help, surely she meant *something* to him. Even if it wasn't the *something* she hoped for.

"The whole thing is weird if you ask me," Maddie said. "Sounds like Kate was right to get herself out of it."

Susan glanced up and down the hall. "She's not here?"

"I haven't heard from her this morning," Maddie said.

"Probably late again," Sarah said flatly. "We'll try calling her at lunch."

"Okay," Susan agreed.

The bell overhead rang. As much as Susan wanted to continue waiting for Luna, she didn't want to be late to class either.

***

CHANCE STIFLED A yawn, thinking about the long boring day ahead of him as he drove to school. Last night, the memories of what he'd done to Kate seemed vague and distant. Like it had only been a dream. This fuzzy, distant feeling he suffered through was the one he usually felt after slipping into *that* mind for an extended chunk of time. He'd killed Kate, but what happened afterward? Had he finished his ritual? How had he gotten rid of the body? What did he do with her car?

As much as his curiosity itched at him, he knew better than to go back to the crime scene. He counted the streets that separated him from school. In spite of what went on in his head, he'd need to be the blithe version of himself that his classmates knew him to be. He pulled into his usual parking spot and slipped on his theoretical mask, hiding all the darkness behind it. As soon as he stepped out of his truck, he spotted Violet in the crowd and all the questions he'd rolled over after the failed date came back.

"Hey!" he called, trotting after her.

She turned to look at him, almost warily, as she said, "Hi."

"Listen, I wanted to say thank you for helping me set up last night. Me and Luna had a nice night, though she probably told you otherwise."

"I actually haven't heard from her yet. I kind of ducked out on walking with her this morning because honestly, I feel *guilty* about the whole thing. I'm worried she's going to be mad at me."

"Why would you feel guilty? It's not like she got hurt or anything."

Violet reached up to scratch the back of her neck. "Well, me and her have been friends forever, and it's not as if we hang out much outside of school anymore. She's leaving in a few weeks, and that might've actually been my last chance to spend time with her. Now she'll probably never trust me again."

Chance barely resisted the urge to roll his eyes. "She'll get over it. Besides, aren't you going to prom? You'll both be there."

Violet stiffened. "No, I can't . . . find a date." She paused as if considering asking him something but instead said, "And last time I checked, Luna hasn't changed her mind on prom anyway." Chance opened his mouth, wanting to ask about Nazir, but Violet continued unperturbed. "I don't want to trick her again, if that's where this conversation is headed."

Chance struggled for a response because that was exactly what he'd planned.

The bell rang, and Violet looked visibly relieved as she said, "Gotta go."

His blood boiled at the dismissal. "I don't need you anyway," he muttered.

Keeping his head down, he went inside the school, trying to get to class before he could unload his anger on someone who didn't deserve it. He was so frustrated, he didn't realize someone was walking at his side until she asked, "Are you ignoring me now, Chance?"

He did his best to wipe all traces of anger away as he said, "Susan! I was lost in my head. Didn't realize you were there. I apologize. What's up?"

"It's just . . ."—she paused to lick her lips, glancing up at him as if she were carefully picking her words—"the girls have their concerns about this situation with Luna. I mean, you've never seemed to be interested in her before, and this sudden fascination is pretty weird."

"What's weird about it?" Chance asked, somehow keeping the irritation out of his voice.

"You've heard the rumors that she's leaving soon for college. Why waste your time?"

Chance laughed. "So? There are rumors about literally everything. They say the lunch ladies spit in the food, but you still eat it so . . ."

Susan set her hand on his forearm. "Fair enough, Chance. I'll see what I can find out. I wanted to make sure it was what you really wanted, is all."

Chance smiled, pleased. "Good."

Chapter Eight

LUNA SET HER science textbook in her locker before pulling out her history book. It was halfway through lunch, and all she could think of was the fact that Violet was mysteriously absent. All morning, Luna had worked around her mind what she would say when she saw her friend, but it was clear Violet was avoiding her.

Of course she is. Luna slammed the door, gasping when she almost crashed right into the girl who'd been standing beside her.

"Hi there!" the girl said in a cheery voice. Her hair was tied into a ponytail with a white ribbon, green eyes similar to Luna's own. Susan Cross. Luna had seen her around school plenty of times, but this was the first time she'd actually spoken to her.

"Um . . . hi?" Luna replied, clutching her book tight to her chest as she spotted the two girls behind Susan. One had dusty blonde hair and dark eyes and the other had dark, almost black hair with bright blue eyes. Luna guessed they were there to enforce whatever tidings Susan had to deliver.

"We're cutting to go dress shopping for prom, and I want to invite you along," Susan said.

Luna looked between all three girls again before she laughed. "What? I'm not going to *prom*." In the back of her mind, she pictured her father's face if she made such a request, and somehow, that made her laugh harder. He would never allow it, and for this once, she was grateful that his stubborn ways could work to her benefit. "Why would you invite me?"

"We've been going to the same schools for years and have barely said more than two words to one another," Susan said, popping her gum. "I feel like officially getting to meet everyone before the year ends. It can't hurt."

"I guess not," Luna said. "But I have a lot of things to do so, if you don't mind . . ." Luna tried to shoulder her way past the three girls.

Susan caught Luna's elbow. "No, I insist you come with us. Really, it'll be fun."

Luna quirked an eyebrow. "Do I look like the type to wear dresses for fun?"

"You never know," Susan said firmly, patiently. "You might not have found the right one yet, is all."

Luna looked from Susan's hopeful eyes to the eyes of the girls behind her. They didn't look as if they cared one way or another. Luna looked back to Susan, uncertainty in her stomach. This had to be a prank of some kind.

"Did Chance put you up to this?" she asked, thinking of the odd statement he'd made before driving off into the night.

Sometimes, it takes real darkness to survive.

A twinkle lit up Susan's eyes at the mention of Chance. A familiar one Luna had seen in Violet's eyes whenever she talked about him. She didn't get it.

He's a chameleon. Making himself into whatever creature will help him blend in best with his surroundings.

Susan tipped her head to the side. "I wouldn't say that, exactly."

"Whatever he's got you signed up to do, you're free, okay? Tell him you took me out and that can be the end of it."

Susan let go of her arm and pulled the textbook out of her hands, looking at it. "What does the reason matter? I think you'd have more fun hanging out with us for an afternoon than reading this."

"There's something *off* about him, and I don't trust him. Do you do everything he says?"

The girl with black hair snorted, and Susan glared at her before turning back to Luna. "Me and him are good friends, but so what? He can't make me do anything I don't want to do. And it certainly doesn't mean we can't be friends too."

"I guess," Luna murmured.

"Come on. You have the rest of your life to be responsible," she said. "And if it'll sweeten the deal, we can get some lunch after. My treat."

Luna chewed her lip, considering. She hadn't eaten the terrible school lunch and would regret it in an hour. She met Susan's eyes, and the girl offered another gentle smile. Luna had a huge dislike for the cheerleaders, mostly because of Kate and her squad of bullies, but there was something about Susan's energy she liked. Maybe they *could* be friends.

Luna grabbed the textbook from Susan and said, "Fine, I'll come. But only if he's not going to be there."

Susan looped her arm through Luna's. "Deal."

Luna shifted her book awkwardly to keep from dropping it as they walked, the other girls following closely behind. How had life gone from studying every chance she got to navigating this weird social chain?

Outside in the parking lot, Susan pointed to a pink car. "That's me right there."

Luna had to keep herself from snorting audibly at the Barbie-like thing. Somehow, it was fitting. Susan slid her arm out of Luna's and opened the driver's-side door without a single care in the world. Susan's two backups climbed into the back seat, and Luna slid into the only seat that was left—the passenger seat.

The engine roared to life and Susan started to pull out of the parking lot when Luna asked, "So where are we going?"

"I know the perfect place," Susan answered.

"You said that before, but the last place sucked," the blonde said from the back seat.

"It wasn't *that* bad, Maddie." Susan rolled her eyes.

Luna zoned out as she listened to them argue. To her, it made absolutely no difference where they went. Luna had never been a fan of clothes shopping, and as the tomboy she was, she wasn't a huge fan of dresses either. She leaned against the door, staring out the window and imagining she was somewhere else.

It wasn't long before Susan parked her car and said, "Okay, we're here!"

They were parked outside the mall. Luna hadn't been there in a long time, her only memories being when she was knee-high and her mother had taken her when they'd first moved to town. Luna hated it. Too many people in such a limited place only served to fuel her anxiety, and so she avoided it.

"The store is a family-owned business. You girls will love it," Susan said, shouldering a tiny white purse as they cut through the parking lot.

Maddie spoke up again, but Luna didn't hear her. Her heart thudded with that usual panic that came from being around crowds. The doors opened to a wide corridor dotted with stores and kiosks. The smells of pretzels and popcorn and sweets reached her instantly. The deeper into the mall they went, the thicker the crowds became.

At one point, they couldn't walk in a line so Sarah and Maddie tagged behind Susan and Luna as they made their way through the food court. Nearly every table was full, and Luna was surprised to see how many people congregated here in the middle of the day. At the end of the food court, they got onto the escalator. Susan offered Luna a gentle smile as they neared the top, and they got off on the next level of the mall.

"How much farther?"

Luna side-eyed her, glad that she asked the question that had been at the front of her brain since they entered the mall.

"A few more steps," Susan said and gestured to the store before them.

There was a sign that said *Midnight Apparel.* Inside were racks of dresses and other formal wear arranged across the brightly lit store. Maddie and Sarah spread out to look at various things, but Luna stayed hesitantly by the door.

This is hell. She hugged herself. *I'm in hell.*

"Come on, silly." Susan reached out to grasp Luna's hand.

Luna didn't like the feeling of her skin against hers, but she didn't fight it as Susan pulled her over to the nearest rack.

"Let me look at you." She tucked a strand of Luna's dark

hair behind her ear. "Hmm," she said and grasped Luna's chin, moving her face from side to side.

"Are we shopping or am I at the doctor's?" Luna murmured.

Susan laughed and let go of her face. "I think you'd look good in a nice summer color," she mused and turned toward the nearest cluster of dresses. She flipped through a few of them before lingering on a yellow one. Finally, she plucked it off the rack and handed it to Luna. "Try this one."

Luna grimaced. "Are you sure about this? It's so . . . *bright*." She preferred darker tones. Grays, browns, and blacks that would assist her mission to not stand out. This yellow dress represented everything she was not.

"I'm positive," Susan said. "Now go try it on, and you'll see I'm right."

Luna wanted to try it on only to show how mistaken she was. At the back of the store, Luna stepped into an open changing room and pulled the curtain shut. It was cramped with a bench and full-length mirror. Luna eyed her reflection, the yellow dress draped over her arm.

Being nice for the sake of being nice is one thing, but why am I actually here?

What happened the night before came back to her, and not for the first time; she felt as if there was a wedge between her and Violet. As much as she didn't like the thought of making new friends, she was going to have to in her new life. There was no way to get through college *without* it happening.

Maybe Violet was right, Luna mused. *Maybe I do need new*

friends.

Susan was nice, and while Luna had her suspicions about *why* she was being so nice, it wouldn't hurt to play along for the day. They would all get bored of her and move on to Chance's next orders soon enough, and then Luna would be able to get back to normal.

Exhaling loudly, she looked at the dress and started to take off her rather boyish clothes before she pulled it over her head. She didn't care for the color, but the fabric was soft and hugged her curves nicely.

Luna eased open the curtain, searching for Susan. When she found her, she was holding up two dresses, a pink one and a purple one, face creased in obvious internal debate. Luna walked to her side, eyes on the floor. Her face burned as she imagined everyone staring at her, and it took all she had not to run back into the safety of the changing room.

"Oh, you look marvelous!" Susan exclaimed when she finally noticed her.

"Really? I don't *feel* marvelous," Luna grumbled. She felt awkwardly outside of her element.

"That's because you can't see how beautiful you are!"

Luna picked at the fabric and kept her mouth shut. Arguing would only draw out the awkwardness.

In the silence, Susan returned her debate to her own two dresses. She held one up in each hand before she asked, "Which one do you think I would look good in?"

Luna had absolutely no idea about fashion and so she picked the one that first caught her eye. "Maybe the pink one?"

Susan tilted her head, staring at it before lifting it higher. "I think I'll try it on. Thanks!" she said as she made her way to the changing rooms. Luna went with her, eager to change back into her clothes when she remembered what she was wearing.

Before she reached the tiny room, Maddie spotted her and called, "Looking good, girl!"

The tiniest hint of a smile graced Luna's face as she pulled the curtain shut.

LUNA STAYED WITH Susan and her friends until the time that school let out. After they ate at a nearby café and chatted, Luna asked to be dropped off at home, worried that if her father was already there, he would notice if she was so much as a fraction late. Part of her feared someone would call and tell him she'd skipped half the day and she'd be in for a lecture for the rest of the night.

I have to get to the phone first, is all.

And so that was how she spent her evening, plodding around the kitchen and waiting to intercept the call that was most likely coming. Abrahim was in the living room, watching television. Luna distracted herself by cleaning, singing to herself as she did so. A kettle of tea roared to life on the stove, and she paused from her tasks to take it off the heat.

Carefully, she pulled two mugs from the cupboard and added a few teaspoons of sugar to each. She left hers on the counter and wandered into the living room to set her father's on the table beside him. He hadn't said much to her since she'd gotten home, and normally, she would've counted that as a win, but she could tell it was one of his bad health days. His normally beady eyes looked dulled and glazed.

As long as she didn't prompt a fight, he most likely wouldn't give one. She did her best to keep him comfortable. The mug clinked when set on the table, and she turned to make her departure when he said, "Luna."

She winced, automatically assuming he'd somehow know that she'd skipped half the day. "Yeah, Dad?"

He gestured to the television with the remote. "Doesn't she go to your school?"

Luna watched the news, a picture of Kate lighting up the screen. Unable to understand what she was seeing, Luna answered, "Yeah, she does."

"She's missing," her father said, squinting to better read the block letters beneath her photo. "Says she's been missing since yesterday. That's what happens when people let their children do whatever they want."

Luna kept her gaze on the television. She had *seen* Kate on Monday, and now she was gone.

A police press circuit came on the screen.

"Do you believe this is connected to the murder of Dahlia Moore?" a reporter yelled from the crowd.

"No," the police chief said into the microphone. "We have reason to believe we're dealing with a runaway-type situation. Nothing more."

The reporter asked something else, but Luna drowned it out. *Dahlia Moore.* She hadn't heard that name in years. When she'd first started high school, Dahlia's name had been everywhere. She'd been the same age as Luna, though she went to school in the next town over so Luna didn't know her. She'd been brutally murdered a mile outside of Lima. The culprit was never caught.

"Such a shame," her father said and changed the channel.

"Yeah," Luna murmured and left the living room, her shock turning to bitterness. What did it matter what had happened to Kate? For as long as they'd gone to school together, she'd been a bully to everyone, not caring how she made people feel. From rumors around school, Kate had a history of running away and then coming back when things with her parents had calmed down. She would show up in a few days and all would be well.

The clock started to chime. Her father had it preprogrammed to chime five times a day, alerting them to each necessary prayer session.

"Just in time," her father said, turning off the television and tossing his blanket aside to stand. "We need some prayers right now."

Luna glanced at the black television screen. Normally, she would've protested or made an excuse to get out of it. Her father was a devout Muslim, but lately, Luna wavered in her faith more and more. Most days, she went through the motions to keep the peace. It was easier that way. In that moment, however, she found she agreed with him.

Chapter Nine

YAWNING, CHANCE TRIED to keep his tired eyes open as he pulled his truck to a halt in his favorite parking spot amid a cluster of particularly creepy trees. It had been a long day. Longer than he'd imagined it would be. He'd expected it to take at least a week for people to notice Kate's disappearance. But Susan was on top of it. To blend in, he'd needed to act equally as worried as she was. As part of that front, he'd spent the afternoon with the Cross sisters passing out fliers and going door-to-door asking people if they'd seen her.

What a waste of a day.

He climbed out of the truck, feet sinking into the thick mud. This part of the woods was miles from town and far from where he'd slain Kate. He came here specifically with the intention of not being found. His house—or the house he *called* his—was abandoned. Had been for years. It was listed for sale, but no one visited. He doubted people in town knew about it anymore and those who did, strongly believed it was haunted. That was enough to keep normal people away.

Everyone but Chance since he was far scarier than any ghost could be. He was real, and he was a monster.

After the hell his life had presented over the past few years, he had no choice but to stay here. There was one other place in town which would welcome him with open arms, present three meals a day and a roof over his head, but that was the exact place he was trying to escape. For a time, it had been his refuge, his safety after he'd been orphaned and forced to move to Lima to make a fresh start. But now he needed to find his own place in the world.

Not for the first time, Chance wondered what he was doing with his life. This lifestyle he'd taken on wasn't sustainable, but until he either failed in his plan or came up with a new one, he was stuck here like so many of his classmates would be after graduation.

Chance gnawed on his bottom lip as he crossed the overgrown field toward the old rundown house. It was a decrepit two-story monstrosity. The windows on the ground floor had been mostly busted out and boarded over. He likened it to a set from a haunted house movie.

It was odd how much he felt like this place was home. If he were capable of emotions, he'd be sad by the path his life had taken him. *I'm past that point,* he reminded himself as he stepped up onto the creaky porch and into the darkness of the open front door.

He crossed through the parlor, route permanently fixed in his brain, and plopped down on the couch, closing his eyes. His mind wandered through everything that had happened over the past few days. Luna's rejection, the note he'd left in her mailbox, the interaction with Nazir, murdering Kate, the way Luna now openly avoided him at school.

How badly he wanted to be honest with her, and yet, he

couldn't. She would never understand. *He* barely understood everything that went into being a Walker, and he'd practiced for years.

The only thing he had confidence in was that she had no knowledge of the Other Side. But it was only a matter of time until she'd learn. She had a tie to that place. An ability that could completely change his life if he could get her to use it for him.

She's never going to do me favors. She doesn't like me, he reminded himself.

She'd made that much clear. He couldn't say he blamed her. He'd been a creep, but he needed her cooperation if he ever hoped to get out of this bind. To earn it, he'd have to be honest. He'd have to be himself. Both in this mind and *that.*

But she's the key, he thought over and over again.

Growling out his frustration, he got up from the couch and walked down the hall to his favorite room in the house. The door swung with ease, revealing a space only slightly brighter than the rest of the house. Two bloodred tapers in golden candle holders threw light onto the wall, highlighting a red inverted pentagram. A series of sigils surrounded it, the same ones he'd drawn in the dirt when he killed Kate. He dropped to his knees in front of it and crept closer, pushing through the bones which covered the floor around the candles.

"Almighty Father of Darkness, I need your help," he whispered, waiting for a sense of *something.* When the answer came, it rioted through him, pounding in his blood, and he understood.

"If I walk on the Other Side, she'll be susceptible to my message, but what if I'm not strong enough?" It was a constant fear of his. Sacrificing Kate had helped but not as much as he'd hoped it would. He needed *more*.

The sensation flooded through him again. He stood up and pulled his trusty dagger from his pocket before he yanked up his sleeve and made a single slit on his skin, watching his blood drip to the floor in a sacrificial *thank you*. When the cut began to clot, he lowered his sleeve, considering his options for the next sacrifice.

Multiple people had made his hate list. He supposed it didn't matter which one he chose. Surprisingly, out of his two top candidates, it was Violet's face that came to mind first.

Chapter Ten

LUNA TOOK TWO tentative steps into the forest and followed it with a full twirl to study the green around her. Sunlight filtered through the mess of branches above. How was it daytime? Hadn't she gone to bed?

Silence engulfed her. The kind that was unnerving rather than comforting. Something in her gut warned her that the quiet was off, that she needed to *escape*. Luna moved forward and listened again. The usual sounds of animals were absent. They could sense that something was off too.

How did I get here?

Luna started to move. A twig snapped loudly behind her, and she moved faster, afraid to glance over her shoulder for fear of what might be there when she did. She screamed, pausing when a scream came back that wasn't her own.

"V-Violet?" she called.

"I'm here!" her friend responded from a few feet into the undergrowth.

With her fear rising up the back of her throat, it was easy to brush off all the petty anger she felt toward her friend. A warning was going off in Luna's brain that whatever this place was, she was in danger. Truth be told, she would've been happy to see *anyone* so long as she didn't have to be alone. When she caught up to Violet, her usually rosy face was pale and sweaty. She stood so rigid that Luna could've believed she had been carved from stone.

"What is this place? Where are we?" Luna asked.

"I don't know," Violet replied, glancing over her shoulder as if she'd heard something Luna had not.

"I have no idea how I got here," Luna admitted, scratching the back of her neck.

"Me either."

"Maybe we should see if anyone else is here."

Violet stared straight ahead as if her brain was a million miles away. Luna started to walk, and at first, Violet kept pace with her, but gradually, she started to lag behind.

Luna hardly noticed as she counted the minutes in her head. No matter how long they walked, they seemed no closer to the edge of the strange forest than when they had begun. Overhead, the sun didn't move, as if it were frozen in time.

Chills went down Luna's spine. "This is getting us nowhere," she said, coming to a halt.

"If anything, I think we're more lost now," Violet replied, eyes glazed with exhaustion.

A click sounded from the undergrowth. The sound of a bullet being loaded into a gun. Luna stiffened with a surge of adrenaline as a figure cloaked in black stepped from the foliage, revolver clutched tight in their hand. Luna couldn't think as her eyes landed on the weapon. She tried to look past the gun and into the eyes of the person aiming it at her, but their hood was up, casting a shadow over their face.

"That's about far enough," he commanded in a voice that sounded more like a snarl.

The gun swung toward Violet, and he took a step forward. Everything moved in slow motion as he pulled the trigger, a bullet sending a spray of crimson into the air and across the green grass. Violet's head snapped backward before she slumped to the ground. Gore splattered the side of Luna's face. She looked at her friend, unable to do more than shake.

"Why?" Luna asked, twin tears trailing down her cheeks as she forced herself to look at the gunman. "Why did you kill her?"

He turned the revolver toward her, and she flinched, staring into the black depths of the barrel. She fully expected him to pull the trigger again, to feel a bullet tear through her skin as well. When he didn't, she somehow found the nerve to ask, "Aren't you going to shoot me too?"

"Not if you be a good girl and follow me," he said, waving the gun for effect.

"I'm not going anywhere with you," Luna said, trying to be brave as she faced down the killer. Inside, she felt nothing of the sort. She felt *sick*. It would be easy for him to shoot her and leave her body in the woods to be eaten by animals. Her heart thumped violently against her ribs, and she worried it would betray her and give out from fear.

When she didn't move, the figure chuckled and approached, frame looming over her. Up close, the weapon looked worse somehow, or maybe it was the reality of the situation sinking in. She wanted to run, she tried to, but her fear had her paralyzed. With the gun hovering an inch from her face, she cowered away.

"I'm not gonna ask again," he said and grabbed her arm. He was strong, much stronger than her. He would win any fight she tried to start. The figure looked into the trees suddenly as if he'd heard someone approach. The gun moved from her temple and into the woods. He pulled the trigger. The *bang* rang through the forest, but to Luna, all she could hear was her blood thundering through her ears.

She screamed out, unable to hear herself after the gunshot but hoping someone else would, and that they would come to save her before it was too late.

"Don't waste your breath," the figure murmured. "There's no one else here."

Luna tried to get a glimpse of his face, but the scene started to slide away to blackness. When her vision came back, the forest had disappeared, and she was left staring at her green bedroom walls. She buried the heels of her hands into her eyes.

It was just a dream, she told herself. Temporary relief washed over her, gone almost as soon as it came.

Luna had never had a dream so violent before.

It's Chance's fault, she decided. Whenever she thought of that night at the restaurant, her mind automatically stopped at what he had done to the bird. Even in her memories, the resounding *crunch* of its body beneath his boot made her ill.

According to her alarm clock, she'd overslept. Bolting out of bed, she hurried through her morning routine and grabbed her backpack off the couch before dashing out the door.

"Bye, Dad! I'm off to school."

When she received no response, she chastised herself. He was most likely already out for the day or asleep. Otherwise, he never would've let her sleep in.

Luna started to run, desperate to get the clinging traces of her dream out of her head. To her surprise, Violet was in their usual meeting spot, waiting for her. She slowed beside her, bending over to catch her breath.

"What's gotten into you?" Violet asked.

As Luna stood back up, she side-eyed her. During the panic of seeing her die in the dream, nothing else had mattered. Now that she knew her friend was okay, everything that had gone down between them the past few days came to the surface, reminding Luna exactly how she felt about her.

"I could ask you the same," Luna said, eye twitching with stress. "Setting me up with Chance? That wasn't cool."

"Why are you trippin'? You said yourself you wanted time outside of the house because your dad is constantly breathing down your neck, so I gave you that," Violet said pointedly. "How'd it go after I left?"

Why were she and Violet friends in the first place? It was clear they didn't understand one another. Hadn't for some time. "As well as you can probably guess."

"Still don't like him?"

"Hell no," Luna said and snorted. "Thankfully, Nazir was there to give me a ride home."

Violet shrugged. "You can't get mad at me for trying."

Luna gave her the stink eye. She *could* and *would* get mad.

If Violet was capable of a trick like that, who was to say she hadn't written the note to Luna's father? Since she was already angry, she added, "You know, after ratting me out to my dad, you'd think you had done enough."

Violet's face twisted with visible confusion. "Ratting you out?"

Luna wanted to believe her friend was lying, but her reaction seemed genuine. "Never mind," she conceded. She would blame her and Chance equally. "Let's just say, all your nonsense has been seeping into my subconscious. Last night, I dreamt someone killed you."

Violet smirked, not seeming bothered by the dream that had so deeply shaken Luna. "Was it you?"

Luna imagined herself in the place of the shooter. "I'd be lying if I said I hadn't thought about it."

Chapter Eleven

ON THE OPPOSITE side of town, Chance awoke at the same time as Luna. A sheen of sweat covered his skin, making him hot and sticky. The adrenaline coursing through his veins made it easy to ignore. He clenched his hands in and out of fists, nearly able to feel Violet's blood on his skin.

That was a hell of a trip.

Light seeped through the dusty black curtain hanging over the window. Chance dreaded what that meant. He would have to be the prestigious Chance Welfrey of Shawnee High School. Sneering, he tried to focus on the positives of his day. School would at least be interesting. Would Luna be upset to see Violet absent the way Susan had been with Kate?

Somehow, he doubted that, but he wouldn't lie that he liked the idea of her being alone. No one to play referee between her and him. Securing his trusty dagger in his pocket, he left his house and slid into the seat of his truck. With a deep breath, he started to drive, speeding slightly to get there faster. He didn't see Luna on the way in and parked in his usual spot toward the end of the lot. He cut the engine and sat in silence, waiting.

Any minute, Luna would be there. As predicted, a tiny figure appeared in the distance. Chance sat straighter, proud of himself, until he realized she was flanked by someone. They passed behind his truck as they cut through the parking lot, and he watched them in his rearview mirror.

It was Violet.

"Son of a bitch," he cursed and punched his steering wheel, a mix of defeat and disappointment bubbling inside him.

It seemed he wasn't strong enough in the Other Realm. Not yet anyway. If he wanted Violet dead, he would have to do it for real. Chance tried to work his way through his shock and anger as he watched the girls part from one another.

He picked the perfect moment to get out of the truck and studied Luna before she became aware of his presence. There were faint bags under her green eyes and a haunted look as if there was something on her mind she couldn't shake. Obviously the dream had worked on *her*.

What had he messed up with Violet?

"What do you want?" she asked, not bothering to look at him as he made his way to her side.

"Prom's tomorrow night. What time would you like me to come get you?"

Luna sneered. "I'm not going."

"Susan told me you were going," he said.

Luna stared at him through half-lidded eyes. "I'm going with *her*, yes. Not you. You're weird, and I'm done having you trick other people into getting us on a date together."

Chance huffed. "Susan's overjoyed to have met you. Did you know that?"

The question caught her off guard. "So? What's your point?"

"So forget that I'll be there. Show up for her. Then we can hang out after."

"You're absolutely insane!" she screamed and stormed off into the building.

"That's not a no!" he called after her, furiously running his fingers through his hair.

There were a lot of moving pieces in this game, and he hated the uncertainty of it all. Everything he did to try to get Luna to warm up to him backfired. If a sacrifice was really the only way to make it happen, that didn't seem to be working out for him either. If he needed to kill Violet on this side of the Realm, would he be able to do it in a way that wouldn't get it traced back to himself?

THAT NIGHT, CHANCE tried to get as far away from Susan as he could. After another day of pounding the pavement, searching for a girl he knew wouldn't come back, he was at his limit. He had other things he needed to figure out, and socializing wasn't one of them. Chance drove out of town, finding the rolling fields of grass at the edge of the woods. There was a hill there, so high that when he sat at the top, looking up at the moon, he felt as if the rest of the world didn't exist.

He dared to feel free. Burying his face in his hands, he was tempted to cry out his frustrations right then and there. He hadn't been *free* for a long time, and all of his resounding failures were only a reminder of that. He'd escaped from the compound for now, but it was only a matter of time before the others would catch up to him. The thought would crush him if he let it.

I'm stronger than that.

"Mind if I join you?" a soft voice asked from nearby.

Chance jumped and looked up, squinting through the darkness. He hurriedly wiped his face, not wanting her to see any trace of tears. "Susan. What are you doing?"

"Thought I'd find you here," she said, settling into the grass beside him. "I wanted to talk to you about tomorrow."

Chance winced. He'd expected this. "Luna tell you she's not going?"

Susan's forehead furrowed. "No. She bought the dress."

Chance started at the information. He'd thought Luna would've been adamant to *everyone* that she didn't want to go, but that didn't seem to be the case. *Interesting.*

Susan peered at the moon. "Can you believe there's only a few weeks left of high school, and then we'll all go our separate ways?"

Chance gritted his teeth. He'd come here to *forget* that he was running out of time. "Feeling sentimental?"

"I suppose. A lot of things are coming to an end. And now everything that's going on with Kate . . . it's hard."

Chance nodded along, but he couldn't relate.

"I've been running you ragged the past couple days, but the truth is, I bet she's fine. Most likely ran away again. I just wish she would've told me this time or waited until we graduated so I could've gone with her."

Chance dared a glance at her from the corner of his eye. When he saw the downcast expression on her face, he *almost* felt guilty. "She'll turn up," he said in his best attempt at consoling.

Secrets always do.

Chapter Twelve

ON THE NIGHT of prom, Luna had forgotten completely about the dance. She'd gotten through a relatively normal day at school and was at home, nestled under a blanket on the couch, bowl of popcorn and a drink nearby as she watched television. Her father was, thankfully, at Friday night mosque, and she was getting in some much-needed alone time after spending the afternoon with Sidra.

When a knock sounded at the door, Luna jumped then frowned. In her mind, she imagined it to be Chance on the other side, stopping by to bother her since he'd been distant in class. Instead, Luna was surprised to find Susan and her sister, Sarah. They were already dressed up, hair and makeup carefully done. Luna's eyes went to the yellow dress draped over Susan's arm.

"Hi," she said hesitantly.

"Don't look so concerned. We're here to make you absolutely *beautiful*," Susan said.

Luna felt her horror rise when she spotted the makeup bag in her hands. "Can I stay home?"

Susan and Sarah exchanged glances before Susan looked back at Luna. "A little late to change your mind now, girlie. If you're worried about Chance, don't be. None of us have dates."

"Oh," Luna said, surprised at the idea that such a pretty girl like Susan preferred to go stag.

The girls pushed their way past Luna and into the house, Susan making a point of eye contact as she closed the door behind them.

Luna's heart started to pound. What if her father came home early and checked on her? If he saw she had company over after dark, he would go through the roof. "For real, you guys don't have to worry about me. Go have some fun. I'll see you at school on Monday, okay?" she said, hoping they could hear the desperation in her voice.

"Oh, *pfft*," Susan said and handed the makeup bag to Sarah. "Can you set the stuff up in the bathroom? I'll be there in a minute."

Sarah took the bag, exchanging another glance with Luna before she disappeared down the hall that led to the bathroom.

Susan turned to Luna, extending the dress to her. "Now, it's your turn. Put your dress on so we can get you ready."

Luna balled her hands into fists, ready to argue again when all the fight left her. Why was she being so difficult? Why not give in, enjoy the little things that made other people her age so happy? Her shoulders slumped, and she took the dress from Susan.

"Atta girl," Susan said.

Luna didn't respond as she went to her room, closing the door behind her. Could she really wear something like this in front of the entire school? She stripped off her clothes and donned the dress. Carefully, she smoothed the wrinkles and with a long glance at the clothes on her bed, left her room. Susan waited for her on the couch.

As soon as Luna stepped into the living room, she stood. "You look great! Come on, so Sarah and I can do your makeup."

Susan wrapped her fingers through Luna's, pulling her into the bathroom. A chair from the kitchen had been set inside, the counter beside it littered with eyelash curlers and brushes, all of which looked like torture devices to Luna.

"Is all this really necessary?" Luna asked as Susan eased her into the chair.

Susan chuckled. "Of course. Don't you want to be pretty?"

Luna scowled, considering. Vanity was something she'd never worried herself with before. It seemed odd to start now.

She must've made a face because Susan said, "Don't answer that. Just relax."

Luna closed her eyes, the light tickling of brushes making her skin crawl. The sensation changed to something being smushed against her skin. She was made to open her eyes, and Susan ran mascara over her lashes.

"All finished," said Susan, at last.

Luna didn't recognize herself in the mirror. Her black hair flowed in thick waves past her shoulders, the light eye shadow making her green eyes glitter. There was a hint of blush across her cheekbones, contrasted well with some bronzer and the natural brown tint of Luna's skin.

"Wow."

"I take it you're pleased," Susan said.

Luna stood up, not taking her eyes off herself. It was

strange how a little bit of powder and creamy colors could make a person look so different.

"You're a magician," Luna said.

Susan giggled, and knocking drifted down the hall from the front door.

"I'll get it," Susan said and disappeared.

Luna glanced at Sarah. The girl was also looking into the mirror, but there was an expression on her face that was hard to read.

"Who's that?" Luna asked, wide-eyed. "She promised she wouldn't invite Chance." She felt ridiculous for believing her.

Sarah didn't look as if she cared much one way or another. "You don't like him either, huh?"

Before Luna could respond, Susan came back into the room with Maddie in tow. Luna didn't know a thing about the girl, but the amount of relief that surged through her when she realized it wasn't Chance was telling.

"It's about to start soon," Maddie told them. "Are you guys ready or what?"

Susan looked over her supplies scattered on the counter. "Almost. We need to get things picked up."

Luna helped the three girls collect brushes and sponges. Somehow, Susan managed to cram it all back into the tiny bag.

"Is that everything?" Luna asked, not wanting to leave a single hint of makeup behind. She could hear her father's rants already.

"Oh, wait! I almost forgot," Susan said, turning to her tote bag. She dug through it, pulling out a pair of yellow high-heeled shoes. "These are for you."

Luna eyed them, not taking them as she said, "What's this?"

"Well, you bought the dress, but I noticed you didn't buy any accessories or shoes or anything. I saw these and thought they would match your dress perfectly, so here."

Luna didn't want to be rude, but she didn't want the shoes. She opened her mouth to say as much, but the hopeful expression on Susan's face killed it.

She's being genuinely nice to me, Luna told herself. *Being girly isn't going to kill me.*

So she accepted the gift, surprised to find that they were the perfect size as she slid her foot into it. She buckled it and moved onto the next foot, wobbling. Susan caught her arm, helping her right herself.

"Is this the first time you've worn high heels?"

"Yeah," Luna admitted sheepishly.

"Well, you'll get the hang of them in no time, I promise." It was then that Luna realized she'd been wearing high heels the entire time yet had moved with such grace. "In fact, let me help you with your nerves," she said and dug inside her big yellow bag again. When she emerged, she held a silver flask in her hand. She unscrewed it and took a sip before burping and passing it to Luna. "Drink."

Luna crinkled her nose at the smell of the booze inside. "What is it?"

"Liquid courage," Sarah said, snagging the flask. She took two gulps and handed it to Luna.

Luna's lip quivered with indecision, thinking of all her father had said about alcohol. Then she took it and sipped. The liquid scorched down to her stomach, and she coughed, handing the flask back to Susan. "That burns!"

Susan chuckled and handed it to Maddie before she capped it and put it back in her bag. "That means it's working."

Maddie looked at her watch. "It's officially time to get on the road."

"Sounds good to me," Susan said, looping her arm through Luna's. "Let's go."

Chapter Thirteen

LUNA WAS NERVOUS about the rest of her night, but in the car with Susan, Sarah, and Maddie belting out "Girls Just Wanna Have Fun" by Cyndi Lauper, it was somehow easy to forget that. Until Susan parked in the parking lot, of course. It seemed there were way more vehicles than she was used to.

Luna felt lightheaded as she got out of the car. The sensation of *What am I doing here?* flooded her mind. Susan didn't seem to notice. She helped Luna walk across the parking lot, keeping her from stumbling. Luna was grateful and found that the longer she walked, the easier it became. By the time they merged with the line outside the gym, she was able to walk without Susan's help.

Balloons, streamers, and lights had been hung around the doors. Beside the entrance, the school's counselor, Miss Lopez, stamped everyone's hands after verifying that they were students at the school. Susan, Sarah, and Maddie got stamped, then it was Luna's turn. She held her hand up, watching the blue ink smear on her skin.

"Have fun," Miss Lopez said and turned to the next in line.

"Ready, girls?" Susan asked, leading the way inside.

Inside the gym, the regular lights were dimmed, strobe lights taking their place. Balloons and streamers lined the walls and hung on the ceiling. There was a table with a punch bowl and snacks along one wall. On the other was a row of chairs. At the far end of the gym was a makeshift stage with a microphone stand, drum set, and guitar. Luna wondered who they would have play.

"They really went all out," Maddie said.

"Wonder if there's any good snacks," Sarah mumbled, making her way toward the table.

Luna wondered the same.

"Let's find out," Susan said. "Coming, Luna?"

Luna looked longingly at the chairs. "I'll catch up. I think I need to fix the strap on my shoe."

"Suit yourself," Susan said, and the three girls parted from Luna.

She stayed by the door, surveying the familiar faces for a sign of Chance or Violet. She didn't see either one and wondered about her best friend. Luna had assumed she would be one of the first ones here.

Must've not gotten a date, she mused and had a moment where she felt guilty for being here without her.

Luna pushed thoughts of Violet aside and crossed the gym, relieved when she plopped down in the chair and took her weight off her feet. The tiny stroll across the parking lot had hurt more than she'd anticipated, and she tried to imagine how she would get through the rest of the night like this. She loosened the strap enough to get the buckle to stop digging into her flesh.

I should've brought my boots to change out of these. There was no telling how long she would be here. Most likely Susan and her friends would want to stay until the end. And they seemed like the type to go to after-parties too. *I didn't think this through.* Her father would be back home long before she was. *Sidra. I'll tell him I was with Sidra.* If he asked, Miss Sidra would likely cover for her anyway.

"You really are beautiful, you know," a familiar voice said from the crowd.

Luna jumped and looked up from her shoe into sapphire blue eyes. The low lights made them more severe. Chance. Luna's gaze wandered behind him to Susan, Sarah, and Maddie at the snack table. None of them came to help. She could've felt betrayed, but she'd made the choice to separate from the group so she had no one to blame but herself.

He must've been waiting. She studied him over. He was wearing a tuxedo, his usually messy blond hair subdued into slick shining locks. He'd actually taken the time to clean himself up for this.

Something about that made her feel weird.

"No one can hear you so go ahead and say what you're really thinking."

Chance slunk into the empty seat next to her. "That *is* what I'm thinking. You are beautiful."

"Instead of bugging me, why don't you go talk to Susan," Luna said, pointing to her on the other side of the gym. "She's beautiful *and* she's crazy about you."

"I guess. She's my friend."

"So that means you can't hang out with her instead of

me?" she asked.

He caught her eye. "It's complicated." Luna was ready to tell him it really wasn't hard at all when he opened his jacket and pulled out a rose. "This is for you. You probably don't want it, but it suits you."

She took it slowly, careful of the thorns. "What am I supposed to do with it?"

He jammed his hands in his pockets. "Thought you might like it."

Luna didn't want to admit that she *did* like it. She'd never had a boy give her a gift before and didn't know how to react. She wanted to sniff the vibrant red petals, but at the same time, she didn't want to do anything that would give him the impression she appreciated the gesture.

She looked at Susan again, hoping that the girl would pick up on how uncomfortable she was and come to her rescue. Instead, she realized there were several pairs of eyes on her. Girls she did and didn't recognize. She could almost *hear* the whispers and swallowed, looking down at the floor.

"What's the matter?" Chance asked, looking where she'd gazed a second before. "Don't like the paparazzi?"

"No," she said. "They're talking about us."

"And?"

"It's uncomfortable."

"Oh, loosen up," he said, smirking at the onlookers before he stood from his seat. He offered her his hand. "How about we dance?"

"I really don't want to," she said.

Chance blinked slowly at her, hand stubbornly still held out.

"You're not going to take no for an answer, are you?" she asked, trying to keep herself from being visibly upset. She wished Nazir were in the same grade as her. He'd never leave her alone at something like this.

"Seems you know me well."

Annoyed, Luna started to reach for his hand and stopped. "If I dance with you once, will you leave me alone for the rest of the night?"

"I'll consider it," he said, grabbing her hand before she could pull it back.

His skin was clammy, as if he'd been sweating. Her instant reaction was to pull away, but he closed his fingers around hers. Gently, he guided her up out of the seat and led her to the middle of the dance floor, smiling as he did so.

Through the crowd, Luna caught a glimpse of Susan looking in their direction. She tried to signal to her, but Susan either didn't notice or didn't care because she turned to her sister.

The music was slow and lilting as Chance pulled her to him. He wrapped his arm around her waist, keeping their bodies pressed together as he propped her hands up on his shoulders. Primarily she was annoyed with the situation, but a new feeling was starting to become apparent. She'd never been this close to a boy before. The places where his hands rested sent electricity through her, and she hated the feeling. She shuffled a bit, hoping to lessen some of the intensity, but it didn't help.

As they stepped to the music, she looked up into his face,

searching for any signs of compassion. "Why do you do this stuff to me?" Luna asked, wondering how he could look so calm, so *content,* when she'd made it apparent that she wasn't happy around him.

"Do what?"

"The date thing with Violet? Getting Susan to lure me here for you? I can't wrap my brain around it. What is it you want from me?"

He breathed out. "I can't tell you."

Luna halted, trying to break free of his grasp. "Seriously?"

"You're going to find out, okay? And . . . you probably won't like it. I want us to be somewhat connected for when that day comes so you won't fight me."

Luna didn't like any part of the statement. Paired with the dead expression in his eyes, it scared her. "What are you planning to do to me? Does Susan know?" she asked. Now she *did* feel betrayed. If Chance *was* planning her harm, would Susan help him?

"No, she doesn't," he whispered. "No one does."

Luna stumbled backward a step, confused. "Does this have to do with what you hide in your pocket?" she demanded and reached toward him, ready to end the mystery once and for all.

The couples who'd been dancing around them looked at her. Chance caught her wrist easily, offered friendly smiles to the crowd, then pulled Luna against himself. He pressed his forehead to hers and whispered, "I don't hide anything, okay? Now drop it."

Luna couldn't shake the uneasiness that he'd stirred in her. His proximity made it worse, and she wondered where Susan and Sarah had gone, wishing they would appear to save her.

"We're ready to start playing," a voice said over the microphone.

Chance's head lifted as he looked in the direction of the stage, and Luna let out the smallest breath in relief.

"Can we get a volunteer to help us out?"

A dozen people shouted for Chance to do it. Luna dared a glance into his eyes and noticed that strange gleam was still there. It was clear he didn't want to, though. What he *did* want to do, Luna had no clue.

"Sure. Why not?" he murmured at last.

Finally, he let go of her and moved through the cheering crowd toward the stage. Luna almost expected him to look back, to warn her not to move, but he didn't. She wiped her sweaty hands on her dress, watching as he took his place on the stage, microphone gripped in one hand. He looked at ease, as if he weren't the center of attention . . . or he was so used to it that it didn't faze him. "Every Breath You Take" by The Police started to play, and Luna inhaled deeply, watching as he dipped subtly toward the mic. As soon as he started to sing, the girls around her swooned.

Luna didn't join in. She continued that detailed analysis of him, but she couldn't pick out anything specific that made her dislike him. From this view, he looked like any of her other classmates.

He sang, eyes flashing in the light when they zeroed in on

her:

> *"Oh, can't you see*
> *You belong to me?"*
> 93

Luna shivered. There was something *off* about him. That much was clear. Something that separated him from the other teenage boys and made him a danger to the people who called him *friend.*

Chapter Fourteen

VIOLET SHOVED THE last three cans of green beans onto the shelf and let out a breath. Her headband was filled with sweat, and she took it off, cramming it in her pocket. Double truck days had to be her least favorite part about working in a grocery store, and if that wasn't bad enough, it happened to coincide with prom night. Not that it mattered much to her anyway. She hadn't been able to get a date, and she'd lost track of how many people she'd asked to go with her.

If it's not meant to be, it's not meant to be, she told herself but it brought her little peace as she lumbered to the time clock.

She punched out and called goodbye to her boss before she gathered her things and started the walk home. Prom had started an hour ago. She considered trying to hurry up and catch the last few minutes but shot it down. It would be over by the time she got home, showered, changed, and made it to school.

I wonder if Luna went, Violet thought as she crossed the street.

She thought her friend had been against the idea of the dance altogether. Then she'd skipped school to hang out with the *"it"* crowd, and Violet felt as if she didn't know Luna at all. If she thought too much about it, she could've hurt her own feelings.

I pushed her away, she thought when she remembered the

night at the restaurant.

At home, she barely had the energy to eat a snack and shower before she collapsed in bed. She tried to sleep, but her mind continued to whirl. To wonder what she was missing out on. Not going to prom was a decision she was going to regret for the rest of her life. Or maybe she was just tired. This was day two of not sleeping. No matter what she did, a headache coursed through the front of her brain.

Violet hoped Luna was having a better time than she was. Settling into bed, she closed her eyes in another attempt to sleep and hoped *someone* would have a good night.

***

WITH THE LIGHTS overhead bearing down on him, it was tough for Chance to see out into the crowd. Luna's shape was easy to decipher. She was the only one standing still, and he almost admired that. While the girls around her were turning to puddles, she stood firm. About halfway through the song, he watched her turn and begin to make her way through the crowd, but he was helpless to stop her. Chance tried to wipe the distress off his face as he finished the song. As soon as he was done, he dropped the mic and ran offstage, ignoring the girls singing him praises, worried that Luna would already be long gone by the time he got outside.

She stood by the edge of the parking lot when he found her, shoes in hand. As casually as he could manage, he strolled to her side. "I didn't think my singing was that bad."

She side-eyed him like he was a dangerous animal she was wary of drawing too close to. "Not that. I'm just ready to go home."

"So you're carrying your shoes?"

She looked at them, frustrated, then back toward the doors of the gym. "Where's Susan?"

The last time he'd seen the trio, Sarah and the brown-haired girl had snuck outside to smoke cigarettes. Susan was somewhere under the bleachers getting felt up by her second choice for a date, but he didn't want to tell her any of that.

"I haven't seen them," he said and stuck his hands in his pockets.

Luna's face hardened as she gazed into the dark parking lot. "This is just great."

"What's the matter? Don't have a ride?" he asked, barely able to suppress his glee.

"No," she said. "I'm not exactly supposed to be here. If I'm late, my dad will kill me. Normally, I'd walk home, but . . ." she trailed off, glaring at the yellow shoes.

"Ah. Quite the dilemma," he said, breathing in a lungful of her perfume on the breeze. "You know, I have a truck. I *could* drive you home."

"I'd rather you not," she said bluntly.

"Suit yourself," he said and started to walk back toward the gym.

Ten seconds later, Luna said, "Wait."

He turned back toward her. She was stiff, her hands balled up into fists, and he could tell she didn't want to ask what she was about to.

"Yes?"

"I'll trust you just this once," she said, and it looked as if it caused her physical pain to get the words out. "Would you mind . . . driving me home?"

"I would be honored," he said, giving her a wolfish grin. He snagged his keys out of his pocket and added, "Come on."

Reluctantly, she started to follow him, and his heart soared. In spite of the questions she'd asked in the gym, she had to have some degree of trust in him to make this request.

She shouldn't, a little voice spoke up.

He ignored it, opened the door and closed it behind her before he got into the driver's seat. As he started to drive, his fingers clenched around the steering wheel. Luna shifted in her seat, piling her shoes and the rose onto her lap. Chance blinked, furiously trying to clear the sensation of losing himself. His foot pushed a little harder on the gas and he took a sharp turn leading out of town.

Luna stiffened. "Chance, this isn't the way to my house," she said, a slight waver to her voice.

Fear. She's scared of me. "I know," he said and dared a glance at her from the corner of his eye. "We're going back to my house."

"What? Why?" Luna asked, some of the fear giving way to anger. "I thought you understood. I'm trying to get home *quickly.*"

"I'm having an after-party at my place," he said.

He didn't look at her again, almost afraid to see what emotion would be on her face. Being alone with her in his truck, in the same place Kate had been minutes before he killed her, made Chance worry he'd slip into *that* mind.

He tried to imagine doing to her what he had to Kate. Luna looked over at him, the rose he'd given her clutched carefully in her hand. While he couldn't tell what she was thinking, she didn't suspect how dark his thoughts were. Or maybe she did. It would explain why she seemed so uneasy around him.

Puffing his cheeks, he turned his attention back to the road and wondered what she would do when she saw the broken-down building he called his home. She already knew something was off about him, but she knew nothing about how deep the rabbit hole went.

Not yet anyway.

Chapter Fifteen

THE RIDE SEEMED to go on forever and ever, made longer by the uncomfortable silence. Luna imagined this was what it felt like to be kidnapped.

He wouldn't do that, she told herself. *He's weird, but he'd never hurt you.*

That brought her little comfort when she remembered how easily he'd crushed that bird beneath his boot. She glanced at him from the corner of her eye. What was going through his mind? Every few seconds, his eyes flashed in the passing streetlights. The same *dangerous* look he'd had on stage was back. She hugged herself, trying to curl closer to the window and away from him.

She wasn't crazy about the idea of going to a party, but it made sense. The popular kids partied a lot. That was why Susan had brought her flask, wasn't it?

This is what it means to be social, she mused, thinking that she hadn't missed out on much by staying to herself for the majority of her high school years.

When Chance finally parked the car, she couldn't see anything beyond the window. She was so lost in her head that she hadn't noticed when they left the city and entered the woods. The night seemed to swallow everything. That paranoid feeling that she was in danger came back, solidified when Chance turned off the engine.

"We're here," he said.

Luna squinted, trying to better see through the darkness beyond the window. "Where's here?"

Chance climbed out of the truck without answering, and she hesitated in her seat. She couldn't see or hear sounds of a party. If there wasn't one, why would he drag her all the way out here? *Nothing good happens in the woods at night,* she thought and looked at the shoes and rose in her lap. They wouldn't make for a good weapon if she needed to fight her way out of this.

The door opened, and Chance grinned at her. "Come on. The house isn't far."

"I don't . . . see a house," she said.

"It's kind of hidden. You gotta walk a little bit."

"Can't you take me home instead?" she asked.

"You can go home later," he said, waving off her concern.

Luna had the feeling that he wouldn't drive her back to town regardless of how many times she asked. She'd never bothered to get her license, so she couldn't do it. Not wanting to show weakness, she said, "Okay," and put her shoes back on. Walking on concrete with them had been a challenge. In the grass? It was nearly impossible.

She wobbled, and Chance caught her by the arm.

"How far of a walk is it?" she asked, pulling herself out of his grasp.

"It's right up here," he said, undeterred.

Luna scrutinized a huge towering oak tree as they passed

it, wondering if there was *anything* up ahead or if this was all part of the plans he'd mentioned in the gym. This was turning into a worse nightmare than getting a scolding from her father. Keeping her concerns to herself, she stayed alert of Chance's movements as they walked through a black gate. Beyond it sat a run-down two-story house. Dark siding nearly blended it into the night. Some of the shingles on the roof were missing, and she could imagine more than that had been stripped away through time.

"*That's* your house?" Luna asked.

He had to be pulling her leg. This was a joke. No one, especially him, could live in a place like this.

Chance said nothing. He continued onward as if she hadn't spoken. Not wanting to be left alone, Luna followed through the knee-high grass, somehow managing not to fall and hurt her ankle. The boards of the porch creaked under her feet, and she could easily imagine falling right through. The door hung on its hinges at an angle that made it impossible to close all the way. Chance propped it open, then met her eyes, expecting her to go first. She peered inside, searching for light or hoping to hear movement. He'd said it was a party, but it was dark and silent. Like staring into the maw of a mausoleum.

"I don't want to go in there," she said, thinking the woods were probably safer.

Rolling his eyes, he grasped her arm and pulled her inside like she weighed nothing. The old door rattled shut behind them, submerging them in blackness. Chance's hand slipped off her arm, and a moment later, a tiny light pushed away the shadows. Chance had lit a candle. It wasn't much, but it allowed Luna to study the inside of the house. They stood in a living room with a high ceiling. Two light-colored couches covered in plastic faced one another near an old stone fireplace. A coffee table sat in the middle of them. Across the room, there was a hallway and beside that, a staircase.

Chance walked through the living room, setting down his candle on the table before he lit another one that was perched on the edge of the fireplace. "Come sit down," he said, leaning against the wall beside it.

Luna couldn't get her skin to stop crawling. "Are . . . are your parents home?"

Chance breathed out, tipping his head to scratch his neck as he said, "I don't live with my parents. Some *unfortunate* circumstances happened, and long story short, I got emancipated from them."

"Oh," Luna said, twining her fingers.

They were alone in the middle of nowhere. *How did I let this happen?* she asked herself, thinking back to how innocent her life had been only a couple hours before.

Chance grabbed a glass bottle from its place beside the candle and sat down on the couch. "It's not much. But it's something."

"You said you were having a *party*," she said.

He took a gulp of the liquid, swishing it around his mouth before he swallowed and said, "Who says there has to be a lot of people for it to be considered a party?"

"This isn't what I pictured."

"This is a lot gentler," he said and sat forward, elbows

resting on his knees. "Besides, I thought you weren't a fan of all that anyway."

"I'm not," she said. While she hated big social gatherings, she might've preferred it to this. This was *awkward*. Painfully so.

"You can stop looking like that," he said. "I'm not going to hurt you."

Luna wanted to believe that, but things had gotten so weird that the only thing she was certain of was that she wanted to be far away from here. She glanced warily down the nearest hallway before she perched herself on the edge of the couch. It smelled musty, and the plastic crinkled uncomfortably beneath her.

Chance picked up the bottle and held it toward her, an offering. "Want some?"

Luna remembered the sip she'd taken from Susan's flask and shook her head. "I'll pass."

"Suit yourself," he said and took a few more gulps before setting the bottle on the table. "Tell me what's on your mind."

"That I want to go home."

"Hmm," he said, letting his gaze wander across the room. "I thought what I said earlier would be on your mind."

Luna didn't think it would help to mention the fact that he was right. When his eyes landed on her, it felt as if he were seeing *through* her, and she struggled to come up with a response. "I-I have to go to the bathroom," she blurted out, desperate for any kind of escape. The intense look on Chance's face was too much for her to bear.

He pointed to the nearby hallway. "First door on the left."

Luna bobbed her head and stood up, disappearing into the darkness of the hall. She set her hand on the wall, following it into the shadows. If he was going to insist on bringing her here and didn't want to answer any of her questions, she would do a little investigating. Once she reached the bathroom, she peeked over her shoulder to see if Chance was watching. He wasn't. She continued down the hallway, but the doors on the right side of the corridor were locked.

When she reached the end, she turned back, checking the doors on the opposite side. One of them swung open quietly, and Luna stepped inside. Like the living room, candles lit the space. Her eyes were drawn to them and the space on the wall that the light illuminated: an inverted five-pointed star with various sigils drawn in bright red. The floor was littered with white things. At first, she thought they were discarded plastic pieces. Maybe old bowls and plates. Then she looked harder and realized they were *bones*. Hundreds of them, varying in size and level of decay. Sucking in a breath, she ducked out into the dark hall, shaking as she tried to process what she saw. As quietly as she could, she pulled the door closed.

Inside her mind, she screamed. When he had mentioned *plans,* did it have something to do with this? *What the fuck?* She eyed the window, wondering if she could get through it to escape. *Then what?* she asked herself. She didn't know how deep they were in the woods and if she could make it out without getting lost.

He's my ticket out of here.

Somehow, she managed to get herself together enough to go back into the living room.

Chance looked up from the bottle. "You were gone a long time. Is everything all right?"

"Yeah, I um . . . fell in the hallway, is all," she said, hating how awkward her voice was. She tried to offset it with a small laugh that probably only made it worse.

He pinned her with his blue eyes, waiting so long to speak again that she thought he suspected what she'd done. "I didn't hear the toilet flush," he said and rose to his feet.

Caught. She was caught. "I uh . . . didn't flush."

Chance crinkled his nose before he glanced up at the wall. A clock was hidden in the shadows. "All right, well . . . it's getting late. I guess I should take you home. Unless you want to stay the night?" Luna shook her head vigorously, and he laughed. "Relax. It's a joke." After what she'd seen, Luna wondered if anything would ever feel like a joke again. Something on her face must've given away her fear because he asked, "Are you okay?"

Luna forced herself to hold his gaze. Each time she looked away, she only made herself look more suspicious. "Yeah. I'm fine. Exhausted," she said and let out a fake yawn. She would've gone so far as to rub her eyes, too, if it wouldn't risk smearing her mascara.

"I'm pretty tired, too," he admitted. "Let's get you home."

As they walked out of the house and through the dark field toward his truck, Luna's mind went from the bird he had killed to the sigils in his back room. Chance was up to something dark, and whatever that something was, it somehow included her.

Chapter Sixteen

AFTER CHANCE DROPPED Luna off, he felt as if he couldn't get home fast enough. His entire body buzzed with anxious energy, and he wanted it gone. He passed by the Cross sisters' home on the way and considered stopping in. A blue SUV in the driveway changed his mind. It wasn't that he *disliked* Susan and Sarah's mother, he just preferred to visit when she wasn't home. So he kept driving all the way out of town and into the woods. On his way through the trees, he passed the spot where Kate had spent her final moments and felt comfort in his misdeeds. At last, he made it home and turned off the truck. He sat behind the wheel for a long time, wondering where the evening had gone wrong.

With a heavy sigh, he slid out of the driver's seat and went into his house. On his way through the living room, he grabbed the whiskey bottle off the table and headed to his bedroom. The room was nearly empty, with the exception of his beat-up old mattress in the far corner. He didn't need anything else. Chance dropped onto the mattress, doing his best to get comfortable on the uncomfortable surface, and propped himself up against the wall.

He took a heavy swig of the stout liquid until his stomach was warm and his throat hurt. He wanted to stop thinking about how he had failed so badly. Something about the way Luna had looked at him bothered him. She was different from other people, and so were the emotions she sparked in him. Her clear disgust for him should've made it easy to loathe her right back, but he couldn't. She *intrigued* him. When he'd first started talking to her, it had been a game. How long would it take to get the ice queen to melt? It was at best, something to pass the time.

That wasn't the case anymore.

What a mess.

He lifted the bottom of the cold glass to his forehead, enjoying the sensation. Chance had been on his own for so long that he'd forgotten what it was like to care about someone else. It felt like a chink in his armor, something that could be exploited. A weakness. What was a snake without its venom?

Caring for her could be a good thing, he tried to tell himself but shot it down when he remembered the look on Luna's face.

It was bogus.

Chapter Seventeen

LUNA BARELY SLEPT a wink, waking long before her father. She made them breakfast as she waited, not so patiently, for time to pass. When the library opened for the day, she was the first one there.

All night she'd pondered her mission, and it had seemed so clear cut. Seeing how massive the library was put things into perspective. Shelf after shelf of books filled the place. She didn't want to ask the librarian for help because if her father or anyone at her mosque suspected she was looking into the occult, she would have a lot of explaining to do. She made her way over to the massive filing cabinet in the middle of the library. The drawers were filled with meticulously organized cards.

Where to begin? she thought, imagining how much time it would take to properly search one drawer, not to mention the entire cabinet.

Religion seemed an appropriate place to start, but pawing through the cards led her to nothing that seemed particularly useful.

I need books on the occult.

But there was nothing under that topic either. Resigned, she closed the drawer.

"Can I help you find something?" a voice asked from

behind her.

Luna jumped and turned to see a woman. She looked to be in her mid-twenties with a purple blouse and matching pencil skirt. A name tag pinned to her shirt read *Dori, Assistant Librarian*. She pushed her glasses up the bridge of her nose and said, "I didn't mean to startle you."

"It's okay," Luna said quietly. This experience was better than the last time someone had scared her. "I actually *do* need your help."

"Of course. What are you looking for?" she asked, sounding more than happy to lend her knowledge.

Luna threaded her fingers together, trying to think of a way to explain herself while receiving the least amount of judgment. "I um . . . have a paper on paganism," she said, not sure if the woman would buy the excuse. "And I need something that discusses the rituals and symbols of their practices."

"Oh," she said, holding a hand to her chest. "What class is this for?"

Luna's heart raced. She hated everything about lying, and she wasn't good at it. So she didn't try to come up with a follow-up.

"Well, um, let me see what we've got," Dori said after an uncomfortable moment of silence. She pulled open a drawer and rifled through the cards so fast Luna wondered if she were reading them or if she'd memorized all the information on each one. She plucked one out and read it over before she pulled a pen and sticky note from her fanny pack, jotting down the details.

"Try this one," she said, extending the note to Luna.

"Thank you," she said, taking it. She narrowed her eyes to read the nearest plaque.

With a patient smile, Dori pointed toward the other side of the library. She wandered from the art books to books about animals and plants to baby books. Eventually she came across a section with titles like *Ghosts and the Paranormal Experience, Tarot for Dummies,* and *The Exclusive Guide to the Occult.*

This seems to be the right place, Luna thought after looking at the note again. She pulled the book from the shelf. It was heavy, and she leafed through it, imagining how long it would take to read all of it. Most likely she'd be in the library all day because she couldn't bring the book home. And if it didn't help, she certainly wasn't going to ask the librarian for other recommendations.

This will *help,* she told herself and settled into a table at the back of the study area. Somewhere she hoped would gather the least amount of attention from anyone passing by.

With a deep breath, she opened it and started to read. The text was so small, so smushed together, she would have a headache by the end of the day. Time passed, and the words started to blur together, none of them making sense. She rubbed her eyes, determined to keep going. She started to get antsy, flipping through the pages to look at the pictures, halting only when she reached a section labeled *Sigils.*

The images showed symbols far different than any of those she'd seen at Chance's house, but this section was the closest so far to answering her questions.

She began to read.

Symbols throughout the years have been associated with worship of various deities, their purposes varying.

Luna stopped reading, staring at the wall. What exactly did Chance believe in? Which *deity* did he worship? An evil being would explain the bones. And how had he *gotten* all those bones? Had he sacrificed those animals? Or had he collected them from the woods?

So many unanswered questions.

Luna sat back in her chair, wishing she *was* crazy and this was all in her head. It would make explaining everything so much simpler. As she returned the book to the shelf, she couldn't forget the fact that she was, as far as she knew, sane.

ON THE WALK home, Luna mulled over all she had learned, not feeling better about any of it. Especially when she took into account Chance's cryptic phrases at the restaurant and prom. If his odd beliefs had anything to do with her, it wasn't going to be good. She was scared, actually *afraid* of what she had seen in his house, and no matter how she tried to talk herself down, it didn't work.

Luna decided to stop by Sidra's rather than going straight home. On the weekends, Nazir was there to look after her, so Luna's presence wasn't *needed,* but she hoped she would be welcome anyway.

She looped around the block, enjoying the stroll through this part of town. Since Sidra lived so close to the park, there were more trees here than in the rest of town. Not like Luna's own neighborhood with houses squished together. On a normal day, she enjoyed it. After last night, though, they reminded her of the forest Chance had taken her to.

Luna crossed the grass toward the house. The front of the building jutted out, marked only with one large window. Beside it ran the deck that led to the front door nestled away from immediate sight. Luna approached the door, smelling the lunch Nazir had cooking inside. She took it all in for a minute—the warmth, the safety, the security. These were feelings her own home should've inspired in her, but they hadn't for some time.

Maybe the space will do you some good.

Maybe it would.

Luna knocked softly.

The heavy wood door popped open, and Nazir raised one confused eyebrow as he pushed open the glass door. "Luna? Is everything okay?"

"Is it okay if I come in?" she asked.

Nazir agreed and stepped aside. "What brings you by?" he asked as Luna sat on the couch. The living room looked the same as it always did when she visited, but with Nazir present, it seemed somehow smaller. As if she was always too close to him no matter where she chose to sit. Before she could answer, he called, "Grandma! Look who stopped by."

Sidra appeared at the end of the hall, her loose nightgown making her look skinnier than Luna was used to. "Luna, dear! What a pleasant surprise."

"How are you, Miss Sidra?" Luna returned politely.

"Good, good," she said and sat in her usual armchair by the window. "How are things going at home?"

"They're fine." In light of her experience the night before, the bickering with her father didn't seem so important.

"That's good. I was watching some TV."

"You know she can't get enough of her cop dramas," Nazir said playfully.

Sidra waved a hand at him. "You hush now."

Luna giggled and relaxed into the seat. An hour or so passed, and they ate lunch. Nazir helped get Sidra seated back in her chair in front of the television, diet pop in her hand. Luna looked up at the clock. So much of the day had gone by already, and her father would be anxious for her to return.

"Time to go?" Nazir guessed.

"Yeah, I probably should start heading back or Dad will worry," Luna said and got up from her seat. "It was good to see you, Miss Sidra."

"Bye, sweetheart," she said, not taking her eyes off the television.

Nazir hopped up from his seat and walked Luna to the door. She took her time getting her shoes on, that usual feeling of apprehension alive in her stomach again. She didn't want to go home.

"I don't mean to pry or anything, but what have you *really* been up to today?" Nazir asked quietly after ensuring that Sidra wasn't paying attention to their conversation.

Luna slid on her other boot, standing to his level. "I was at the library."

Nazir followed her onto the porch, pulling the door shut behind him as he asked, "Why? Most people sleep in on Saturday morning."

Luna looked at her hands, stomach twisting with the idea of telling someone what she'd seen.

He must've sensed something was off because he added, "Does it have something to do with the situation at the restaurant the other day?" He made a face. "Are you actually sneaking around with that guy?"

"No!" Luna blurted out, hating the heat that flushed her face. It only made her look guilty. "I'm not."

"Really?" Nazir asked, not looking as if he believed her. "Cuz prom was last night, wasn't it? Now here you are acting weird."

Luna sighed. There was no use trying to lie to Nazir. He was at the age where he could get information from her classmates if necessary but also old enough to hold weight with the adults in her mosque at the same time. If he really wanted to find something out, he could and *would*. "Yes, it was. And yes, I did go, but not with him. At least not on purpose. I thought I was going with friends, but they kind of abandoned me."

"That happens to you a lot, doesn't it?"

Luna cut her eyes at him, not in the mood to be reminded.

"Okay," Nazir said. "I feel like I'm missing part of the story here. How does being ditched at prom lead to you going to the library?"

Luna tucked her lip in her teeth, imagining the room with the sigils and bones. *He's going to think I've lost my mind,* she told herself. "It's . . . hard to explain."

"Ah," Nazir said, not looking as if he understood, but he

didn't push the conversation further, much to her relief. "Whatever the case, be careful walking around town alone, okay? They have no information about what happened to that Kate girl."

"I will," Luna said. But it was a promise she didn't have the power to make.

Chapter Eighteen

WHEN MONDAY MORNING came around, Luna's head pounded with a fresh migraine, courtesy of the poor sleep she'd gotten over the weekend. Saturday *and* Sunday had gifted her with nightmares that made it hard to sleep longer than a few hours. Both nights she'd found herself awake before three in the morning and unable to go back to bed to rectify it. That, coupled with what she'd seen at Chance's house and the conversation she'd had with Nazir, made her feel disconnected from her daily routine as she forced herself to walk to school.

I have four more weeks of this. That's all, she told herself as a sort of pep talk. She didn't feel better. A lot of things could happen in a month.

Luna made it to the usual meetup place with Violet, but her friend wasn't there. That didn't surprise her. Several times throughout the weekend, she called Violet, but she hadn't answered.

She's avoiding me. Sure, Luna had been upset about the restaurant thing, but not so upset that she wanted to cut contact.

The sound of footsteps came from behind her, and she looked up, heart hammering until she realized it was Violet. "There you are," Luna said, turning her gaze back toward the road as they started to walk. "Thought you were avoiding me again."

"No, just running late," Violet said, struggling to catch her breath. "I had a late shift last night.

"Ah," Luna said, feeling guilty for her earlier assumptions. *Assume ignorance before malice,* she told herself.

Violet adjusted the straps of her backpack and said, "So . . . elephant in the room. How was prom?"

Luna side-eyed her. "Don't get me started."

"Oh, come on. Hanging out with the popular girls? Had to be a hoot. Especially since I thought you *weren't going* to prom."

Luna huffed, thinking of how the girls had seemingly abandoned her. "You heard a lot for not actually showing up. Which, I have to say, boggles my mind since you talked about it every day for the past month."

Violet looked away. "I wanted to go, but my schedule changed. Besides, you know how I felt about going alone."

"You could've come with us."

"I didn't want to do a friends date, Luna."

Luna couldn't keep the venom to herself. "Yeah, well, I didn't want to go at all."

"Oh, come on. You can't tell me you didn't have any fun," Violet insisted.

Luna wanted to stay firm in her argument, but the start of the night, before she wound up alone, *had* been fun. It'd been a taste of what life could be like if she had a different, less studious personality.

"Did you go to any after-parties?" Violet continued. "There had to be at least *one* good one."

I'm having an after-party at my place. Chills ran down Luna's spine.

"No. The *after-party* Chance took me to wasn't a party at all. It was me and him alone in this abandoned house," Luna said, mentally chastising herself for getting in the truck with him to begin with.

"Weird."

"That's putting it lightly," Luna said, unamused. "Color me disturbed because *he's* weird. He said it was his house."

Violet made a face, and Luna hoped that meant her words were finally registering. If she could get *one* person on the same page as her, it would make coping with what she saw a lot easier. "His parents weren't there?"

"According to him, he's emancipated from them."

Violet quirked her lip into an awkward grimace. "What does that mean?"

"It means he legally has responsibility for himself. For whatever reason, his parents must've been deemed unfit or unsuitable."

"Huh," Violet mused. "I should ask him how he did that."

Luna tried to ignore the pity in her gut—the feeling that came from hearing the sadness in her friend's voice. It couldn't be easy to love parents who simply didn't love you back. Luna was lucky for the fact that at least she could guarantee she had her mother's love. That might've been true for Violet once upon a time, but she'd died when Violet was young, leaving her under the care of her abusive father for the majority of her life.

"The whole thing was weird." Luna continued, remembering the uneasy feeling of the place. "I doubt that's actually where he lives. I mean, there wasn't any electricity or running water and . . ."

Violet furrowed her brow. "And?"

"I think he was trying to scare me or something," Luna said. "It's the only thing that makes sense. The popular girls invited me to prom so he could take me out somewhere and scare me."

Violet shrugged. "Maybe. To me, it just sounds like he was trying to get you alone."

Luna ran her tongue along her teeth, wondering how much she should push the subject. Nazir hadn't been fazed, but she'd not been willing to tell him she'd gone to his house alone. She considered Nazir her friend but also worried that if she crossed the wrong boundaries, he would report it to her father. She didn't have those fears with Violet. *I told her this much,* she reminded herself, *might as well put it all out there.* "There was this creepy room in the back of the house. With candles . . . and stuff."

"So?"

Luna felt her cheeks flush with frustration. She was selling the room short, but she couldn't bring herself to share what she had seen, what she had *learned.* In the light of day, it all felt ridiculous. Unreal. That house was old, maybe the sigils and bones had been there before Chance moved in.

The candles were lit. He keeps up on it.

"I think you're stressed out and had a bad dream, is all," Violet said with an apathetic shrug. "It happens."

"Yeah, except that wasn't what happened because I remember my dream that night. It was the one where I saw you die. I had it a lot this weekend actually. It's been hard to sleep."

"Okay, that was funny the first time you mentioned it, but now it kind of bums me out," Violet said, jutting out her bottom lip.

"Not like I can control what I dream about."

"They say whatever you think and talk about the most comes out of your subconscious through your dreams. I know there's been some tension between us lately, and that's probably the reason for it."

Luna opened her mouth to make a rebuttal. There was more she could say to make her point, a *lot* more, but it was clear that Violet didn't believe her.

No point in beating a dead horse, she thought, and the words she'd been about to say crawled back into her throat.

Awkward silence fell on them, and it stayed until their splitting point. Today, Luna was glad to see Violet go. Maybe when she saw her at lunch, she'd be able to better articulate her thoughts.

As Luna started to ascend the stairs to the front door, she noticed the hush that passed over the group of popular kids hanging out at the base of the staircase. Her skin crawled under their stares. She'd had nightmares like this where people watched her everywhere she went until it felt like she was being hunted.

Luna wasn't in the mood. She dared a glance at them, but they openly stared back as if she were some kind of otherworldly creature. She had prom to blame for this. Dancing with Chance in front of everyone had been a statement. People were going to look at her differently. Maybe expect different things from her too.

Whatever. She brushed off the looks and approached the set of double doors.

Right before she pulled them open, a pair of arms snaked around her waist, bringing her backpack against solid muscle. Heavy cologne flooded her nostrils and her mouth, and she screamed in surprise before laughter filled her ears. She broke free and spun around to see Chance laughing at her.

"You scared the hell out of me. That *wasn't* funny!" she yelled, holding onto the edge of the door for balance. The kids at the base of the stairs stared up at them, and her entire body shook with adrenaline. She hated Chance a little more.

"Depends on who you ask."

Muttering a string of curses under her breath, Luna turned away and took two steps into the school as she said, "Geez, what did you do before coming to school? Bathe in cologne to hide the smell of death?"

She didn't hear him coming. One moment, she was walking, and the next, Chance grabbed her. One arm was wrapped around her waist and the other on her wrist in a way that looked almost *playful* to the people they passed, but his grip was tight enough to hurt.

She tried unsuccessfully to free herself. "Ouch! You're hurting me. Let me go!" she demanded, but when he didn't let her go, she froze.

Chance kicked open the door of the nearby girls' bathroom and dragged her inside. No one was in there, and he took advantage of that, pinning her against the beige wall. Her head cracked against the hard white tiles, and she winced at the pain.

Chance brought his face close to hers, blue eyes flashing. "What did you mean by your comment?" he demanded. He was so close she could see each individual eyelash. Her mind went blank. When a minute of silence went by, he pressed closer to her, their bodies touching as he closed the gap. "Answer me."

Luna forgot every word she knew. Her brain raced, coming to the bird outside of the restaurant and the bones in his "house." "I-you . . . the bird," she stuttered lamely.

There was blue fire in his eyes.

"I don't think that's what you were talking about," he said in a mock sweet tone and brushed a lock of hair out of her face. "You started acting strangely after you *went to the bathroom* at my house, and you're not acting right now. So tell me what it is you *really* saw before I find out myself."

"I-I-" Luna started to ramble. Chance cupped her jaw. The predatory gleam in his eyes scared her more than anything else. "I found a room with sigils and bones," she said in one great gush of breath.

Chance's nostrils flared, grip loosening as he said, "I thought that might be it. So here's the deal. You are to tell *no one* what you saw, okay? If you do, you'll regret it."

"I don't know what I saw," Luna admitted.

Chance let go of her and took in a deep breath, shifting backward to ruffle his hair. "Good. You'll know the truth soon, but in the meantime, act as if you never saw it."

Trembling, Luna opened her mouth, but he walked away

before she could say anything else.

***

THROUGH THE CRACK in the stall, Violet watched Chance pin Luna to the wall. That look on his face was the one she recognized from her encounter with him in the school parking lot.

He can be scary when he wants to be.

That look was the only thing that came to mind when she thought about him. It was hard to believe she'd ever had a crush on him.

Swallowing, Violet shifted, trying to better see out to the bathroom. Chance pressed closer to Luna, growling words that Violet couldn't quite make out. Luna's words were as hard to hear since they were stifled by her fear.

Violet considered rushing out to help, but her own fear rooted her in place. Chance grabbed Luna by the jaw, and Violet couldn't tell if he would strangle her or kiss her. A second later, he dropped her and stormed out, leaving Luna standing there rubbing her sore wrist.

Violet put her hand on the lock, ready to undo it and go greet her friend, to ask if she was okay. Then she thought about the possibility of Chance coming back and finding out that she'd witnessed the whole thing. She stayed in hiding until Luna wiped the tears from beneath her eyes and left the bathroom.

What kind of friend am I? she scolded herself. *A real friend would've helped. A real friend would've intervened.*

But Violet simply couldn't bring herself to do either of

those things.

Chapter Nineteen

IT TOOK EFFORT for Luna not to have a complete breakdown in the middle of the bathroom. The back of her head hurt from where it had smacked against the wall, and her wrist was bruised. She felt *violated.* Nearly every encounter with Chance had left her feeling that way, but this was the worst.

Luna looked at herself in the mirror, grasping either edge of the white basin beneath it for balance. Her green eyes looked distant, far away. She prodded the skin on her neck in search of marks, but there were none. Luna rinsed her face with cold water and persuaded herself to go out into the hallway, partly convinced Chance would be right there waiting.

He wasn't, but it felt like everyone she passed knew what just happened. She kept her eyes on the ground. On a daily basis, she made it a point not to make eye contact, but the need was especially strong now. She peeked up once and accidentally locked eyes with a girl who had blue eyes similar to Chance's, and the incident came flooding back. How was she supposed to make it an entire eight hours like this? She stopped walking in the middle of the hallway. How much trouble would she get in if she skipped the rest of the day?

Rage washed over her. Who did he think he was to try to scare her? To manhandle her where anyone could see?

I can't let him win like that, she thought.

She would make him face her. She would make him think about what he had done. For him to have such a volatile reaction, she liked to think that meant that she was getting under his skin as much as he was hers.

That was the motivation she needed to hightail it to class. By the time she got there, it was already almost full. Her usual seat was a desk positioned at the front of the room, so of course it was one of the last ones remaining open. Gratefully, she slid into it, tossed her backpack at her feet, and set her notebook down. She looked at the board, but Miss Kessler hadn't written anything on it yet. As she waited for class to begin, she started to doodle absentmindedly on the cover of her notebook. Miss Kessler strode into the room thirty seconds after the bell rang, beginning her lecture.

"What're you drawing there, Luna?" a voice whispered from behind her.

Luna dropped her pen with a *clang,* hating that the sound of Chance's voice had been enough to give her a scare. She hadn't heard him come in, but he must've been watching her for a while. The corner of the blue notebook cover was littered with sigils— the same ones she'd seen in his house.

"Nothing," she said, scribbling over them.

"Mm-hm," Chance murmured, then went silent. A *creak* let her know he'd settled back in his seat.

Luna was relieved until she felt something hit the back of her head. She reached up and ran her hand down her hair, pulling out a crumpled wad of wet paper. *Spit wads, how disgusting!* She shook her hand, watching the paper fall onto the floor.

She wiped her hand on her clothes, trying to focus on the lecture, when another piece hit her hair. Then another. She gritted her teeth, telling herself not to give in. One more splatted into her hair, tipping her over her limit.

She whipped around in her seat. "Stop doing that!"

"I haven't done anything," Chance whispered, smiling innocently. His desk had nothing on it, and she guessed he had it all on his lap, out of view.

"Then how—" she began.

"Miss Ketz!" Miss Kessler boomed.

Luna winced, turning away from Chance and back toward the front of the room.

"Do you have important information to share with the rest of the class?" she demanded, arm frozen mid-movement of whatever she was about to write.

"No, I don't," Luna whispered, sinking into her chair with a blush on her cheeks. "I'm sorry."

Miss Kessler gave her one last warning glare before turning her attention back to the board, her lecture the only sound filling the room.

"Nice going, kitten," Chance whispered.

Luna doubled her hands into fists. She wanted so badly to unleash all her anger on him, but now wasn't the time. She looked down at the scratched-out drawing on her notebook, remembering what he seemed to be so desperate to hide.

SOMEHOW, LUNA MADE it through the rest of the day without getting into further trouble, and by the time she returned home that afternoon, she was exhausted. She sat at the kitchen table with her head down, thinking about all that had happened. Particularly the confrontation with Chance in the bathroom. In the back of her mind, she could feel his hand on her jaw, the way his hot breath fanned over her lips as he threatened her. How much worse would the incident have been if he had snapped like that when they'd been alone at his house?

Never be alone with him again, she told herself.

Lifting the sleeve of her sweater, she dabbed at her face, stopping when a knock came from the door. She stopped, considering her options. Her father wasn't home. Since it was one of his better health days, he was out working on a project he'd put off the past week. Peering out the peephole, Luna was surprised to see Violet on the porch.

That morning, their walk had been awkward at best, and Luna had the feeling she hadn't been the only one relieved to part ways. So why would she choose to come over?

Hesitantly, Luna pulled open the door.

Before she could say a word, Violet said, "We need to talk."

Luna kept her emotions off her face, stepping aside to let her friend into the house as she asked, "Do we?" Part of her wondered if it had something to do with Chance and their newfound friendship.

Violet's eyes darted around the kitchen as she clasped and unclasped her hands before her gaze finally came to rest on Luna.

"I guess I'm just gonna say it. I saw what Chance did to you today at school."

"Oh." Luna felt as if the floor disappeared beneath her feet. What had happened was embarrassing enough, but the idea of a witness who didn't bother to help made it worse.

Violet continued. "I was in one of the stalls. What . . . happened?"

Luna bit her lip. "I don't know. One minute, he was teasing me and the next, we were there. It was like he . . . *snapped.*"

"What did you say to him before that?"

"I sort of brought up what I saw the night he took me back to his house."

"You should tell someone what he did," Violet said.

Luna shook her head. To admit what happened would mean admitting all that had led up to it. If her father found out that she'd not only gone to prom but to a boy's house afterward, she'd be done for. "No."

Violet gaped at her. "I'm sorry. Did you say *no?*"

Luna inhaled a deep breath through her nose and held it before she said, "I think *telling* someone is only going to make it worse. We graduate at the end of this month and then I'm not going to have to see him again anyway. I can . . . I can avoid him until then, and it'll be like it never happened."

Violet reached up to scratch the back of her head. "I don't like it. What if he goes off on you again?"

"I'm not going to give him the opportunity," Luna said, eyeing her friend. She could've been angry at Violet, blamed the situation on her. But she wouldn't do that. Violet would never act out of malice toward her. The entire thing with Chance had been stupid, but she hadn't meant her harm by it. That's why she was here now. In a way, she was attempting to make amends.

Violet pushed her lips into a tight, disapproving line. "Okay. I guess I can't *force* you to report him if you don't want to. But be careful, okay? Chance's temper is . . ."

Maybe she spoke too soon.

Violet looked more sad than angry as she said, "I know I have no defense for what I did. I'm sorry for tricking you, but I promise I tried to make up for it. He wanted me to help get you to go to prom with him, but I said no. He didn't handle it well. Kind of yelled at me in the school parking lot. I haven't talked to him since."

Luna was floored by the information. At least now she understood why he'd called on Susan to help. "Why didn't you tell me any of that?"

"I didn't think it would matter," Violet admitted. "And honestly, part of me felt like I deserved it for letting him get the best of me in the first place."

"I think we should *both* avoid him for the rest of the year then," Luna said, barely resisting the urge to tell Violet, "I told you so."

Violet made a face. "So you're really just gonna let this go?"

"Yes. I want to forget all of it. Everyone's heard the rumors about him. He's trouble. So if we stay away from him, he'll pick a new target and lose interest in us."

"I guess you're right."

Knocking sounded at the front door, and the girls exchanged confused glances. Violet was the only one who ever paid Luna a visit at home. Her father had a few friends who occasionally stopped by, but none of them would bother to knock without seeing his car in the driveway first.

"Who in the world?" Luna asked, peering through the peephole.

On the porch was a smiling Chance.

"Speak of the devil," she murmured and pulled open the door. She kept her hand on the knob, prepared to slam it closed the second he moved a way she didn't like. Through the opening, she asked, "What do you want?"

"Thought I'd leave a little note for your father," he replied. "Someone should tell him how you've been acting up in class."

Rolling her eyes, Luna made a move to slam the door.

Chance put his boot in the way, easing it open. The corners of his lips turned up, and he stepped toward her, hand snaking around her waist. She froze as she remembered how he'd held her in the bathroom. Luna had never cared for him, but she was finding that simple dislike was turning into something else. She was starting to become *afraid* of him. Chance easily pushed past her, giving him enough space to slide into the house.

"Hey!" she called after him.

He plopped on the couch, arm resting across the back. "Hey, yourself." He picked up the remote, channel surfing.

"Is he serious?" Violet asked.

Luna had no idea what to do. A sick feeling bubbled in

her gut, echoes of the conversation she'd had with Violet playing through it. Maybe she was wrong in her theory that avoiding him was the best solution.

Soft footsteps sounded as Violet came up beside her. "You can't let him in here after what he did."

"You saw what happened. He didn't exactly give me a choice," Luna said, unable to keep her annoyance to herself. She wanted them *both* gone.

"I'm worried," Violet said, reaching for Luna's wrist.

Luna pulled her arm free. "Don't be." She stormed into the living room, snatching the remote out of Chance's hand. "You need to go."

Chance rolled his shoulders, settling himself against the couch. "Nah."

Luna closed her eyes, counting to ten to try to keep her emotions under control.

"Luna," Violet said again softly. "What are we going to do about him?"

Luna glanced at him from the corner of her eye. That was a good question.

Chapter Twenty

CHANCE HAD BEEN surprised to see Violet inside Luna's house, but he tried not to make that obvious. He wanted to look calm, cool, and collected after the scare he'd given Luna earlier that day. From the corner of his eye, Chance watched Violet, wondering what they had talked about and why they were watching him with nearly mirrored expressions. Had she told Violet about what he'd done? He tried to think of something to say that would come off as casual but nothing came to mind.

"What were you two talking about?" he asked finally. Maybe he'd get lucky by being direct.

"None of your business," Luna said, hands on her hips. "I don't want you here. And you need to leave before my dad throws you out."

Harsh. He kept flicking through the channels, finally settling on the news.

"In tragic news, the search for high school senior, Katherine Red, came to a close today when a local man walking his dog made a gruesome discovery. It has been reported that ritualistic markings were found on the body and at the scene of the crime. Police are asking anyone with information to contact the Lima Police Department," the reporter said.

Chance sat forward, resting his elbows on his knees. They'd already found her body; that was a double-edged sword. The cops would question him soon because he'd been there the night she disappeared. But at least he wouldn't have to spend his afternoons passing out fliers with Susan anymore.

Susan. He imagined the show he was going to have to put on for her later. When she heard the news, she would be a mess. He started to sink into one of his darker moods when Luna and Violet crept into the room, watching the television screen. It displayed a patch of woods with *CAUTION* tape around a white tarp. His eyes were on Luna, scooting subtly closer to her.

"Wasn't she your friend?" Luna asked.

He glanced at the television, frowning at the thought of the terrible things Kate had said to him the night he killed her. She'd always been so bitter and narcissistic. No one in the world could be as self-absorbed as she had been. The more he thought about her, the more he realized he didn't have a single positive thing to say. "Yeah, good ol' Kate."

Luna and Violet must've heard the lack of emotion because Violet looked at him exasperated. "Doesn't this upset you?"

"Oh, of course it does," he said, voice just as flat.

The reporter continued. ". . . three years after the mysterious disappearance and murder of high school freshman, Dahlia Moore."

Luna exchanged a look with Violet before both of them made a move to leave the room. He could read that look. They'd both lost a little more respect for him, if they'd had any in the first place.

"What, you're not going to stay and watch TV with your boyfriend?" he asked, laughter in his voice to cover up the worry that he felt.

Luna whipped around to face him, knee colliding with the coffee table. Wincing, she said, "Never say that again. You are *not* my boyfriend. We're not even friends."

He pretended to look hurt, though he had to admit he *was* stung. "I'm offended, Luna."

"Who cares? You should be concerned that your friend's been murdered, you heartless asshole," she murmured as she limped back into the kitchen.

Chance watched her go, rolling his bottom lip in his teeth. He could've acted better, except he didn't care enough to try. It would bite him in the ass later. Luna already suspected something was up with him, and it would only be a matter of time before she connected the dots.

Chapter Twenty-One

LUNA NEARLY SHOOK with frustration as she sat down in a chair at the kitchen table. Violet followed her, standing near the other chair, but she didn't sit. Her gaze remained on the living room, monitoring Chance's location.

Luna focused on the lack of concern Chance seemed to have for Kate. A normal person would've been shocked or sad to find out their friend was dead, but he was stoic. The phone rang, and she jumped, holding a hand over her chest until her heartbeat evened out.

Violet watched her with questioning eyes as she stood and scooped up the handset.

"Hello?" she said, prepared to give the speech that her father wasn't home.

"Hi, Luna," a voice said. "It's been a while."

Her heart dropped to her stomach, and a flutter of joy and surprise came back up. It was a voice she knew well but one she hadn't heard in years. Max Cazmea, one of her oldest friends. They'd been close in middle school until his family moved out of town, promising to stay in touch, but their weekly phone calls had tapered to every other week, then to once a month, then to not at all. She couldn't remember the last time he'd called.

"It has," she managed to say.

Violet tipped her head to the side, questioning with her eyes. Luna turned her head to look at the wall instead. She'd explain later.

"I heard about Kate on the news," Max said.

"Yeah, I just saw it. They're thinking it has to do with Dahlia Moore."

"I saw that," he replied, then went silent until he eventually asked, "Are you okay?"

How to answer that question? "I'm fine. Stressed out. Counting down the weeks until graduation, though really *everything's* been so stressful lately, it's making me have this reoccurring dream." She furrowed her brows. "Or I guess I should call it a nightmare."

"Oh?"

Her cheeks flushed. She didn't know why talking about it embarrassed her, but she didn't want to pass up the opportunity to get *some* of her troubles off her chest. "Yeah. It's weird. There's this forest. Me and Violet walk for a long time before we're stopped by a figure in black. He's got a gun, and he kills Violet before he makes me go with him. I always wake up before finding out where he wants to take me."

Max was quiet on the other end of the line for a full minute before he asked, "Is Violet okay?"

Scrunching up her face, Luna met her friend's blue eyes and said, "Yeah."

"Good," Max said, sounding relieved. "How many times have you had the dream now?"

"I had it last night, Saturday night, and one time before

that," Luna said, counting off the occurrences on her fingers. "Why?"

"I . . . may have had the exact same dream."

Luna wasn't prepared for that answer. She opened and closed her mouth, but she choked on anything remotely coherent. "You're pulling my leg," she managed finally. Max always had been a jokester, the class clown.

"Mine's not to the exact same detail," he clarified. "But it's like a different perspective of the same thing. For me, the dream starts with Violet dying. I try to help you, but I get shot."

"That's so weird," Luna muttered, thinking of the way the figure stopped to shoot into the woods for seemingly no reason before dragging her away. "Who's the figure?"

"I have . . . theories, but we can't talk about it now. I have to go. I really just wanted to call and check in, considering all that's going on in town right now."

"I'm fine but . . ."

"Talk to you later," he said.

Luna didn't want to let him off the phone. She wanted to curse at him, demand he stay for a few more minutes and tell her what the hell was going on, but he would hang up with or without her consent. "Okay. Talk to you later. Bye."

"What was that about?" Violet asked.

"I'm . . . not sure," Luna admitted and hung the phone up.

"So who was on the phone?" Chance asked, coming into the kitchen to look between them.

"An old friend of mine," Luna replied and gave Violet a look that said, "Is he serious?"

"Someone I know?"

"Maybe. Maybe not."

Chance flared his nostrils. "Look, if this is about the whole business at school this morning, I'm sorry."

Luna looked up at him, at the blank emotion on his face. The same that had been there when he'd talked about Kate's death. "Why can't you tell me what's going on instead of giving fake apologies?" she demanded. "You can choke on your sorry for all I care. Just tell me what the hell is wrong with you."

Chance looked from her to Violet and back to her. "Look, can I talk to you in the other room? Without an *audience*."

"If I agree, will you leave?"

Chance reluctantly said, "Fine."

Violet gave Luna a long look that said, "I don't think this is a good idea." Luna wasn't sure about it either, but if there was a possibility Chance would leave after, it was worth trying. She followed Chance into the living room, just out of Violet's line of sight.

"Okay," Chance began and reached out to touch her shoulder.

Luna wasn't having it. Her wrist burned from his grip when he'd pinned her to the wall, and she stepped backward so that his hand fell through open air. "Why do you keep putting your hands on me? Didn't you get enough earlier?" When Chance said nothing, she added, "You should be less concerned about me and more with the fact that your friend is dead."

"The truth is . . . things happen that I can't always control," he replied, voice even, calm. "As for Kate, she and I were never exactly *close* so it's not like her death is going to rock my world."

"You're a heartless bastard," Luna said and scoffed. "But I should expect nothing less from someone who thinks he can do dark magic, right?"

Anger flitted across his features. "You don't know what I'm capable of."

"Yeah? Then why not tell me? My guess is that you wanted me to see that room. Your . . . your *altar*. That's why you took me home, right? It was never about the dance. And it was never about an after-party. You were showing me something without actually showing me. Why go through all that trouble and not explain any of it?"

Chance took a step closer, bringing his face an inch from hers. She was ready to call for Violet when he started to speak, "It's like testing out the temperature of the water before going for a swim. You don't jump in, you dip your toes in first and adjust before you submerge yourself."

Chance pressed himself closer to her, lips nearly brushing hers as he said, "I've shared a special part of myself with you. Consider it a gift. One that can't be returned or *shared*." His eyes bored into hers, deep sapphire to emerald green as he dipped the slightest bit closer. That glint was there again. The one he had in the bathroom when he said, "Understand?"

"I understand," Luna managed to squeak, but she was more confused than she'd been that morning.

"Thank you, "Chance said, backing away when Violet peeked around the corner at them.

He reached out to grasp her jaw, moving her chin to the side to examine her neck and the blotches that were starting to appear. "For what it's worth, I'm sorry about this."

Luna used her all to pull free, back hitting the wall as she glared at him. "You'll understand if I don't believe you."

"That's fine," he said and glanced toward Violet again. "As promised, I'll leave now." One more second of eye contact, then he turned away. The next second, Luna heard the front door slam.

"What . . . the . . . *fuck?*" Violet asked the same thing Luna was thinking.

There was no way Luna could prove he had anything to do with Kate's death, but the more she learned about the enigma that was Chance Welfrey, the more certain she became that he was nothing but trouble.

Chapter Twenty-Two

OR A FULL minute after Chance left Luna's house, he sat in the driver's seat of his truck, staring out the windshield and thinking about that morning in the bathroom. The trail of red scratch marks he'd left on Luna's light brown skin. How foolish he'd been to assume that she was completely immune to *that* mind. As soon as his anger had started to get the best of him, he lost control, and it didn't matter that it was Luna in front of him, he wanted to subdue her. To make the accusations stop. Except they weren't accusations. Not really. She was onto the truth, and from the looks of it, she wasn't going to handle it well.

She just needs time, he thought. Beating himself up about it wouldn't help anything.

It hadn't made things better that Violet had been a witness to the entire ordeal. That only meant he needed to deal with her sooner in case she decided she wanted to turn him in.

As a distraction, he turned his mind to the evening before him. He could go home and call it a day, but it would only be a matter of time before Susan and her group saw the news about Kate. He needed to be there for them. To pretend to be the version of Chance she believed him to be. So he started to drive. On the way to her house, he stopped to pick up a bouquet of flowers, practicing what he would say over and over in the back of his mind.

By the time he pulled up in front of her house, the worries with Luna were buried deep. He slipped into character and out of the truck, flowers clutched tight as he walked up to Susan's house and right inside. When Chance reached Susan's room, he peeked inside to see her lying on her stomach on the bed, knees bent as she scribbled in the notebook in front of her. Sarah was situated in the beanbag chair on the floor, gently running a nail file over her freshly polished black nails.

"Knock, knock," Chance said.

Both girls looked up, Susan nearly beaming. He assessed her bright eyes and rosy cheeks. She hadn't been crying.

She doesn't know.

He was fine being the bearer of bad news. Flowers held out, he entered the room. "These are for you. I never got the chance to properly thank you for helping me out with Luna."

Susan took them, smiling as she held the petals to her nose. "It was no problem, really. She's a sweetheart."

Chance had been under the impression she'd been being nice to get the event over with. He hadn't considered that she might befriend Luna. "You like her?"

"Yeah. I mean, she *is* your girlfriend, right? Why wouldn't I?"

Chance mulled that over. He chose not to correct her. After the next sixty seconds, she would forget all about it anyway. "So uh. Did you guys see the news today?"

Susan raised a thin eyebrow. "No. Why?"

"They found Kate," Chance said, doing his best to seem

sorrowful. The exact expression he should've worn at Luna's but didn't. "Or I should say, they found her *body*."

Susan gasped and dropped the bouquet onto the bed with a soft *thump*. One hand covered her mouth. "Oh my God."

"I know," Chance said, sitting on the bed beside her. He did his best *sad* voice, glad to see they were falling for it. "I couldn't believe it."

Sarah stood, face more passive than Susan's but with a hint of sorrow in her bright blue eyes. "I'm gonna call Maddie. See if she's heard."

When Sarah was out of the room, Susan dabbed her face with her white sleeve, careful to avoid smearing her makeup. "Did they say what happened?"

"They're thinking a homicide," Chance said. A scene-by-scene playback of her murder flashed through his mind.

Susan opened her mouth to respond when a loud knock came from downstairs. Through her tears, Susan managed to look irritated. "What is she doing down there?"

The sound of Sarah's muffled voice came mixed with a new one. A much deeper one. Male. Chance's skin crawled with foreboding as footsteps creaked on the stairs. *Two* sets, he guessed right before two cops appeared in the doorway, both of them staring at Chance and Susan with hard-to-read expressions.

"Susan Cross and Chance Welfrey?" one of them asked.

"Yeah," they replied at the same time, Chance's voice much stiffer than Susan's. He didn't recognize either of the officers and couldn't decide if that would work for or against him.

"Good afternoon to you both. I'm Officer Smith, and this

is Officer Novak. We'd like to ask you some questions about Kate Red. Miss Cross, we already phoned your mother and got permission to talk to you."

"I'm happy to help however I can," Susan said, clasping her hands together over her heart.

Chance stayed silent, calculating the situation. He considered running but it would only backfire on him, so he stayed put.

"Okay, well, Mr. Welfrey, you come out here with me," Officer Smith commanded, gesturing to the hallway. "And Officer Novak will stay here with you, Miss Cross."

Chance gritted his teeth but obeyed. He could keep his cool around them, but that didn't stop him from feeling nervous. He never knew when a comment would send him into *that* mind, and it would be disastrous if it happened around a cop. Chance licked his teeth and studied the back of the man as they walked down the hall. He was tall but thin. On the younger side so Chance didn't think he had much experience. He thought about what he would do if Chance decided to attack him. How well would he fight back?

They went into the first room they came across, Sarah's bedroom. It was the opposite aesthetic of Susan's. Her lights were off, highlighting the red lava lamp in the corner of the room. The bedspread was black, and heavy metal posters were pinned on nearly every inch of the wall.

Officer Smith flipped the light switch and pulled the chair away from Sarah's desk to sit on. Chance plopped down on her bed, getting satisfaction from knowing that she would hate this.

Would hate to know he had invaded her personal space.

"Don't you need someone's permission to talk to me too?" Chance asked, but there was no one who could vouch for him.

"Normally, we would. But you *are* eighteen years old, and you were an emancipated minor, isn't that right?"

Chance felt some of his smugness slide away. When did they add that to his file? As far as he knew, everything tied him back to the one place he didn't want to be associated with. This information was new.

Cody has been busy, too, he realized.

"I'll dive right into this then," Officer Smith continued. "What was your relationship with Miss Red?" The walls were so thin that he could hear Susan and the other officer as he asked her nearly the exact same question.

"She was a good friend to me and Susan," Chance lied, listening as Susan replied almost verbatim.

"And do you mind accounting for your whereabouts last Tuesday evening?" both officers asked.

"Me, Kate, and my sister, Sarah, hung out here for a bit, then went to go get smoothies," Susan said.

"I was here with them for a while. When the girls decided to go out, I went home."

"When was the last time you saw Miss Red?"

"When she stormed out of here," Susan said. "We were talking about prom, and she got upset when she found out Chance was taking someone else. He went out to talk to her. That was the last time I saw Kate."

Chance tipped his head. "When she left in the middle of us talking."

"No one went after her?"

Chance jutted out his bottom lip, appearing deep in thought. "Nope."

Officer Smith tapped his pen to his notepad. "So you say you split off from the Cross sisters and went home. Do you have anyone who can verify your alibi?"

Chance clenched his hands into fists. "I'm an emancipated minor, Officer Smith. What do you think?"

"Humph," Smith grunted, tucking his pen into the spiral binding of his notebook. "I have a feeling we'll be meeting again, Mr. Welfrey."

Not too soon, I hope.

He could barely contain his relief as Smith got up, joining his partner at the top of the stairs. Chance watched them go out the front door. He hurried downstairs, parting a curtain to watch them talking to Sarah on the porch.

How much time did he have before they came back? His story and Susan's had been different. The cops would notice that, and they'd be back for another round of questioning. Once Susan stood by her story, all the suspicion would fall on him.

I can't let that happen.

A predator bleeding through his mask, he rushed back up the stairs and into Susan's room. Her eyes were wide and green in a way that reminded him of Luna's and that only brought a fresh wave of anger.

"That was scary, huh, Chance?" she asked, hugging

herself. "I never thought I'd be questioned by the police."

"I got something scarier for you, *sweetheart*," he growled and pulled his dagger from his pocket.

She tried to cower away, but he was faster, wrapping her beautiful long hair around his fist. "Listen up, and listen good. The stories we gave the cops were different, and they're gonna realize that. When they do, I need you to do something for me."

She winced, staring up at him through watery eyes as he gave her hair another particularly rough yank. "Chance, what are you talking about? What did you do?" Then understanding dawned across her face, her eyes widening to meet his. "Oh my God! When you went outside . . . you . . . It was you . . . you killed Kate."

He held the blade to her throat. "Maybe I did, maybe I didn't, but when those cops come back to question you again, you're gonna say that what you told them was a lie. I never went after her. I stayed with you and Sarah until you two went out. Then I went home."

"But— That didn't happen!" she protested.

"I think this knife says it did. Now, are you gonna be a good girl and do as I said or would you like to join Katie?" he purred, yanking her hair so hard that she was forced to look up at him. "I'm sure she's lonely."

"I-I'll do what you said. I promise!"

"And this little incident here? It *never* happened!" He rubbed the blade of his trusty dagger against her throat. It left a tiny incision—the smallest reminder to Susan that what was happening was as real as his threat.

Tears streamed down her face, and she blinked, trying to clear her vision. "I promise I won't tell anyone. Please, please don't hurt me."

"'*Anyone*' includes your sister."

"Of course."

"Good." He glanced at the phone on the table beside her bed. "He give you a business card?"

Susan nodded weakly.

"Call him back," he ordered. "And retract your statement."

Slowly, he pulled his knife back, not fully trusting her not to try and make a bolt for it. His fingers stayed wrapped in her long brown locks as Susan pulled the phone toward her. She dialed the number with shaking fingers. It rang and rang, and Chance watched expectantly. She didn't take her eyes off his as she hung up.

The rage on his face was clear, the knife raising to her throat as he asked, "The fuck you hang up for?"

"It went to his answering machine," she said quickly.

Chance rolled his eyes. "So leave a damn message then. Christ, it's not rocket science."

Susan swallowed hard and picked up the handset again. When the voicemail played this time, she was silent for a long while before she said, "Hi, Officer Novak? This is Susan Cross. We just spoke. Um, I wanted to say that I mixed up some things in my statement. I'm sorry."

She hung up quickly, peering up at Chance through her lashes. He wasn't displeased with the performance but disliked that she hadn't gone into more detail.

"I-is that good?" she asked.

"Should suffice." He sneered as he leaned slightly closer. "While I have you, let me clear up something else too. No more of this befriending Luna nonsense. I don't like to share. Understood?"

Susan did her best to bob her head against his firm grasp. Growing bored, Chance let go of her, but Susan didn't move from the position she'd been in.

"Glad we got that all straightened out," he said, walking toward the door. He paused before passing through, holding the knife up so that the blade flashed in the light and added, "I'll see you at school tomorrow."

CHANCE DIDN'T GO far. He sat in his truck a few doors down from Susan's house, carefully wiping her blood off the blade with a rag and counting down the minutes until she decided to run and try to go for help. While he wasn't thrilled at the idea of killing someone who had been such a good friend to him, he didn't think she'd listen to him so he was prepared. He held the knife up, observing the beautifully carved cobra in the silver handle before he tucked it away into his pocket.

He started up the truck, staring into the rearview mirror for another full minute. Susan didn't make an appearance, but he had the uncomfortable sensation that he was being watched. He flexed his fingers around the steering wheel, aware of how clear all his senses were. When he'd attacked Susan, he hadn't slipped into *that* mind. He had been fully himself. It was almost as if he were incorporating traits from that side of him into this one.

Breathing out, he started to drive with thoughts of the fear in Susan's eyes. Something about having control over another person made him feel powerful. Complete.

He wished he could bottle the feeling.

Pulling his truck into its usual place on the outskirts of his land, he cut the engine, sitting in his own company. From the corner of his eye, he spotted Luna's rose in the passenger seat. He didn't realize she had left it. As he stepped out of the truck, he snagged it, feeling close to her as he moved through the woods, heavy black boots flattening the grass in his path. Inside his grotesque house, he pulled a matchbook from his pocket, struck a match, and lit the small white candle he kept near the door.

He stood in the doorway of his ritual room, trying to see it as Luna must have. There was no way to innocently write it off. He'd known that when he sent her this way. Yawning, he scooped up the nearest bone, so aged and worn that it was hard to tell what it originally was. A femur perhaps. Carefully, he wrapped the stem of the rose around it, kicking the remaining bones out of the way to make enough room to set his creation between the two candles.

He admired the way the candlelight made it look as if the bone was bleeding. Bowing his head in respect, he uttered a little prayer before he turned and left the room. The tiny candle he'd abandoned in the living room burned ominously. He picked it up, carrying it into the room he used as his bedroom. The old beat-up mattress in the corner looked as unwelcoming as it felt. Chance settled on it, bending his back so the broken springs weren't pressing too hard into his spine. Licking his fingers, he put out the candle with a tiny hissing sound and clamped his eyes shut.

Work here was done, but there was plenty more to do on the Other Side.

152

Chapter Twenty-Three

IT WASN'T OFTEN that Luna was glad to see her father, but when he came home that day, she was. He might not be there for her emotionally, but he would protect her in the case of someone threatening her with physical harm. After everything that had happened with Chance, Luna was forced to accept the fact that she was weak. Her skin hurt in the places where he'd grabbed her, and she knew they would bruise. Hopefully, the worst of the damage would stick to places that could be hidden beneath her clothes.

Violet refused to leave, staying with Luna until they heard the sound of her father's car in the driveway, just in case Chance decided to come back. Luna thanked her, and she slipped out before her father made it inside. He knew Violet and wouldn't be upset about her coming over, but Violet preferred to limit her interactions with him. Luna couldn't blame her.

Luna sat in the armchair near the door, waiting for it to open so she could greet her father. When he came inside, his dark eyes were red-rimmed, face pinched tight as if he were barely holding himself together. Luna's heart dropped to her stomach with the anticipation that something terrible had happened. Rarely did that face ever show emotions. Now his eyes were glassy, as if they were full of tears threatening to spill over.

Concerned, Luna jumped up from her seat and asked, "Dad, what is it? What's happened?"

His father somehow managed to go more downcast as he set his hand on her shoulder. "Luna, I'm so sorry to tell you this, but Sidra has passed."

Luna stared without comprehending. Sidra . . . *passed.* The words had no meaning. Sidra was fine. Luna had just seen her. "Wh-what do you mean?"

"She's with Allah now," he said and took in a deep breath, most likely to hold back a sob.

"No," Luna said, trying to process what he was saying. Sidra . . . dead. It made no sense.

A loud sob came from her father, and the sound flipped a switch in Luna's head. Grief came all at once, a great weight that crushed her. Sidra was *dead?* Luna started to sob, too, but no tears fell. A painful hitch in her breathing made her gasp.

It didn't matter that they had gotten close only because her father had pushed Luna to be more integrated with Nazir's family as a possible way to arrange a marriage. She cared about all of them as if they were her extended family. In a way, they were. They'd become her haven, a little place of normality.

Luna had been a little girl the first time she'd met Sidra. It had been during her family's first gathering at the mosque. Luna couldn't have been older than five. Sidra had been young and healthy, her hair black rather than the silver that Luna associated with her now. And she'd been so much more mobile. She'd picked Luna up, helping her see the selections on the table for a lunch buffet.

In her younger days, Luna supposed that part of her considered her to be a replacement for her own mother. As Luna aged and became more complex, so did her relationship with Sidra.

She tried to remember the last time she'd seen her. The morning after prom when she'd hastily stopped in for the sole purpose of avoiding going home. She had been so wrapped up in what she saw at Chance's house that she hadn't properly spent time with her.

What had she said to her?

Had it been anything meaningful?

She hadn't worried about it, positive she would see her again on her Tuesday visit. *We always think there will be a next time until there isn't.* Gut-wrenching sorrow tore through her.

Sidra was *gone.*

Nazir. How was he handling the news? As one of the few remaining members of Sidra's family, he would be expected to help wash and shroud the body while processing her death at the same time. Luna had not yet been made to partake in one of those ceremonies, but she'd heard about them, and she couldn't imagine the grief.

"We need to go offer our condolences," Abrahim said.

Luna readily agreed and put her shoes on, forgetting all about the mess her day had been.

SOMEHOW, LUNA MANAGED to fall asleep that night with her eyes and cheeks raw from crying. She wanted nothing more than to slip into the blissful nothingness of a good sleep, but she wasn't so fortunate. When she opened her eyes, she was faced with the powerful hands of her dream abductor. Struggling with everything in her, she kicked and clawed, trying to elbow or bite him. It was all in vain. The harder she fought, the tighter he held on.

As he dragged her through the strange forest, the thick trees thinned away to dead ones bared of all their leaves. The air was thick, the blue overhead turning into a dusky gray. They ended up on a remote trail lined with dense undergrowth. Luna's eyes darted around, desperate for anything that could tell her where they were, but all that surrounded them was unforgiving wilderness.

At last, they came upon a clearing. In the center of it was a cabin. The wood was degraded in some places as if maintenance wasn't kept up on it. Next door to that was an enormous temple with ivy growing through the cracks in the stone wall. The cabin didn't look much better. From where they stood, she couldn't see inside because there was something black covering the windows.

Luna stiffened as the dream figure started to lead her forward. She didn't want to go inside either of the buildings, positive that when she did, she wouldn't come out alive. Luna dug her heels into the dirt, trying to get him to slow down. He nearly picked her up to keep moving, setting her on the porch as if it took no effort at all. With the rotten wood wall less than a foot from her face, her abductor reached around her to push open the door. Holding her breath, Luna peered inside. The only source of light was a candle sitting in the middle of a table.

A strong shove came from behind, and Luna stumbled forward, trying to catch her balance. By the time she regained herself, her abductor slammed the door, concealing them both inside. The fear she'd felt until that point was nothing compared to what she felt now. The darkness suffocated her like a cloth over the face. The man wasn't perturbed, edging her closer to the wall across the room.

Two shackles lay at her feet.

"Sit down," the voice growled in her ear.

Luna jerked away, trying to glare into the shadowy face, but she couldn't make out any features beneath the hood. She remembered what had happened to Violet, the violence he was so clearly capable of, and sat down with her back pressed to the wall.

The man crouched before her. She couldn't see his eyes, but she could *feel* them scanning her as though he was searching for something. He grabbed one of her slender wrists, wrapping it in one of the shackles. When she realized what he was doing, she tried to pull free, but he was quick to disable her other wrist as well. She pulled on the chains, but they were tightly bolted to the floor. The man stood up, and she dared a peek at him through her lashes. He said nothing, but she had the distinct feeling that he was watching her, studying her like artwork on display.

"I'll be leaving now," he said and turned to begin walking toward the door. Before he left, he called, "Don't go anywhere!"

The cabin rattled with the effects of the slamming door. Left alone, Luna's eyes darted in all directions, desperate for an escape. The door seemed to be the only way in and out. There was a hallway that led deeper into the cabin, and she wondered about the possibility of a back door. During her search, her eyes came across a small table pushed in the corner. On top of it was a dagger with a cobra carved into the handle. The blade glistened with fresh red blood.

Luna screamed and bolted straight up in bed, the cabin gone as quickly as it had appeared. Her own walls didn't bring her much comfort when she remembered her reality, but it was enough to stop screaming. Sweat drenched her face, her black hair matted thickly to her forehead. She wiped the sweat off, shaking from the aftershock of her nightmare, and knocked the covers away.

It was only a dream, Luna told herself, but part of her wasn't convinced. Not only had it been visceral, but this dream was strange, considering that it seemed to have simply continued from where the other one left off.

I've never continued a dream before.

Standing on shaking legs, she did her best to compose herself. While her body yearned for sleep, she didn't want to see the bloody dagger again. Maybe cold water would help her calm down. As she headed to the kitchen and filled a glass, her mind started to wander. She thought of Max and the new dream, diving down any rabbit hole that could possibly provide any explanation.

Luna set the cup in the sink and headed back to her room. She settled in bed, staring up at the ceiling with those lingering few seconds of the dream at the front of her brain. The blood on the blade.

Someone had died.

He had killed them.

Who is he?

The voice in her head whispered, *Chance.* He checked all the boxes. She shot it down. *This is all craziness. It's just a dream.*

She pulled the covers up to her neck and turned onto her side, trying her best to get comfortable, her eyes raw from crying. Tomorrow would be hard enough as it was. She needed to get all the rest she could. She managed to fall back to sleep, the vivid dream waiting for her.

Chapter Twenty-Four

MAX STIRRED IN bed, caught in the same powerful dream trap as Luna. He was back in that bloody forest at exactly the place where the other dream had left off. He lay behind the bush he'd used as cover. Phantom pains coursed through his upper body from the bullet. Fresh trails of blood found their way free, and he wiped them away absently.

The dizziness gave way to a fainting spell, and he let himself drop to the forest floor. When he came to, he was moving. A sharp tug on his collar pulled his shirt against his throat, and it took effort for him not to gag. He tried to glance up at whoever was there with him but only caught a flash of black.

If he was right in his thinking, this was the man who had killed Violet. For Max to have his attention now wasn't good. The tight grip loosened, and the back of Max's head slammed onto the ground without warning. Somehow, he muffled the groan. Subtly, he tried to glance up at the man again and instead, found himself taking in details of their surroundings.

There was a cabin and a giant stone building. A dog's frustrated howling rang out from somewhere nearby, and Max flinched, wary of anything that sounded so feral coming toward him when he was vulnerable.

Max closed his eyes, wishing the dream away.

***

AMY DRAGGED HER feet over the threshold and into her house, lugging her backpack with her. She was tired and hungry, but her mind was focused solely on the anatomy notes she needed to study. She'd never struggled so much with a class before, but since she refused to do the frog dissection her teacher had been so excited for, her grade took a massive hit. In order to pass, she needed to get perfect grades on every test from now until the end of the year. And each one seemed harder than the last.

Her sister, Michelle, greeted her from the kitchen, and Amy called some words back before going up to her room to start the process of studying. She'd crammed nonstop for days already but worried she wouldn't remember the important stuff when the time came. Her solution was to study more. Eventually it *had* to stick with her.

In her room, she closed the door and threw her backpack onto her bed. A voice whispered in her ear when she bent down to slip off her shoe, and she froze. She whipped on her heels, searching the corners of her room, but no one was there. Amy huffed and slipped off the other shoe. When the voice came again, she realized it was in her head. To block it out, she started to hum and climbed onto her bed, digging for her textbook. Leaning her elbows on her knees, she started to read. She didn't finish the first page before exhaustion hit her, and she nearly face-planted in her book.

Focus, she scolded herself.

Amy didn't like to sleep, and for good reason. Sleep brought dreams and in those dreams, she had to be someone else. A responsible Keeper with duties that only she could achieve. She didn't like to think of that part of herself, but it became impossible to ignore anytime she grew tired. It was an ordinary part of her life, like school.

Amy had been little when she'd been initiated into that world. So little, in fact, that she couldn't remember *how* little she'd been. In her dreams, she'd been chasing a butterfly through a meadow, entranced by the vibrant markings on its tiny yellow wings. It felt as if she chased it for hours yet was no closer to catching it than when she had started.

Somewhere during her travels, the meadow changed to a forest, and the butterfly disappeared. Not liking the darkness of the shadows, Amy trudged onward along the path that dumped her into a clearing. It was littered with items, including a masquerade mask, a sword, toy handcuffs, and a metronome. Each item had a significance that she hadn't been aware of at the time. She had been drawn to the masquerade mask due to the sparkling purple sequins along its edge. As soon as her tiny fingers made contact with it, a burst of knowledge was shot directly into her brain. She knew what the mask was for and that what she would be doing with it was *important*.

That night, she'd met her first partner, and things had gone from there. Years had passed and nothing had changed. She watched the town. She reported odd activity on the Other Side. So on and so forth.

It was easier to stay awake for days straight than deal with any of her responsibilities. Part of her hoped that if she ignored it long enough, someone else would be chosen to replace her. She never *wanted* to have this position. Never asked for it. What she wanted was to be a normal teenager.

You are normal, she told herself. She supposed in a way, she was. There *were* others like her in this town and others nearby.

Amy tossed a long lock of brown hair over her shoulder and focused on the textbook. Her eyes crossed and the words blurred to nonsense. She was tired. So very tired, but she refused to give in.

Focus, she scolded again, thought about brewing a pot of coffee, and leaned toward the textbook.

The next thing she knew, she was awake in the Other Realm. "Son of a . . ." She wanted to curse in a manner that was unlike her.

Her first reaction was to try and wake herself up. She pinched her arm and closed her eyes, trying to wish herself out of this Realm. It failed. The only way out would be to handle her responsibilities. The sooner she finished, the sooner she'd be able to get on with her life. She sighed and accepted her fate. Admittedly, she *was* curious about Luna and why she seemed to be so tired lately. Every time she saw the girl, she looked as if she wanted to do nothing more than go to sleep.

If she's not sleeping, is she awake here?

She supposed this place would be the easiest way to get answers without simply asking Luna herself. Amy navigated familiar neighborhoods. In the fog, it looked surreal. Sometimes, she saw other Keepers and Walkers who didn't realize they were in a completely new Realm.

She envied their naivety.

When Amy made it to Luna's house, she didn't feel as confident. She'd never been here in the Real World, and it almost felt as if she were invading by walking inside. On the couch, a man was asleep with a remote clutched in his fist. She assumed it was Luna's father, judging by his resemblance to her friend.

Amy made a move to start down the hall, stopping when she considered where her friend might be. An uncomfortable feeling settled in the pit of her stomach as she found the archway to a bedroom. When she peered inside, she recognized the name on the awards on the wall. Mostly they were academic achievements, but there were a few ribbons and mentions for choir too.

Amy was impressed, scanning the space until she came to the bed. Her hope for a quick and easy mission plummeted when she realized Luna was gone.

She's traveling. Amy did another search around the room, but there was nothing to indicate where she was or where she would go.

Breathing in, Amy closed her eyes and pictured her partner in the front of her thoughts. When the image was clear, she reached out to him. The signal she received back was powerful, telling her that he was awake in the same Realm. However, he couldn't come to her.

He was trapped in a dream cycle.

Chapter Twenty-Five

VERTIGO.

Chance had felt it a number of times while traveling through worlds. It usually happened upon entering the Other Realm. Rarely did he find it unsettling. On the return trip, the transition was seamless. He never had vertigo happen upon waking. He wasn't sure what that meant, if it meant anything at all. Rubbing his eyes, his stomach sloshed with clinging traces of nausea. Carefully, he climbed to his feet, taking deep breaths.

He tried to distract himself from his nausea by thinking of everything that had happened on the Other Side. From what he could remember, nothing happened that should've left him feeling so *gross*. Luna. The cabin. It had all been pretty standard. Then he froze.

It's not possible, is it?

Getting up, he lumbered to the bathroom and splashed water on his face, trying to get the worst of the nausea to disappear, and dared a glance at his reflection in the cracked mirror. He looked almost *radiant*, nothing like the way he felt inside.

Snap out of it, he scolded himself and wandered through his house. He almost wished he would throw up already so the feeling would leave.

Chance slipped outside, the cool night air soothing his clammy skin. He climbed into his truck, sitting in the driver's seat with the door open for a long minute before he bent over and hurled into the undergrowth. With an undignified groan, he wiped his mouth and got back into his seat, plucking one of the old water bottles out of the middle console. He sipped it, wincing at the taste. It was awful, but not as awful as the taste of his own vomit. When the bottle was empty, he discarded it, then sat, relieved that the worst of his symptoms were gone.

You have to check.

The idea of driving through the woods so late at night wasn't his favorite thing, but he wouldn't be able to sleep if he didn't. So he started his truck. He drove erratically, angry at the decision to get out of bed. The deeper into the woods he traveled, the harder it became to navigate. Worried about the possibility of crashing, he parked and got out, deciding to scout for a while on foot.

I'll be quick, he told himself and shut off the engine.

In the middle of the night, this could've been a much more difficult mission, but it was easy for him to move through the undergrowth. He was so used to the woods that he didn't trip on any of the sticks beneath his feet. Tilting his head, he felt the pop in the base of his neck and walked toward the looming clearing.

It's going to be empty, he told himself, picturing that same clearing from his dreams.

By the time he reached his destination, he was so wrapped up in denial that he couldn't handle the fact that he was wrong. Time didn't seem to move as he stood in the darkness, staring at the massive outline of the building.

The cabin from his dreams was as real as Chance himself.

Up until this point, he'd been uncertain of everything. While things seemed to be moving into place with Luna, there were other players in the game. The mysterious boy he'd found in the dream, the one he had shot. The fact that Violet hadn't been affected by the cycle.

He'd been close to writing off the plan. But this? This was confirmation it was *working*.

If Luna could pull this off by being afraid on the Other Side, what could she be capable of with other emotions? Happiness? Determination? *Love?*

Chance balled his hands into fists, determined. There were a lot of loose factors, but in the grand scheme of things, Luna was the only one who actually mattered. And he had her where he needed her in the Other Realm. On this side, all he needed to do was stick to her like glue, and he had faith that the rest of his problems would sort themselves out.

Chapter Twenty-Six

IT TOOK A long time for Luna to get out of bed the next morning. She was tired, her body ached, and her brain felt full of fuzz. She was not in the headspace to go to school. Islamic tradition called for a person to ideally be buried within twenty-four hours of death. That meant Sidra's funeral would be today. Luna tried to get her father to let her stay home so she could attend, but he declined, sending her on her way.

Luna wanted to be angry for his callousness, but she was too tired, too numb. She operated on autopilot, going through her morning routine, and didn't come back to herself until she reached school. There had been no sign of Violet during her walk, and she didn't ask anyone where she was.

The exhaustion seeped into her bones as she trudged up the stairs. Luna used the handrail to help keep herself steady, cursing when she tripped over her foot. Irritation filled her. She shouldn't be at school right now. She should be at home, grieving. Most parents would grant their children that mercy.

Not *her* father.

Luna considered going to the office to see if she could find more leniency with the secretary when she spotted a familiar figure wandering toward her.

An oversized, long-sleeved white sweater covered her

hands. Her gaze was on the floor, her long brown hair greasy and unwashed, loose without a sign of the white ribbon that normally held it in place. Perhaps the strangest thing about the scene was the fact that the girl was alone, not flanked by any of her friends.

"Susan?" Luna asked, surprised. The last time she'd seen her was on prom night. Remembering how she'd been ditched brought her anger and embarrassment back to the surface.

Susan looked up and caught her eye. Instantly, she turned on her heel and tried to hurry down the hall the way she'd come.

"Susan!" Luna called and hurried after her. When she didn't slow down, Luna picked up the pace and cut her off, forcing the girl to acknowledge her. "What's your damage? You haven't spoken to me since prom. Thanks for ditching me, by the way. What happened to wanting to be my friend?"

Susan sniffled and lifted her sleeve to wipe under her nose. That was when Luna noticed how red her eyes were—she'd been crying.

She's grieving a death, too, Luna told herself, remembering the news about Kate. Instantly, she felt guilty for her harsh approach and took the smallest step backward to give her some space.

"I'm-I'm sorry," Susan said, voice trembling with an odd mix of sorrow and something else. Fear? "I can't be near you right now."

She tried to step around Luna, but Luna didn't let her go so easily. "Why? What did I do to you?"

"Nothing," Susan said and pulled the neckline of her sweater up.

That was when Luna noticed a thin red line on her pale

skin. A perfect slice. Luna gasped. "Did somebody *hurt* you?"

Susan swallowed hard and looked down at the floor, emotionless.

"If someone is threatening you, we should go to the police."

"They won't believe me," she whispered.

"I'll go with you," Luna said, having an odd moment of déjà vu remembering her conversation with Violet in the kitchen.

Susan shook her head. "I . . . can't do that."

Luna could understand the girl's stubbornness. Pleading with her wouldn't get her to change her mind. "Okay. Well, I'm here for you if you need me."

"Thank you," she said. Her ice-cold hands reached out, grabbing and squeezing one of Luna's. "But you need to help yourself."

Luna looked down at their entwined hands and startled when she noticed a mark around her wrist. With more force than she meant to, she shook off Susan's hand. "What?" she asked, pushing up her sleeve to better see it. A purple, nearly black, ring encircled her wrist, standing out against her light brown skin. Had it been there this morning? Luna remembered the dream, the shackles that had held her in place.

That's impossible.

When she looked back up, Susan was gone. Luna was torn between going after her and figuring out what had happened to her during the night. Someone had attacked Susan, that much was clear.

But who? Chance?

Why would he attack Susan?

Had she found out about his angry side? The more questions Luna asked herself, the less things made sense. Then she had a lightbulb moment.

If Susan found out some sort of connection between Chance and Kate's death, why didn't she want to go to the police?

Then Luna felt like a hypocrite. She'd chosen not to go to the police either. As foolish as it seemed, fear was a powerful emotion.

Luna looked at her wrist again, at a loss for how she'd gotten injured. *There's no way.* Did Susan's wound have the same mysterious origin?

Overhead, speakers crackled to life. "Everyone, please report to the gymnasium immediately for a morning meeting," Principal Wilson said.

Luna stared up at the ceiling. An assembly? *Now?*

It must be about Kate, Luna thought and made her way down the hall.

Once she stepped foot into the gym, she saw she was correct. There was an officer sitting in a chair at the edge of the stage and a woman beside him that Luna didn't recognize. She wore a suit and scanned the teenagers as if she were used to addressing crowds. Beside her, a stand held an enormous poster board with a picture of Kate. On the bottom, *R.I.P.* had been written in fancy script. It was like stepping into a funeral, except there was no casket present.

Unnerved, Luna climbed up the bleachers and took her seat. She surveyed the crowd for Violet but didn't see her. She spotted Amy, but she was on the other side of the gym. By the time Luna made her way over to her, the spots around her would be full. Luna gave up, settling into her seat for whatever would come. When her classmates filled the bleachers, Principal Wilson stepped up to the picture of Kate, a microphone clenched in her hand.

"Good morning. I wish I had good news to share with you all today, but I wanted to talk about the recent tragedy that's befallen our town."

Luna zoned out, focusing on the other side of the gym. Susan, Maddie, and Sarah sat together. Out of everyone, they seemed to be the only ones openly showing grief. Susan especially. She held one hand over her mouth, her sleeve nearly covering her entire face.

Principal Wilson continued. "We're asking for anyone who may have information about the tragedy to please come forward. Before I let you all go, I want to take a minute of silence to remember Katherine Red."

Luna looked at Susan again. Not too far away from the trio, Chance sat at the end of the bleachers. He glanced over at them once or twice, but his face and posture were stone, gaze locked on the giant picture of Kate. He was a gargoyle overlooking tragedy.

ALL MORNING, THE look in Susan's eyes haunted Luna. The raw fear. Luna couldn't wait for lunch. She planned to confront Susan again and see what other information she could get out of her.

When the lunch bell rang, Luna stood and gathered her books. Behind her, Chance's chair scraped the floor. The brush of his fingers on her shoulder caused her to tense. She didn't look at him, hoping he would lose interest if she paid him no attention.

"Luna," he said softly.

She met his eye—an action she'd avoided all day. Up until this point, he'd been surprisingly withdrawn. All she could think about was what had happened yesterday. Not only the incident in the bathroom but his visit to her house as well.

You don't know what I'm capable of.

"What?" she asked, her voice surprisingly even.

"You going to lunch or study hall?" he asked.

She stuck her tongue in her cheek, somehow able to still find him annoying. "Lunch."

"I'll come with you," he said.

Luna shouldered her backpack but said nothing. It didn't matter if she replied or not. He'd follow her anyway. Side by side, they walked down the hall, Luna pulling away whenever he drifted too close. Curious eyes watched them go. Popular and unpopular alike couldn't believe she was walking to lunch with Chance. Luna chewed her lip, thinking of the rumors that they were dating. Going to lunch together certainly wouldn't help make those disappear.

Luna was the first in the cafeteria, Chance a step behind. When Luna took her place in line, she expected Chance to get bored and wander off to his friends, but he stayed by her side. She tried to ignore him at first, but his presence overwhelmed her.

If Susan believes the rumors, that's probably why she doesn't want to talk to me, she thought. *She's worried I'll tell Chance what she said.*

It made sense. Luna did a survey of the cafeteria, searching for Susan, but there was no sign of her. Sarah and Maddie sat at a table near the front of the line. When she was close enough, Luna poked Sarah, getting her attention.

"Have you seen Susan?" Luna asked.

Sarah blinked her big, pale blue eyes, emotionless. "She wasn't feeling good. Went home."

"What's going on with her? Is she okay?"

"You haven't seen the news?" Sarah asked, turning back to her lunch.

Luna *had* seen the news. A pit opened in her stomach. With Sidra's recent death, Luna felt safe in saying she knew exactly what Susan was going through. But that didn't explain the mark on her throat or why she'd been so afraid to talk about it. Her grief didn't explain the glint of fear Luna had spotted in her eyes.

Chance watched Luna curiously. Before he could question her, she spotted a table on the other side of the cafeteria and said, "Those are your friends. Go *there.*"

"Nah. I'm good right here," he said, replanting his feet to make a show of staying in place.

Rolling her eyes, Luna grabbed a Styrofoam tray from the pile, filling it with food before paying the lunch lady. Violet had a table near the windows all to herself, and Luna joined her, Chance right by her side. She noted the fact that he hadn't bothered to get himself any lunch.

Luna sat down across from Violet, Chance sliding into the

seat beside her. "Hey, Violet."

Violet glanced up at her, eyes glossing over when they took in Chance. "Hi, Luna."

"Sorry I missed you this morning. I had a late start," Luna said, taking a small bite of her food. "Sidra died last night."

"That old lady your dad made you help take care of?" Violet asked, pausing mid sip.

"Yeah."

"I'm sorry. I know you two were close."

"It's . . . expected," Luna admitted, thinking of the last time she'd seen her. How thin the nightgown had made her look. "I guess part of me wishes she could've held on until after graduation. She would have been proud of me."

"She *was* proud of you," Violet said. The sentiment made Luna's eyes well with tears. Violet must've noticed because she turned to Chance and said, "Why the hell are you sitting with us?"

He snagged a soggy French fry off Luna's plate and plopped it into his mouth. "Free country."

"Whatever," Violet murmured, hiding her displeasure by taking a bite of her burger.

The silence that came next was almost too much for Luna to bear. Normally, she liked quiet, but with her mind wanting to sprint in all the directions she *didn't* want it to go, she was desperate for someone to say *anything*.

Violet must've felt the same way because she said, "So it was weird randomly hearing from Max again. I don't think I asked you what he called about."

Luna forced herself to swallow a bite of fry. It squished

between her teeth, the cold grease causing her stomach to turn. "He told me some . . . weird stuff that's been going on with him lately."

"Weird how?" Violet asked, giving Chance a disgusted look when he scooted a little closer to Luna.

Luna attempted a bite of her burger. It wasn't much better quality than the fries had been. "He saw the stuff on the news with Kate and wanted to see if we were okay."

Violet bobbed along.

"And . . . he said he had the same dream I did."

Violet looked back down at her food, interest clearly leaving. "Not this again. Why worry about this, Luna, when you have real problems? Problems that are much more prevalent?" She pinned Chance with her glare.

Chance made a mocking face at her in return.

"You don't care at all, do you?" Luna asked.

"Nope. I don't think you've got your priorities straight."

"You can't deny that there's been a lot of weird stuff going on lately, Violet," Luna said. "Kate's death? They said there were markings on her. What if the dream is connected to that?"

"It's not," Violet said flatly. "Because it's a *dream*. Hasn't anyone ever told you they can't hurt you? I mean, didn't you say I died in the first one you had? If they were real, I'd be dead now, right? Case closed."

"B-but Max described it in detail," Luna stuttered.

"Did he tell you these details *after* you told him yours?"

Hesitantly, Luna said, "Yes."

"Then he's *lying!* He came up with something to trick you.

He always did think it was funny to pull your leg because, I hate to tell you this, but you can be pretty gullible."

That had been Luna's initial thought, but things had only gotten stranger since that phone call, in ways she couldn't explain. "I don't think that's what this is," she said. It had been such a long time since they'd last talked that she found it hard to believe he'd call now just to prank her. Considering Kate's death, Susan's disheveled state, the sigils in Chance's house, and the odd dreams, she was willing to lean toward something major happening, even if that something was beyond her understanding. "I had another dream last night."

Violet rolled her eyes, glancing toward the other side of the cafeteria as if contemplating getting up and walking away. "Of course you did."

"Wait! You don't understand! This one started where the other one left off, and—"

"I think what happened was you had a hard night," Violet said, voice going much softer. "You lost someone you care about, and you're grieving. That never gets easier, but the first few days are the worst. I think you'll be in a better headspace when you get some real sleep."

Luna had one more ace up her sleeve . . . literally. She'd been afraid to mention them at first, but now she was angry enough not to care. "Look!" she growled and yanked her sleeves down revealing the deep purple-black splotches underneath. Violet gasped, and Luna flexed her wrists, watching the marks rumple. Chance grabbed her arm, holding her wrist close to his face. She tried to pull herself free, but he wouldn't let go, saying nothing by way of an explanation before finally releasing her.

"How did you get those?" Violet demanded, eyes stuck on the ugly blotches.

"I woke up with them this morning," Luna said with an exaggerated sniffle. "And I get it, okay? This *doesn't* make sense. Not at all, but there's something to this."

"It makes no sense at all," Violet said, then finally moved her eyes to Chance. "I'd believe it more if you told me he was responsible."

Chance snarled, and Luna expected him to spit his rage at Violet when he got up and stormed away instead.

"Now that he's gone, are you gonna tell me what really happened?" Violet asked, concerned.

"I already have," Luna said and pulled her sleeves down to hide her ghastly marks.

Chapter Twenty-Seven

THE REST OF the day, Luna's mind volleyed between Sidra's funeral, Susan's haunting words, the marks on her wrists, and her weird dreams. Something about the look in Chance's eyes at lunch stuck with her too. A cold fascination that was almost . . . chilling. It was the same look he'd worn when he killed that bird.

As Luna walked home, she subtly moved her sleeve aside to glance at her wrist. To say she felt helpless was putting it lightly. Up until now, she'd always relied on science, on *logic*, to help her figure things out. This situation, just like the room with sigils and bones, seemed to be beyond both.

"Hi."

Luna jumped at the sound of Max's voice and turned to see him walking beside her. He was bigger than she remembered, with a tuft of brown hair and a square jaw. "M-Max?" she stuttered, a slow smile spreading across her face. "What are you doing here?"

"I promised you some answers, remember?" he said, staring down at her with an absence of emotions.

"I remember," she said, excitement dimming. He was here on business.

"You look like you're lost."

That was an understatement. "My friend's grandma died yesterday. She and I were close. It's not been an easy day."

"I can imagine. You're brave to go to school."

"I didn't have much of a choice. Dad wouldn't let me stay home."

"That sucks," Max said. "Especially with what's been going on with the whole Kate thing. Makes the most sense that he'd want to keep you nearby if possible."

You'd think.

"Things have been weird since she disappeared," Luna said.

Max raised an eyebrow. "Weird how?"

Her heart raced with the desire to spill everything she'd learned. Would he listen or would he brush off her concerns? "What if . . . I told you I think I might know who's responsible for what happened to Kate?"

Max's brown eyes went wide. "I'd ask, what have you found out?"

Desperate to unload the weight of all she'd learned about Chance, Luna started to talk. "I don't know if you remember him or not, but Chance . . . from elementary school? Well, he stays in this weird old house in the woods that has this room full of bones and sigils. I tried to do some research to figure out what they mean, but I couldn't find anything specific. Rumor around town is that when Kate was found, she had ritualistic markings carved into her skin. I can't help but think that's a hell of a coincidence."

"That *is* pretty compelling," Max said. "But how did you find that room in his house?"

"He kind of took me there after prom. I didn't have a way home so he offered me a ride, except he didn't take me straight home."

"If you're right, and he did kill Kate, then you're lucky he let you go."

"It's intentional," Luna said, thinking of the cryptic things Chance had said. "I think he wanted me to see it. He keeps saying how it has something to do with me and that I'll find out what it means. I'm scared, Max."

"Have you reported any of this?"

Luna shook her head. "Violet thinks I should."

"For once, she's right."

Luna shot him a scathing look. That wasn't a conversation she really felt like getting into again.

Max sensed it and graciously decided to change the topic. "All that is really weird shit, but it doesn't prove he killed anyone."

"It's a feeling in my gut. I can't explain it. Kate was friends with him, but he didn't care when she went missing. I heard he passed out fliers with Susan and her sister, but I think that was only for show," Luna said. "The icing on the cake is that now Susan is also going through something. She won't tell me what, but I think someone tried to hurt her. I tried to get her to go to the police, but she wouldn't."

"This is really serious."

"That's why you're here, right?" Luna asked. "Something else happened?"

"Yeah. The new dream. I'm thinking it's also not a coincidence."

Luna wanted to believe him, but Violet's doubts swirled around the back of her mind. She felt like she had five hundred out of a thousand-piece puzzle and had to somehow put the pieces together. She would be smart about how she approached the conversation. "What happened in your version?"

"In the dream before, I get shot, and it normally cuts off there. This time, I woke up after that had happened, and I was dragged to this place—a clearing in the woods with this creepy-ass cabin."

Luna stiffened, trying to remember if she'd told him about a cabin before. *I didn't even know about it the last time we talked.* "That's the cabin I'm in. It's one hundred times creepier inside. There's shackles and bloody knives."

"Shackles?"

She nodded.

"Probably safe to say he's not going to kill you if he's keeping you hostage," Max murmured as if he were talking to himself. "But why?"

"I don't know," Luna said and pulled up her sleeves to reveal her wrists. "But I woke up with these today."

Max's eyes went wide. "You said there were knives in the cabin? The dream figure has one on him too. I saw it sticking out of his pocket."

Luna came to a halt, speechless. She knew someone else who had something silver in his pocket. Someone who always seemed to be around when she least suspected it. The center of all the strange happenings.

Chance.

"Are you okay?" Max asked, stopping to look at her.

His voice broke her out of her reverie. "I think I connected the dots. The sigils . . . could they be controlling this dream stuff? Is that possible?"

"You wouldn't believe what's possible. Truly."

You don't know what I'm capable of.

"Explain it to me. I can handle it," she said.

Max side-eyed her. "Okay, but if you laugh once, I'm gonna stop talking."

Luna stayed quiet, eager to hear what he had to say, even if it *was* ridiculous.

"You've heard of universes parallel to our own," he began. "There are a lot of them that happen to be in the same Realm where our dreams happen. A place I call DreamWorld, but I've heard it called the Other Side."

Luna bit her lip to keep from saying something. The names sounded so impossible that she wondered if Violet *was* right about him. *Any explanation is better than nothing,* she reminded herself and waited for him to continue. She'd promised him a chance to explain, and she would give it to him.

"No clue what your stance is on magic, but yeah, that's basically what happens there. People sort of . . . do what they want to do."

"I've had dreams before," Luna snorted. "But I would *not* classify them as magic."

"It doesn't work that way for everyone," Max said, scratching the back of his head. "Some people are stronger than others. To the point where what they do can have effects in this world too."

Luna twitched. "So in theory, someone is purposefully dreaming of killing Violet, shooting you, and kidnapping me?"

"Exactly."

"Why would someone do this?"

"That's the million-dollar question, isn't it?" Max asked, pulling the corner of his lip up to show his teeth.

"Is there at least a way to get out of the dream someone else has created?"

Max shook his head. "Not until they're done with it."

"This is really not how I thought my last month of high school was going to go," Luna said, holding a hand to her forehead. "Graduation? Check. Scholarship applications filled in? Check. Glorified Freddy Kreuger? Fucking check."

"Yeah, this isn't exactly a thing *anyone* can really plan for. The upside is that at least you can do whatever you want *inside* the dream. I mean, have you tried breaking your restraints and escaping?"

"Yeah, but they're too strong."

Max ran his tongue along his teeth before he said, "Honestly, I'm not surprised. In that plane, your biggest fear is your biggest weakness, and it can be used against you fairly easily. You're scared of dogs, right?"

Luna hesitantly bobbed her head, looking at the scar on her arm. When she was little, her father had taken her to the park one day and someone's dog had gotten free. Not knowing any better, Luna had tried to approach it. The dog bit her, requiring a series of stitches in her arm that had taken weeks to heal.

She hadn't trusted dogs since.

"You're there in dog chains most likely," Max said. "Whoever is behind this knows you well enough to manipulate your fears."

"Well, that's great," Luna said, punctuating each word with venom. They knew everything about her, and she only *suspected* who they could be. It didn't seem like much of a fair fight.

"This is probably as good a time as any to mention that if you die there, you die here too."

"That's a bullshit rumor," Luna said. "I mean, Violet died in the dream, but she's alive."

"That's the part that's got me confused," Max admitted, running his hand through his short hair. "There are a few things at play that don't quite add up."

Luna shrugged. "Maybe she wasn't fully asleep? I mean, she told me she'd been in and out that night."

Max scratched his head. "Maybe. It's really curious."

That wasn't the word she'd use for it, but at this point, she was too rattled to come up with something better.

"If we can get this to stop, then we should be fine," Max said in an attempt to console her.

"And how do you propose we do that?" she asked. "You're telling me I could go to sleep tonight and get murdered."

"I doubt it. It doesn't seem like he plans on killing you. Not if he went through all the work of taking you away from where he killed Violet," Max reasoned.

"That makes sense." There was silence between them before Luna tilted her head and added, "How do you know all this stuff, Max?"

He breathed out slowly, careful to avoid eye contact. "It would . . . take too long to explain. You have a funeral to get to."

"I have time," Luna insisted, hating that he would use Sidra as an excuse for anything.

"Look, I'd rather not say, okay?" he snapped.

Luna recoiled, caught off guard by the anger. If he was that determined to keep his secrets to himself, pushing him wouldn't change a damn thing. "Fine, but I can't help but think there must be other people who can stop this."

"They're called Keepers. Like the Peace Keepers of the Realm. When something goes wrong, they're the ones to take care of it and clean up any residual issues so common people don't figure out the truth."

"If there are people who can do that, why don't they err on the safe side and keep *everyone* out?"

"Some people are too powerful. Not to mention the fact that there are more of them than us."

"*Us?*" she echoed. "What do you mean?"

"Nothing," he said quickly and ran his hand down his face to hide his expression.

Luna pursed her lips. If she hadn't been suspicious of him before, she was now. There was something about his tone that had her believe there was something major he didn't want to tell her. Somehow, she forced away the uneasiness and asked, "What *can* we do?"

"We fight," Max said as if it was the most obvious answer in the world.

Luna sighed as they came to a halt in front of her house. She wanted to argue. To tell him that it would be impossible to fight when she had no idea what was going on, but she could see her father peeking out the window.

"We'll talk some more later," she said, glancing toward her house. "I have to go."

Max's face hardened, but he said nothing else before he waved goodbye and walked away. Luna trudged up the path and into the house. She braced herself, ready for Abrahim to barrage her with questions about who the boy was that she'd been walking with. Her father moved around the kitchen, not calling so much as a greeting. Curiously, Luna set her bag down and crept to the entrance, watching him. It wasn't often that her father cooked—Luna was normally the one responsible for dinner.

So the casserole on the kitchen table unnerved her.

Luna took her seat and dropped the question she already knew the answer to. "When is Sidra's funeral?"

"It was earlier today," he said, turning away to dig through the cabinet full of baking dishes.

He couldn't even look at her to tell her the news. A dozen emotions swept through Luna. Anger, hatred, sadness, and hopelessness. She closed her eyes, holding in her tears. It would be a long time before she forgave her father for making her miss it.

"Why couldn't I go?" she asked, trying to keep herself from having a full-on meltdown.

"You don't need to remember her like that," her father said, putting the lid on his dish.

Kindness. Her father thought he'd been acting out of *kindness*. He didn't understand how cruel the decision actually was.

"You had no right to deny me the chance to say goodbye," Luna said pointedly.

Her father stopped and looked at her. She couldn't identify the emotion in his eyes as he said, "You can visit her grave at any time."

Luna had already planned on it. "If the funeral's already done, what's that for?" she asked, pointing to the casserole.

"We're visiting with Sidra's family," her father said. "They haven't had time to eat a proper meal."

Luna opened the lid on the casserole, observing what was inside. "This doesn't exactly count as *proper*."

"What's wrong with it?"

Luna poked the unmelted cheese on top and guessed the middle was cold. "I'll make something," she offered. If she couldn't attend the funeral, the least she could do was give Nazir a presentable meal.

She ignored her father's protests as she went to work cooking a plate of her own. "Here," she said an hour later.

He looked at it, then at his own creation and said, "Okay, this is better."

Luna packed it up, and they got into the car. It wasn't often that they took trips together. The majority of the drive was silent. The warm travel plate burned her lap, but she didn't move it. The pain almost felt good in a way, reminding her that she was alive.

Outside of Nazir's place, a maze of vehicles forced

Abrahim to park halfway down the block. Luna climbed out of the car carefully so as not to drop the dish. An odd sense of foreboding washed over her when she looked up at Sidra's house knowing she was no longer inside it.

Before they reached the driveway, Abrahim set his hand on Luna's shoulder. Snapping back to reality, she wiped her face with the back of her hand, not wanting to be vulnerable around her father.

"Are you okay?" he asked.

The compassion in his voice surprised her. "Yes," she said because she didn't want to go in-depth about all the emotions she actually felt.

Abrahim nodded and took the lead. He knocked on Sidra's door and an adult Luna vaguely recognized from the mosque opened the door. He greeted them, but Luna kept her eyes on the food in her hands.

"The kitchen is through there," he told her.

Luna nodded curtly and went into the other room, adding her dish to the pile of others. Awkwardly, she stood near the table. Her father had already been led away toward a group of men on the other side of the house.

Luna knew better than to follow. A few women she recognized from the mosque flitted about the kitchen, rinsing out cups and preparing beverages. She could've joined them, but their chatter seemed like too much for the mood she was in.

Luna drifted out of that room and into the living room. She looked at Sidra's chair by the window, remembering the last time she'd seen her. There was a man seated in it now, and when he looked her way, she quickly averted her gaze.

Luna didn't see Nazir in the living room or the kitchen, so she went in search of him. When she finally found him, he was sitting on the back step, staring up at the changing colors of the twilight sky.

"Hey," Luna said softly, and she sat beside him.

He cut her a sideways glance, his eyes and face red. "Hi."

"How're you holding up?"

"As well as you can probably imagine," he answered and sniffled.

"I'm sorry," she said. And she was. Out of everyone she knew, it seemed so unfair that Sidra had to die. She wished they lived in a world where the good could simply live on forever.

"It's all part of life, right?" But his words sounded hollow, without emotion, as if he were practicing some script he'd been told to follow.

Comforting words escaped Luna, and Nazir buried his face in his hands, resuming his sobbing. Luna sat awkwardly beside him. She wanted to run her hand over his back, but the action would most likely be frowned upon. Instead, she offered him silent companionship.

When the tears started to slow, he looked up and said, "I'm really going to miss it here."

Confused, Luna asked, "Where are you going?"

"Don't know yet. Guess I'll be staying in the dorm full-time now. Dad's got it in his head to sell this place."

"That sucks," Luna said bluntly. Her friendship with Nazir felt like the only real relationship she had. The one with her father was always strained and her friendship with Violet was on life support. Things were always easy with Nazir.

Effortless.

The thought of losing not only Sidra but Nazir, too, left her hollow.

"Yeah, it does," he said. "I have so many memories here, but I can understand why Dad wants to get rid of it."

Luna stayed silent. Memories would be a reason to hold on to a place like this. A place that connected you to family who are no longer around.

Nazir ran a hand through his hair and looked up at the sky. "But it feels too soon."

"Way too soon," Luna agreed and forced out a question she was hesitant to hear the answer to. "Will this be the last time we see each other for a while?"

Eyes glittering with tears that were yet to fall, Nazir said, "I think so."

Forgetting about proper etiquette, Luna pulled Nazir into a tight hug, feeling complete when he hugged her back.

Chapter Twenty-Eight

I T WASN'T OFTEN that Amy received messages from her partner when she was awake. It was an awkward kind of tickle, almost annoying, and if she tried hard enough, she could ignore it. Except, the sensation persisted. Agitated, she allowed the connection to open.

Meet me in the woods tonight, her partner said, sending coordinates along with the message.

Okay, she replied, already knowing what it was about.

She'd felt the ripple, the change in atmosphere over their entire town as something had been pulled from the Other Realm and into this one. She put her textbook away and got her room in order. Michelle was asleep in the other room, so Amy had to do her best to sneak out while making as minimal noise as possible. Once that was done, the rest was easy.

She slid into her sister's red car and eased it down the road. A heavy yawn left her mouth as she drove, and she thought longingly of brewing a big pot of coffee.

She made it out of the town and to the edge of the looming woods. She parked the car in a spot off the road, where she hoped it wouldn't be spotted by anyone passing by, and grabbed her mask before she wandered into the woods. It was so dark it was nearly impossible to see. Animals hooted and chirped around her, but she couldn't tell how close they were. With the mask, it was hard to see much of anything at all.

She followed the compass in her head, the pull of her magic toward her partner's. When she finally found him, he was in a part of the woods where the plants overhead were thinner and moonlight reached the forest floor.

"Ready for tonight?" he asked as soon as she approached. The gems in his masquerade mask sparkled in the moonlight.

She shook her head. "Never ready for this. Why are we in the woods?"

"Someone pulled something out of the Realm. A cabin."

***

FOR THE ENTIRE afternoon, Chance ruminated on the cabin. The one Luna had been able to pull clean from the Other Realm and into this one. He hadn't had the proper chance to explore it yet, but today, he vowed to do that.

After he finished his responsibilities for the day, he drove out there, parking his truck in a place where it wouldn't be noticed should anyone happen to come looking. He crept into the clearing, taking in every detail on the outside of the building.

It's uncanny, he mused and pushed his way inside.

He traveled through the main room, impressed with Luna's work as he wandered deeper into the cabin. Impressed with *her.*

She'll be quite the asset, he told himself.

He paused in the doorframe to the bedroom, feeling the

sturdiness of it beneath his fingers.

Before he heard their footsteps, he could *sense* them coming, picking their way through the undergrowth outside as if the plants were an extension of himself, warning of oncoming danger with a hivemind.

Keepers.

Shit. Chance bolted out the back door.

The surge of Luna's magic had been huge. Something that everyone who was sensitive to the Other Side could pick up on. Of course they would come to investigate. But if the Keepers found him, they would think he was responsible for this, and he'd need an explanation. Without him, they could chalk up the incident as nothing more than the result of accidental Dimensional Theft, which happened from time to time.

Swallowing heavily, Chance crept through the foliage to get his first real glimpse of the Keepers. There were two, a guy and a girl, both of the top halves of their faces covered with masks. The girl was small with a clump of thick, bushy brown hair running midway down her back. The guy was large, hefty. Probably the muscle. They muttered to each other in voices too low to pick out any particular words and with one last glance at the cabin, they started to wander back through the trees.

Chance had the urge to follow but let it pass. They would be back, and he would have more opportunities to face them. Next time he'd be ready.

Chapter Twenty-Nine

THE FIRST THING Luna did upon waking in the dream that night was to look for something she could use to break her way out of the shackles—a hammer, a nail, a piece of wood. *Anything.* She clawed at the wall, at the floor, until her fingertips were raw and threatened to bleed, but nothing came loose. After exhausting all her ideas, she had to admit defeat. There was no way out except for the key.

Faced with that fact, she turned her attention to studying the rest of the cabin. There was a pile of boxes in the corner that she hadn't noticed before. What was in them? The only difference between this dream and the dream before was that the dagger was gone from the table. Did the figure have it with him?

He's not here.

That thought gave her sufficient room to breathe. Maybe tonight, she wouldn't have to see him and could have all the time she needed to come up with an escape plan. As the thought came, the door rattled and dashed her hope. It inched open, bright light filtering in from outside as the man shambled inside. She tried to catch a glimpse of his face in the sunlight, but the everlasting dark shadows beneath the hood kept his face hidden.

Then her eyes went to the body he dragged with him. He took it to the corner of the room near the boxes, dropped it, and stood up straight before closing the door.

Max's words played through her head. *If you die in a dream, you die in reality.*

The body in the corner was a boy who looked to be her age. She didn't recognize him with the spiky blond hair and shining ivory skin. Luna looked away, then a tiny flash of movement made her look back. Had one of his hands twitched? She narrowed her eyes to get a better look, but the hand didn't move again.

Of course it didn't, she thought numbly and pulled her eyes away. The figure sat in a chair at the table, watching her. As soon as her eyes landed on him, he stood and approached her. He knelt before her, a foot away.

Luna's heart started to pound, mind racing with a dozen possibilities of what could happen next.

"I think it's time for you to know the truth," he said and pulled the hood down.

Luna's insides twisted when her eyes met Chance's. *All* her suspicions had been correct. Dread filled her. Why would he confess now?

Chance smirked. "Cat got your tongue?"

Luna blinked, speechless at her own stupidity.

"You're not proud? You were right about me," he said.

"I don't . . . understand," she admitted. If she'd been right about Chance, then that meant everything Max had told her was true too. The Other Realm. The *magic.* She felt faint.

Chance moved closer, studying her. She pulled back as much as she could, but the wall kept her from going far.

"It's a lot, I know," he said and sat before her cross-legged. "You have many questions, but first things first, let's fix this," he said and pulled two pieces of white cloth out of his pocket.

She gagged when she saw the fresh blood splattered on one. Considering the body in the corner, it wasn't a surprise. He grabbed her right wrist and tucked one of the cloths around her skin, creating a cushion against the cuff. He did the same for the other one, and as she watched him work, she suddenly understood his reaction in the cafeteria. He hadn't thought the marks would follow her out of the dream.

"You have a lot to learn, kitten," he said and touched her chin affectionately. "Until then, these cloths should lessen the marks you seem so eager to show off."

Luna jerked away in disgust. "Don't touch me."

"You're cold even in my dreams," Chance said, chuckling as he stood up before crossing to the body in the corner. "Imagine that."

"Is he dead?" she asked.

Chance gave her a scathing look. "What do you think?"

Luna thought a lot and liked none of it. "I think this is how you killed Kate."

"I was *not* responsible for what happened to her."

"No one else had a reason," Luna said softly.

Chance smiled, but she could see he used it to hide something else by the way he ducked his gaze. "All right, you got me," he said. "I killed her, and you know what? I'm not even sorry."

He didn't wait for her to reply before he grabbed the boy's shirt collar and started dragging him down the hallway, leaving a trail of blood behind. She heard a door open, then a loud *thump* as if he'd thrown the body like it was nothing but a bag of dirty laundry.

Chapter Thirty

CHANCE'S EYES FLUTTERED when the first of the day's rays hit his face. He sat up, groaning at the various pops as his muscles stretched. His trip to the Other Side had been taxing, but he'd learned something vital. Luna knew that he was responsible for Kate, and she could only have learned that if Susan had told her.

I let her make it. Chance hated what he'd have to do next. It'd been a bad choice to keep her alive in the first place, but he had hoped she would listen.

Chance dragged himself out of bed. There was a lot on his itinerary for the day and little time to get it done. It was Wednesday, but he was fortunate in the fact that it was Skip Day. He didn't plan on going to school and guessed none of his friends would be there either. Luna might be the only one. Part of him ached at how innocent she was.

Chance smoothed back his messy hair and pulled on clean clothes, tucking away his trusty blade into his pocket. First things first, he'd have to pay Susan a visit. It would be difficult, and he strained his mind trying to think of an alternate course of action.

Either her or you.

That decided it.

He made his way through the house and into his truck.

Yawning, he pondered what he'd snag for breakfast from the café after it was over. Fifteen minutes later, he parked in front of Susan's house. Breathing in, he leered at the front door of the perfect home. His plan was straightforward with one exception. Sarah was a variable. If she was in the house, he couldn't do what he wanted to do. If not, it was go time.

Susan's car wasn't in the driveway. Had she driven it or had Sarah? Cautiously, he got out of his truck and made his way up the walkway. The door was unlocked, and he pushed it open, listening for movement anywhere inside. It was quiet. Eerily so. Encouraged, Chance pushed it open the rest of the way and crept up the stairs. First, he peeked into Sarah's room, verifying that the bed was empty. Then he made his way to Susan's room. Her door was shut so he pushed it open as quietly as he could. Susan lay in bed, face serene as she slept, a heavy white nightgown over her frame.

Chance approached her and whispered, "Rise and shine."

She woke gradually, face clouding with fear when she saw him. She jerked away until her back hit the wall. "What are you doing here?"

"Someone didn't keep her mouth shut, did she?"

Susan's face morphed into something animalistic, and she lifted her comforter, throwing it at him before she tried to make a dash for the door. Chance was quicker, and he wrapped her in a bear hug, pinning her arms to her waist. She growled and kicked, desperately trying to land any blow she could. Chance hoisted her an inch off the ground before she managed to wiggle free. She lurched forward, but before she could make it to the door, Chance intercepted, ramming his shoulder into her. She lost her balance, the side of her head slamming onto the corner of the dresser.

The blow immediately knocked her out.

Chance huffed for breath as he hovered over her unmoving body. "I didn't think cheerleaders could fight so well."

He watched her as he regained his composure, certain she didn't have any other tricks up her sleeve before he scooped her into his arms and made his way out of the house, grateful that at least she wouldn't be conscious for what would come next.

Chapter Thirty-One

WHEN LUNA OPENED her eyes to the safety of her bedroom, she stared up at the ceiling and thought through everything that had happened in the dream. She looked at her wrists, the marks darker now. The cloths Chance had forced into the shackles had done nothing.

At least you're alive.

Who had been Chance's unfortunate victim?

Doesn't matter now.

Sunlight streamed through her window, and the clock on her bedside table said it was a few minutes before she was due to get up for school. She hit the button to turn off the alarm. Today, she *didn't* have to go. It was Senior Skip Day. Her father didn't know about it, and Luna planned to keep it that way.

If only Skip Day had been yesterday.

Luna rubbed her sore eyes and kicked off her covers, stumbling over to the closet to get dressed. Her father wasn't awake yet, so she was silent as she crept across the linoleum floor to where the phone hung on the kitchen wall. Clumsily, she dialed Max's number, listening to the line ring and ring.

"Hello?" Max's voice croaked on the other end.

Luna realized she must've woken him up and immediately felt a bit of guilt that was easy to assuage. "You had a new dream last night, right?"

"I did," Max said, sounding instantly more alert. "You were right about Chance."

Luna furrowed her brow, opened and closed her mouth, and tried to figure out how Max could know. "You knew?"

"The *body* Chance brought into the cabin? That was me."

That statement only created more questions. "You look nothing like you."

"That's intentional," he said. "I tried to get your attention. Didn't you see me wave?"

"I thought I *imagined* that."

"You didn't. I couldn't make a big show of it because I didn't want him to see that I was alive," Max said. "But I think he knows anyway. He put me inside a closet and the door is locked."

"So he's keeping you hostage, too," Luna said, clenching the phone tighter. He'd been at the table when she'd talked about Max to Violet. Did he seek him out *because* he was someone she knew?

He's really been playing the long game, Luna thought despondently.

"I guess so," Max agreed. "Or he's got something else planned for us."

"I don't know how much more of this I can take, Max. I feel like I'm falling apart. I tried to push all my problems away until I graduate, then have this grand new life, but that's not going to work anymore."

"Unfortunately," Max said. "Look, we should talk in person. Meet you at the regular place."

"All right," Luna agreed, glad she wouldn't have to spend the day alone.

"See you soon," Max promised and hung up.

Luna did the same, considering everything the day would bring. *The regular place.* That was a phrase she hadn't heard in some time. In elementary school, Luna used to sneak out of the house to spend time with Max at the park on a regular basis until he'd moved away. It had been a place of peace for her ever since.

Her stomach rumbled with hunger. The past few days, she'd eaten only a few bites of dinner, enough to get her father not to bug her about it. Half-heartedly, Luna opened the fridge and pulled out an apple. As she took a bite of the fruit, she curled her lip at the ugly marks on her wrists.

What did Max have to say that he couldn't tell her over the phone? Considering everything he'd been through on the Other Side, she wondered if he had some wounds of his own he wanted to show off. That would explain the need for the in-person visit. Shuddering, she turned her back to the kitchen and slid her shoes on, hid her backpack in the closet, and traveled to the park with her head bowed low as she finished her meager breakfast.

On the way, she passed a copse of trees. Luna tried to hurry past them, but the morbid part of her brain made her stop and stare. Three years ago, they'd found Dahlia's body there. A bit of sun-bleached *CAUTION* tape hung from one of the branches. That was all that was left of her.

Now the town has two ghosts, Luna thought, imagining that Kate's final resting place would look similar to this.

Unnerved, Luna forced herself to move on. At the park, she wandered through the playground equipment and to the stretch of woods at the back of the lot, plopping down next to the base of a tree. As she sat there, dark thoughts creeping in, she watched the sky, losing track of the time until, at last, Max appeared, red in the face and out of breath from his jog. He plopped down beside her.

"All right, what is it you have to tell me, Max?"

Ragged breaths tore from his chest, and he held up one finger. As his breathing started to even out, he pulled up the sleeve of his T-shirt to expose his shoulder and a deep purple wound with a yellow bruise around it.

"What is that?" Luna asked, squinting as if that would answer the question.

"It's the bullet wound I got from the dreams."

Luna gasped, raising a hand to her mouth. Her bind marks were nothing compared to his injury.

"This isn't going to stop. *He's* not going to stop anytime soon," Max said. "We need to figure out a plan."

"If we have magic like you said we do, then why don't we confront him and put an end to this?" Luna reasoned. "Two against one."

"You're biting off more than you can chew there," he countered.

Luna humphed and folded her arms. "You got a better idea?"

"Maybe. You're onto something with the group thing. We shouldn't forget that we weren't the only ones in these dreams.

Violet is part of this too."

"I've tried to tell her about the dreams, but she thinks it's ridiculous. She's thought that since the very first time I brought them up."

"We should talk to her anyway."

"I don't think that's a good idea."

"What have we got to lose?" Max asked. "Who knows? Maybe she'll decide to talk to *me* about it. And maybe we'll learn something. She got out of the dream cycle. Which potentially means we could get out too."

There were a lot of *ifs* in his plan. A lot of uncertainties. But he spoke with confidence. Confidence that made Luna more suspicious with each conversation they had.

Had something like this happened to him before?

Chapter Thirty-Two

CHANCE PULLED THE ribbon out of Susan's hair. While he'd worked, it held her long brown locks out of the way, but now they were a mess around her unmoving body. He tucked the ribbon into his pocket and lay her head down gently on the dirt. He'd managed to complete this ritual, thankfully, without her waking. When he was finished, he cut her throat and let her die. Then he was faced with the problem of her body. He didn't want to leave her in the open and risk her being found like Kate, but he hadn't brought the supplies with him to make disposing of her simple.

He ruffled his curtained blond hair. Moving her would only end up drenching him in her blood. In *that* mind, he always knew what to do with the corpse, but for whatever reason, he hadn't slipped into it.

Chance searched through his truck for anything that could help. In the back seat, he found an old duffel bag and pulled it out. Dusting it off, he opened it up, trying to gauge its size. It wouldn't be a permanent solution, but it would do for the time being. Once nightfall came, he'd be able to dispose of Susan properly, but until then, he needed to keep her hidden.

Bag in hand, he went back over to Susan and arranged it beside her. He picked up her tiny body, carefully bending her arms and torso before dropping her inside. It was a tight squeeze, but when he pulled the zipper, it closed. He picked it up by the handle, straining under the weight, but he managed to lug it over to his truck, setting it in the back seat. He stripped off his shirt and stuffed it into the bag as well before carefully tucking it beneath the seats.

Rooting through a pile of old hoodies, he selected the one that stunk the least and pulled it over his head before plopping down in the driver's seat. He was already tired and hungry, and his to-do list was barely half-completed. Chance rolled his shoulders and turned the engine on. With Susan taken care of, he'd fix the Violet problem next.

He cruised down the street, taking his time on the drive. He stopped at the café and ate as he plotted out the rest of his day. With a full stomach and a plan, he made his way to Violet's house. He doubted she knew that he was aware of her address, but he kept notes on *everyone*. Most of the time, the information was useless, but in this case, it worked in his favor. With one glance at the back seat to see if the duffel bag was hidden from anyone walking or driving by, he got out of the car and stormed up the walkway. He pounded on the door with the side of his fist, not worried about the possibility of her parents answering.

From what he'd heard, Violet's parents were similar to the Cross sisters' in that they were practically ghosts, coming by only when it concerned them. Or at least that was true of her father. Her mother had died some years back. Violet took care of her brother and worked a part-time job at the grocery store to support them both.

When the door opened, Violet's eyes went wide, and she made a move to close it in his face. Chance held his hand out, preventing that. She backed up as he stepped inside. The house stunk. Dirty dishes and discarded beer cans littered the furniture and the carpet. The heavy smell of cigarette smoke and other acrid odors hung in the air, and he wondered when it had last been cleaned. Carefully, he shut the door behind him. "Hello, Violet."

"What do you want?" she growled and backed into the living room, stopping only when she bumped into the couch. "You're not welcome here."

"Too bad. I've got some things to say," he began and pulled out his dagger. Slowly, he ran his finger along the blade and said, "I really don't appreciate how you've been bad-mouthing me to Luna."

Violet folded her arms over her chest. "And? I'm not scared of you."

He turned the tip of the blade toward her. "You should be. I could be your worst nightmare."

"More like *Luna's* worst nightmare. I saw what you did to her in the bathroom. I never would've agreed to help you if I knew you'd hurt her. I just wanted to give her a chance to get out of the house. I didn't mean for any of this to happen."

"I suppose we're past the point where my charm is enough to woo you so . . ."—he grabbed her wrist—"let me try another tactic." He pulled the blade across her skin, opening a deep gash with such speed that it took a full five seconds before it started to bleed.

Violet gasped and pulled her arm away. She clenched her

hand over the cut, blood seeping through her fingers.

"Imagine that on your throat," Chance said.

Violet's eyes stayed on the blade. Indecision crossed her face as if she wanted to continue arguing but knew how serious the situation was. "Fine. I'll listen," she said at last. "What do you want?"

"I want you to stop talking to Luna."

"But she's my best friend."

"That didn't seem to matter to you when you decided to unload her on me. So keep being you. Be *distant*. You're good at that."

She weighed her options, eyes on the gore seeping between the spaces of her fingers. It would be selfish to abandon Luna when her friend was clearly in such a bind, but this was Violet's fate if she didn't obey Chance. "Fine."

"Good," he said pleasantly, as if they were chatting about nothing more than the weather.

A knock sounded at the door, and he winced, panic washing over him. A witness wasn't part of his plan. He crept over to the window nearby, parting the ridiculous frilly curtain to peek outside. Luna stood on the porch beside a boy he didn't recognize. Chance squinted. Or *did* he?

"Who is it?" Violet asked, trying to peer through the window over his shoulder.

"Luna and some kid," he said without taking his eyes off them. "Go out there and see what they want."

Violet glanced down at her arm, at the mess of blood, but didn't say anything.

"Ugh," Chance groaned, then pulled a cloth from his pocket. "Don't say anything about me being here while you're out there."

Violet said nothing as she wiped up the blood. Shuffling it to show the least amount of crimson, she pressed it to the wound and moved to open the door.

"Luna and Max, this is a surprise!" she greeted before it closed behind her.

Chance took up his position at the window, staring at her with such intensity that he'd bet money she could feel it.

Chapter Thirty-Three

"GREETINGS, VIOLET, IT'S been a while," Max said almost as soon as Violet stepped out on the porch.

Violet's eyes went from him to Luna before her bottom lip jutted out. She didn't look *happy* to see them. "Yeah, it has."

Luna eyed the bloody rag on her arm, concerned. "What happened?"

"Oh, burnt myself on the stove while I was making lunch. It's nothing," Violet said, but she didn't let Luna see what was underneath the makeshift bandage. "What's the occasion? I can't remember the last time either of you came over."

Luna ducked her gaze away, guilt flooding through her. It was easy to blame Violet for how much their friendship had deteriorated this year, but she certainly hadn't done her part to keep it alive.

"I have some questions for you," Max said, not breaking eye contact.

"For me?" Violet asked, confused.

"Yeah. About that dream you had."

"The dream from a week ago?" Violet rolled her eyes. "Seriously? What is it with you guys?"

"It's just a question," Max said easily. He smirked.

"Answer it."

Violet sighed, looking suddenly exhausted as if Max's words had taken all her energy. "I didn't *have* the dream. Luna told me about hers, and I told her I couldn't remember anything from that night. My insomnia's been acting up lately so I can't really tell you a thing about dreams. At this point, I'd be grateful for *nightmares* if it meant getting a decent night's sleep."

Max looked at Luna. "It's like I thought. He couldn't pull it off for some reason."

Violet puffed her cheeks. "Pull *what* off? What are you—You know what? I don't care. Is this all you wanted? Cuz I'm busy."

Luna's shoulders slumped. She couldn't think of a thing to say. She'd known Violet wouldn't listen, and even if she did, it didn't seem that she had much useful information anyway.

"I guess that's all." Max sighed, disappointed.

"It was nice to see you again." Then Violet disappeared back into the house with a crash of the screen door.

"That . . . went exactly as expected," Luna said as they stepped off the porch.

Max shrugged. "It was worth a shot. The more hands on deck, the better."

"If you say so," Luna muttered, thinking Violet wasn't really much help at all. "Now we're right back to where we started."

They walked the next few feet in silence. A tear ran down Luna's face, and she wiped it away. Max eyed her, waiting for it to happen again before he commented on it, "Are you crying?"

She shook her head. "No, my eye does that sometimes. It's allergies, I think."

"How so?"

"Huh?"

"Is it like one tear or more than that?"

"Why does it matter?"

Max said nothing, waiting for her answer.

"One," she said slowly.

"Hmm, okay," Max said, then shook his head. "Before I forget, there's something I should tell you before you go back to DreamWorld."

Luna winced, trying to imagine how much farther the rabbit hole could possibly go. Every time she thought she'd hit the bottom, it fell out from beneath her feet. "*More?*"

"Chance has a pack of dogs fenced in at the back of that cabin. He must really want to keep you there . . . or keep others out."

"A pack?" Sharp teeth and flashing eyes flooded her mind, and she looked at the crescent scar on her arm, imagining when it was fresh.

"Unfortunately," Max said, "if you do get out of the shackles, the danger doesn't end there."

Luna shuddered. She needed to find a permanent way out of the dream. Until then, she was stuck until Chance finished with her or she finished off Chance.

Chapter Thirty-Four

A S SOON AS Violet stepped back into the house, Chance emerged from his hiding place. One last glimpse out the window gave him a final peek at Luna and Max as they walked down the street. He'd overheard the entire conversation. It had been about the dreams. Max knew something about them. That led Chance to wonder if he was the mystery kid Chance had managed to trap in the dream with Luna. Of course he *looked* drastically different, but that was always a possibility in the Other Realm. Especially when it came to Keepers. Some people didn't want to be identified, but it wasn't so difficult when the idiot made it blatantly clear who he was.

Violet eyed him warily. "Did I live up to your expectations?"

Chance turned his gaze to her, almost forgetting she was there. "Yeah, you did great."

"Fantastic," she murmured.

"Why does Luna keep talking to you about dreams?" he asked, trying to downplay how desperately he wanted to be in on the loop.

"Wish I knew," Violet said and tossed her bloody rag in the trash. "Honestly. It's all she talks about. She acts like I'm holding something back, but I keep telling her I got nothing. I've had insomnia for a while now."

Chance felt himself blanch, so he reached up to scratch his jaw, hiding his reaction. Could the reason for his spell not working be so simple as Violet not being fully asleep when it occurred? *No, there are bigger forces at play here.*

"Whatever. Stay away from Luna, okay?" He patted his pocket twice to remind her of his threat before slipping out of the house and into the afternoon sun.

***

WITH THE MAJORITY of her classmates not at school, Sarah spent most of the day going to her classes and watching movies. It was a peaceful sort of day, but she yearned to get home and check on Susan. That morning, she'd tried to convince her to come with her, but Susan had insisted on staying in bed. More and more, that was where she spent her time, and Sarah was worried. Grief did things to people. It was never easy to lose a friend, but Susan seemed to be taking Kate's death harder than everyone else. If Sarah had been close to her, she would be in the same boat.

When Sarah made it home, she dropped her backpack by the door and made her way upstairs to her sister's room. "Susan?"

No response, so she peeked her head inside, but she wasn't there. Susan's blanket was crumpled near the door, a picture frame lay broken beside the dresser. Sarah crossed the room and picked it up, swiping the remaining shards of glass onto the floor. She set it back on the dresser before she crept down the hall.

Maybe she's in the bathroom.

Her sister wasn't there either.

"That's weird," Sarah said out loud.

Then she shrugged it off. Her sister was a fan of the smoothie bar down the street. Most likely she probably slipped out to get herself one. Probably didn't realize she'd knocked the picture down. She'd be back soon.

***

VIOLET SAT IN the living room for nearly an hour after Chance left, debating what to do next. The wound had thankfully stopped bleeding, but her fear was very much alive. What were her options here?

Go to the police.

She'd been mad at Luna for not doing it, but now that the ball was in her court, she was hesitating too. What if they didn't take her seriously?

What if they do? What if they put him away and you and Luna can live in peace?

That was all the convincing Violet needed. She went to the phone and pressed three buttons. When a woman answered, Violet said, "I'd like to report an assault."

Chapter Thirty-Five

AFTER THE CONVERSATION with Violet, Luna and Max spent some more time at the park before getting lunch at the café, then she saw him off on the bus. Luna spent the rest of the day walking through familiar places in town and waiting for the appropriate time to go back home. She desperately missed Sidra and wished she could spend the afternoon with her but had to remind herself that those days were behind her.

Out of habit, she walked past her home anyway, saddened by how corporate and cold the house looked with its matriarch no longer inside it. Luna considered going to school for the rest of the day but didn't want to risk an encounter with Chance, so like a specter, she roamed the town.

Her father was still out of the house so Luna started on dinner. When he returned, the sun was already below the horizon, and he asked her no questions as they ate. They went through their evening prayers and said their good nights.

Luna lay in bed, staring up at the ceiling. This was the hardest part of the night. She didn't know what to expect when she woke in DreamWorld, and she imagined the worst.

As soon as Luna's eyes opened, she glanced around the cabin to see if anything looked different. It was dark, but she could make out Chance seated in a chair across the room. He sat beside a table. On it was a bone wrapped in a rose. Her eyes moved from it to Chance. He hardly paid her any attention as he ran a white rag along the blade of his dagger, polishing it carefully. There were no traces of blood, and Luna wondered why he'd taken the time to clean it.

"Wh-what are you doing?" she prompted, finding the silence unbearable.

A smile crossed his face as he looked at her, continuing to polish the dagger. "I think your friend has been locked up long enough. Time I take him for a little walk next door."

The ugly temple with the sigils and runes carved into the bricks. *If you die in a dream, you die in reality.*

"You can't do that," Luna said.

His smile grew as he rose from the chair. "Really, kitten? *I* can do whatever I want. You only have yourself to blame for bringing him here."

"I didn't," she said weakly.

Chance snorted. "He's not here for me." When Luna said nothing, he continued. "Now if you don't mind, I have some business to take care of." He whistled a jaunty tune as he crossed the room, dagger in hand, to disappear down the hallway.

"Max!" she hollered.

Luna pulled on her chains, shifting to put her weight into the movement. They didn't break. If Chance stabbed Max, it would be game over for both of them. Grunting with the effort, Luna pulled until the metal sank into her skin, freeing two thin lines of crimson.

A crash sounded from the hallway followed by a loud

thump. Quick, uneven footsteps approached, and she opened her eyes in time to see Max—the spiky blond-haired dream version—running out of the hall. He dropped to his knees beside her, Max's brown eyes boring into hers from the unfamiliar face. "I have to get you out of here."

"Don't worry about me. Get out while you can," she said. "You said yourself he won't hurt me. If he catches you, he's gonna kill you."

She couldn't tell if he was listening or not. One hand was on her shackle, his eyes following its length to the wall as he muttered curses under his breath. "But you're bleeding."

"I'll be fine," Luna said with a confidence she didn't possess.

The echo of movement sounded down the hall, and Max didn't seem keen to argue anymore. He stood up, and with one last fleeting glance at Luna, ran through the front door. When Chance appeared, his hand was pressed to his face. He moved it to reveal fresh blood. It seemed Max had gotten in a decent punch before escaping.

"Felix! Sniper!" Chance yelled. Two large Rottweilers appeared, standing side by side outside the open door. "Tear him to pieces!"

The dogs took off after Max, howling with excitement. As Luna watched them disappear, she prayed for Max's safety and then her own when Chance's attention turned to her. Blood dripped down his face from a cut underneath his eye. He stalked over to her, dagger clutched tight.

She imagined him sinking it into her when he knelt, blade

resting on her knee. She looked away, swallowing the nausea caused by his bloody face. The corner of his lip pulled back, and he ripped the white cloths from beneath her shackles. At his silence, she followed his gaze. Ugly gashes were left in her skin. He said nothing as he wiped away his blood with the cloth, crumpling it in his fist.

"Your friend will pay for this," he snarled. "Tell him to run as far as he can and as fast as he can, but I'll get him."

Chapter Thirty-Six

MAX RAN FOR his life, literally, with the two huge hounds right behind him. *Thump-thump, thump-thump . . .* Their paws struck the ground to the rhythm of his heart, their panting breath urging him onward. He tried his best to wake himself up. If he couldn't do it in time, he never *would* wake up. Every stride brought them closer, and Max was growing desperate. He pinched the skin on his arm, but the forest stayed around him.

"Wake up!" he yelled. He'd never come this close to death before and didn't want to imagine how much it would hurt.

Hot pains radiated from his calf when the first dog made contact, its sharp teeth locked onto his leg.

With a jolt, he pulled out of the dream and into the solitude of his own room . . . and so did the dog. Max screamed and rolled over, kicking the beast in a desperate attempt to get it to loosen its grip. It growled, and he kicked its nose again. It let go, snapping its teeth before it lunged, aiming for his throat.

With as much force as he could manage, Max managed to land one more kick to the dog's face. With a *yelp,* the dog flew backward against the window. Glass rained onto the ground as it went through it, landing in the grass outside.

Max watched warily, waiting for its next attack as the dog

climbed to its feet, shook the shards off its pelt, then turned tail and ran, leaving Max shaking and bleeding alone in his room.

223

Chapter Thirty-Seven

"LUNA!" A VOICE growled.

Her eyes shot open with the fear that Chance was in front of her. All her mind could offer was the look on his bloody face as he snarled his rage at her.

"Luna!" the voice said again.

She startled and sat up when she realized her father stood next to the bed, hands on his hips. "You're going to be late for school," he said, pointing at the clock.

Luna tried to appear normal, but after what had happened in the dream, she thought she would be sick. She didn't want to go to school but also didn't think she could face up to any probing questions from her father. So she said nothing as she stood up and moved to walk past him, expecting him to go about his morning.

Instead, he asked, "Are you okay?"

The genuine concern surprised her. It wasn't something she was used to hearing from him. "Fine, Dad," she said. "Had a hard time sleeping."

"With everything going on, I can't say I'm surprised."

Luna clenched her hands into fists, waiting for him to turn it into a lecture.

"All right, well, I'm helping Henderson again today. If you

need me, the number is on the fridge."

"Okay," she said, knowing she would never call that number.

Luna wandered into the kitchen for a glass of something cold to cool her down while Abrahim went to gather his things from the other room. She pulled open the curtains, the bright pink of dawn filling her eyes. She had never been a big fan of the color, but there was something so mystical about a sunrise. Drinking her juice, Luna bid her father goodbye and went to the bathroom, brushing her teeth and getting herself together.

While getting ready, she turned on the television for background noise, freezing when she heard, "Another teen disappearance."

The orange juice she'd downed sat like a rock in her stomach as she turned up the volume.

"Less than a week after the brutal discovery of high school senior, Katherine Red, reports are coming in of another missing girl. Susan Cross is described as being five-foot-six, with brown waist-length hair, emerald green eyes, and a distinguishable heart-shaped birthmark on her arm. If anyone sees her or has information about her whereabouts, they are asked to call police immediately."

Luna stared at the picture of Susan, barely able to process it. *He got her.*

The trip to the mall flashed through her mind. In spite of her initial thoughts of Susan, she'd warmed up to her in the end. Whatever happened, she didn't deserve it.

A knock at the door brought Luna back to the present,

and she turned off the TV. Had her father forgotten something? *He wouldn't knock, he'd come in,* she told herself.

Could it be Chance? She was already late for school, and since they shared first hour, he would notice if she wasn't there. Shaking, she peered through the peephole, confused to see no one beyond it.

"Luna! For Christ's sake, open the door!" Max bellowed.

Baffled, she pulled it open and Max rushed in, slamming the door behind him. Before she could ask what he was doing or why he was even in town, he pulled her into a hug so tight he nearly squeezed the breath from her lungs.

Uncertainly, she hugged him back. *Something must be really wrong,* she decided. "Are you okay?"

"No. Everywhere I go, hellhounds are trying to kill me! I barely escaped that dream alive. I mean, look at me!" He pulled his pant leg up to reveal a bloody gash on his calf. Rugged punctures marked the outline of the wound, the middle covered in clumps of congealing blood that made it nearly impossible to tell how deep the dog had managed to sink its teeth.

Her stomach twisted. "Is . . . is that from the dream?"

"Yeah, the dog bit me before I woke up," he said, dropping his pant leg to cover the injury. "And I pulled it out."

"You . . . you *what?*"

"I. Pulled. It. Out. The dog is *here.* In this Realm."

"Where?" she asked, wondering if maybe Max had somehow managed to trap it. The idea of it being free was terrifying.

"It got out of the house and ran off," Max said.

"Does this . . . happen a lot?" Luna asked. Between the story about Susan and this new tidbit of information, she didn't think her brain could process anything else the day had to offer.

"No," Max said. When Luna's eyebrows furrowed, he added, "As far as I know."

"As if we're not dealing with enough," Luna said and looked at Max, doubting he'd had a chance to see the news—the newest development. "Another girl was reported missing this morning who also happened to be one of Chance's friends."

Max shook his head and moved past Luna to sit on the couch, burying his face in his hands. "This situation is spiraling."

Luna watched him. "Should we go to the police?"

Max didn't look any better as he dropped his hands. "And tell them what, exactly? We can't tell them the dream stuff. They'll never believe us."

Luna huffed and looked down at the floor.

"Let me see your wrists."

She sat down beside Max, pulling up her sleeves to reveal the blackened marks beneath. They were worse than they'd been two days prior, and she was glad her father hadn't noticed them when he'd come into her room. She would've had no way to answer his questions.

"These look awful," he said at last.

Something pounded against the front door, the silence afterward loud. Max and Luna exchanged glances, faces equally ashen. Shakily, she stood to her feet and crept over to the door.

"Luna, don't open it," Max called.

She barely heard him as she stood on her tiptoes, trying to

peer out the peephole. On the other side, there was darkness, as if someone had pressed their finger directly over it. Aggravation swirled up in her stomach. She was tired of feeling afraid, especially at home—the one place where she was supposed to be guaranteed safety. With a huff, she whipped the door open to reveal Chance. His eyes were glazed and unfocused, and in his right hand he clutched a mostly empty bottle of whiskey.

"Hi . . . Luna," he slurred in a way that made it clear he had whiskey in his stomach.

"What are you doing here?" she snarled.

He took a step forward as if he intended to wrap her in his arms, and she slammed it shut before he could. Heart pounding, she put her weight against the door to keep it closed.

"Help me!" she called to Max.

He rushed over to her, and they switched places as Luna did the locks. Once the door was secured, they moved to the kitchen window, looking outside to see what Chance would do next. Why had he come here? And how had he known her father wouldn't be home?

"Hard to believe he's pure evil," Max said, snorting as Chance took a backward step off the porch and nearly toppled over.

"Believe it." Luna hugged herself, recalling the memory of all she had seen and all he had said. She remembered how his eyes had smoldered with rage that day he'd pinned her to the wall in the bathroom. The way Susan looked during their final encounter. He was planning something. *Something that involves me,* she reminded herself uncomfortably. "I've seen exactly what evil he can do."

Chance toppled over on the lawn, face-first. The bottle stayed in his hand, pointing up to the sky.

"And he's out," Max said.

"For now," Luna shot back, dropping the curtain.

"This dream stuff, on the other hand, isn't going to stop anytime soon."

"So what do we do?" Luna asked, turning away from the window. "If we strike first and incapacitate him on this side, no one would believe it was in self-defense because he does most of his business on the Other Side."

"Not all of it, though. Look at Kate," Max reminded her.

Luna drew her eyebrows together. "I really thought he would be a suspect for that, but so far, it seems like he's not even on the police's radar. How is he not getting caught?"

Max shrugged. "Seems to me like he's not working alone. I mean, he's not the only one who's ever thought of using the Other Side for bad things. There are others."

Luna hated the sound of that. "We need proof to tie him to Kate's murder. That would help us make our case to the police."

"Maybe," Max said, sounding wholly unconvinced. "But even if you do prove he did it, and he goes to prison, that wouldn't really stop things. Dreams are everywhere."

"You're right," Luna agreed with a sickening feeling in her gut. The only real way to take him down would be to do so on the Other Side, but that's where he's the strongest. "What do we do with him in the meantime?" Luna asked, peeking outside and seeing that he hadn't moved from his spot on the grass. "I have to go to school. I'm already late."

"Leave him there," Max said. "He'll recover, and we'll be long gone by then. He can explain to your father why he's here."

"Fair enough," Luna said, studying Max and noting the bags under his eyes. Last night had been a lot rougher on him than she could imagine.

"Be careful, okay? Things are getting crazy," he said and slipped outside, closing the door behind him.

Luna watched him go, each step a struggle. The wound on his leg was horrific, and it was only by luck that it hadn't ended up on his throat.

The dog is still loose somewhere, she thought. Would it come back for him? Would it come for her?

Luna got her shoes and backpack and went out the door. As she passed Chance, she glanced his way to see if he'd woken. He'd shifted so that his profile was in full view. His silver-blond hair was swept off his face, and she had an odd moment where she realized he *was* handsome.

Satan was beautiful too.

His charm would spell out doom to the girls who fell for it like some kind of siren song. That made her think of Susan again. What had happened in her final minutes of life? Had she tried to go to the police, or had Chance decided she had simply outlived her usefulness?

Chapter Thirty-Eight

CHANCE'S EYES POPPED open as soon as Luna was a safe distance away. He got up, checking to make sure he hadn't spilt too much of the whiskey on his fake fall, and approached the door.

He had a plan. When he'd noticed that Luna hadn't turned up to school, he decided it was time to act on it. In his opinion, she was spending too much time with Max, and that could be his doom.

But that's okay, he told himself, positive that once he put his plan into action, it would put a divide in their relationship and ultimately, their plans.

He slipped a bobby pin out of his pocket and rattled it in the lock, popping the door open. Inside, he took a deep breath, catching the lingering fragrance of Luna's perfume as he sought out the perfect location to leave his gift. Carefully, he set his whiskey bottle between the cushions on the couch, enough for the neck to stick out, and stepped back to admire his work.

Smiling, he turned and left. His truck was parked two doors down, in the perfect position to spy on Luna's father when he got home. Chance slid into the driver's seat and waited. The only thing that could make this better was if he had some sort of snack to go with his entertainment.

Woo-woo.

Police sirens sounded, red and blue flashing lights blinding him, as a cop pulled onto the side of the road behind him. Heart pounding, Chance wrapped his fingers around the steering wheel, trying to better see in his rearview window. The cop got out of the car and approached the truck. Chance's shoulders slumped, relief breezing through him. His lip pulled back into a sneer before the officer opened the passenger door and slid into the seat beside him. Chance ran his tongue along his teeth as he watched the man.

They sat in silence before he asked, "Could you be any more obvious?"

"Ah, Morgan, I'd say it's nice to see you again, but it's not," Chance said passively. "Still playing the role of obedient puppet for Cody?"

Unamused, Morgan answered, "You belong to him as much as I do."

"Hardly," Chance replied in a bored drawl as he studied his fingernails.

"You should show some gratitude," Morgan said. "They know you were the one who killed that girl. The only reason you haven't been arrested is because he gave you an alibi for that night."

"I didn't ask him to do that."

"No, but he'd do anything for you," Morgan said. "What the hell *are* you doing anyway? I got a report from a girl that you attacked her yesterday. Had a bleeding cut to prove it."

"Doesn't sound like me."

"You're lucky I was around to intercept that call."

"I wasn't worried about it."

"Well you should be. One assault and two murders in less than a month? You're drawing too much attention to yourself and by proxy, that brings too much attention to *all of us*. Novak and Smith already have it in their minds to talk to you again about this new girl."

Chance rolled his eyes until it hurt. "Look, if what I was doing was such a *problem*, Cody would stop covering for me. Hell, he'd tell me so himself. But I haven't seen hide nor hair of him."

Morgan scoffed. "That's because he hasn't been able to find you."

"*You* found me. Couldn't be that hard."

"If you don't come back, he's done covering for you."

"That's not going to happen," Chance said, thinking how he'd barely managed to escape this time. "You might be happy with that place, but I'm not."

"After all he's done for you, you're nothing but a brat."

"Is that all?"

"I can't make you do anything," Morgan said, clenching his fingers in and out of fists. "My only job is to pass along a message: Whatever it is you're planning, you're going to regret it. Cody's patience is running thin."

"I don't need a lecture from you. You wanna be a gopher? Tell Cody I said he can get bent. I'm not coming back," Chance said and waved a hand. "Now kindly get the hell out of my truck before I call the *real* police."

Morgan scoffed and opened the door with a soft *pop*. "Suit yourself. Remember that Cody is watching. Whatever you decide to do next, he'll know."

CHANCE WAS CONFIDENT the situation with Luna was under control, but he had a new problem. If Morgan was right, Chance's resources were running thin, and he'd have to start cleaning up after himself. With the news out about Susan, his next stop was to talk to Sarah. He needed to know if Susan had told her anything before he'd taken care of the situation.

Chance gave one last look at Luna's house. He'd find out how this wrapped up later. For now, he had other work to do. Chance drove around, waiting patiently for the day to end. When people were at work and school, the town had an odd sense of peace about it that was absent during the bustle of the day's later hours. He considered going to school to pass the time but thought Officers Novak and Smith might look for him there, and he wanted to put off that encounter as long as possible.

The time came, and he made his way to the Cross home, ensuring Sarah would have had ample time to make it home first. He parked out front as she pulled in the driveway in Susan's pink car, parking behind their mother's SUV.

"What are you doing here?" she asked as soon she climbed out of the driver's seat.

"I wanted to stop by and see how you're doing. I heard about Susan this morning."

Sarah glared at him with a gleam in her eyes that spoke of suspicion. It didn't come as a surprise that she didn't like him. He'd heard it a while ago but never considered it to be a problem until now.

"Funny you should pretend to care about her now," she said, folding her arms over her chest.

"How could you say that?" he asked, holding a hand over his chest. "I've always cared about her."

Sarah opened her mouth to utter what he expected would be a bitter reply, when a police car pulled into the driveway behind hers. Chance breathed out slowly, mentally cursing his luck as Officers Novak and Smith climbed out of the cruiser.

"Just the two we were looking for," Novak said as the officers approached.

"Of course. Come right on in. Mom's in her room," Sarah said, leading the group inside. Novak followed her down the hall, and he expected Smith to do the same, but he didn't.

He stood there, studying Chance from his head to his feet. "You again, huh?"

Chance stayed silent, gritted his teeth.

"Well, we've got another missing teen and no leads," he mused.

"Sounds like you should get to work then."

"I've been doing some digging," Smith said. "And the funny thing is, Mr. Welfrey, you were friends with both victims."

Chance tipped his head. "And? Sarah was friends with both. Maddie was friends with both. A lot of girls, *and guys,* were friends with both. You can't just look at the goth kid. That's stereotyping."

"What I find particularly interesting about this situation is the sobbing voicemail my coworker received from Miss Cross shortly before she disappeared."

"Sucks."

"Right, Mr. Welfrey. So do you mind telling me where you were yesterday?"

"I paid a visit to my good friend, Violet," he said.

Officer Smith wrote down his words, but there was a look on his face that said he didn't believe him. He flipped the tiny notebook shut and looked back up at Chance. "You know, things don't look good for you."

"Oh, really? Cuz you have no proof I did a thing," Chance said.

***

WHEN OFFICER NOVAK sat with Sarah after fully questioning her mother, it was so silent in the house that one would be able to hear a pin drop. The room without her mother's sobs seemed empty. *Too* empty.

"When was the last time you saw your sister, Miss Cross?" he asked at last.

"Yesterday before school. It was Skip Day, but I went anyway because I like the peace and quiet. Susan's been staying home since the news about Kate."

As Novak jotted down her words, he asked, "Do you know what she had planned for the day?"

"No," Sarah replied. "I assumed she'd probably sleep in and chill at home, but when I got back from school, she was gone."

"What's your relationship with Mr. Welfrey?"

Sarah ran her thumb over her knuckles. "Is he a suspect?"

"I can't answer that," he said.

Sarah huffed. "Okay. I don't have a *relationship* with him. He was friends with Susan, so he came over a lot."

"That's how you know him?"

"Yeah," Sarah replied. "He's not *my* friend. Personally, I can't stand him. There's something off about him."

"How so?"

"He seems . . . *fake*. Like he uses people. Susan always had the biggest crush on him, and he dangled her hope. That's a huge part of why I never cared for him," Sarah said. "Susan would've willingly jumped off a bridge for him, but it was never enough."

"I see," Officer Novak said, resuming his writing.

Sarah tried to read some of it, but she couldn't make out the scribbles. "Do you think you'll be able to find my sister?" she asked after another minute of silence.

Officer Novak set his pen down. "I'll be honest with you, Miss Cross. We suspect the person responsible for Miss Red's death may be in possession of your sister."

Chapter Thirty-Nine

"LUNA!" ABRAHIM BARKED from the couch as soon as she came home from school. She closed the door and froze, staring at her father. He stood in the middle of the living room, arms crossed. "Is there something you need to tell me?"

"No?" she said, trying to sound firm but it came out as more of a question. What she considered *wrong* and her father considered *wrong* were different so there was no telling what could've set him off this time.

"Really?" he asked and turned to grab something off the table behind him. He held it up. Chance's empty bottle.

Luna's heart sank. Hadn't she locked the door on the way out? This was the note thing all over again, a reminder that if he wanted to, he could control her life both inside *and* outside of dreams.

"Mind explaining this?"

Luna floundered. How could she possibly explain everything that had happened that morning? She couldn't tell him about Max or the dreams. He would never believe her.

He seemed to take her silence for an answer. "These past few weeks you've really shown your true colors. Smoking, swearing, and now drinking?" He punctuated his sentence by tossing the bottle into the trash with a heavy *thud*. "Teenagers have a tendency to rebel, I get it, but this seems like more than that. You're going to destroy your life if you continue with this behavior."

Luna breathed out slowly, trying to keep her cool. "This is going to be hard to believe, but it's *not mine*," she insisted, wishing she could make him understand by her desperation alone, but she and her father had never been on the same wavelength. And this time, she couldn't blame him.

"Then where did that come from?" he demanded.

Luna racked her brain for an explanation that could assuage her guilt, but there was none. Frustration rolled over her, the corners of her eyes burning with barely restrained tears. Her father stared at her with disappointment she didn't deserve but would receive anyway.

"What am I going to do with you?" he asked, shaking his head. "You're grounded until further notice."

"Dad, you can't. I graduate in less than three weeks!"

"You haven't given me any other choice."

"Dad, please. We can wo—"

He put up his hand, done with the argument. Luna collapsed into the armchair adjacent to the couch, sick to her stomach. She was a fool for thinking that she and Max had the upper hand. Somehow, Chance had known they were planning something, and he was making sure to stay one step ahead.

AFTER THE SCOLDING from her father, Luna retreated to her

room, sick and angry. All she could think about was how much Chance was ruining her life, and she was tired of lying down and taking it. As if the terror he'd inflicted on the town wasn't enough, he was going out of his way to ruin her life as well.

He's not going to stop, she heard Max say from their conversation earlier. *Dreams are everywhere.*

Prison might not be enough to stop the nightmares, but it would certainly keep Chance away from her home, from her *father*. She sat in her room for hours, stomach roiling with indecision as she considered the pros and cons of her next move.

I can't ignore this any longer, she decided and pushed open her window.

Cool air came in to greet her, and she stood there, breathing it in. There was something soothing about spring air that made her feel nostalgic for better days. Glancing over her shoulder, she stuck one leg out the window and then the other, landing in the grass outside with a soft *thump*. From the outside, she pulled the blind down so only a crack was visible. That way, if her father did happen to peek in the room, he wouldn't think anything was amiss.

Her heartbeat was all she could hear as she walked down the street. She stuck her hands in her jacket pockets, thinking of how great it would be if Chance *did* happen to get arrested. So caught up in her thoughts, she didn't realize a car had pulled over to the curb beside her until a familiar voice called her name.

"Luna!"

"Huh?"

Nazir peered at her from the shadowy interior of the car.

She approached to hear him.

"I said, you're lucky I was passing by."

"What are you doing in town?" Luna asked.

"Getting the last of my things. Why are you out here alone? There's another missing girl, you know," he said and pushed open the door. He didn't ask if she needed a ride, and she didn't ask if he would help. She accepted the gesture and climbed into the passenger seat. Nazir started to drive down the block before he said, "I thought we talked about you being more careful."

Nazir watched her without judgment, waiting for her to speak. Something about the look told her how much he cared about her. How patient he was willing to be with her because he sensed she needed it. She wished he could understand the intensity of her emotions through her gaze alone.

"I can't let it go," she said, looking down at her hands once eye contact became too much.

"Let go?" he asked.

"I . . . didn't tell you everything about prom," she admitted. "My friends ditched me so I didn't have a way to get home. Chance offered so I risked it. Except he didn't take me straight home; he took me to some old place in the woods."

Nazir quirked an eyebrow. "I don't really want to hear—"

"That's not where I'm going with this," Luna said, cutting him off. "There was a room in that house. It had bones and sigils and stuff. *That* was why I went to the library the next morning. I . . . wanted to know what they meant."

Nazir sighed, sounding truly disappointed in her as he said, "I hate to tell you this, but it might not mean anything at all. A lot of those goth kids think being edgy is cool. He was probably just trying to scare you and doesn't know what any of it means. Even if he does believe in all that, so what? If he's not hurting anyone—"

"That's the thing. I think he *is* hurting people," she said, unable to hear the end of that sentence. "Those two girls. They were his friends."

"He sounds weird, but it could be a coincidence." Nazir opened and closed his mouth, carefully searching for his words before he said, "Then again, if you're right, and he *is* delusional and thinking he's performing rituals, he could be an actual danger to people."

"I know. That's why I'm out here. I was going to the police."

"Do you have some evidence to show them?"

She had a confession. *But he told you in a dream.* She imagined telling the police that. They would laugh her out of the office.

Tears welled in the corners of her eyes, and she wiped them away with her sleeve, thinking about the marks underneath. She considered pulling them down, letting him see, but how would she explain how she had gotten them?

No matter what I tell him or anyone else, they're going to think I'm crazy because it all ties back to the dreams.

"No," she said finally. "Nothing concrete, at least. I could show them the house, but that's all I have."

Nazir pulled the car to a halt next to the curb. "Luna, I admire your spirit, but you need to think about what you're saying. What the ramifications could be if you go through with this."

"I have to," she said, thinking about everything Chance had done, everything he planned to do. If she didn't put a stop to it, who would?

"Look, as it stands, it's unlikely the police will listen to you. And word will get back to him. If he *is* dangerous, he might come after you. Not to mention there's a possibility that they'll call your father and tell him everything you tell them. Are you prepared to deal with him finding out everything that's been going on between you and that boy?"

She wasn't. She *really* wasn't.

The look in her father's eyes a few hours before had been terrifying. He was close to giving up on her. If he found out about all of this, it would be the straw that broke the camel's back. He would send her away. She would have to uproot her entire life and start over somewhere else.

"No," she said and buried her face in her hands.

Nazir set a hand on her shoulder. "I'll take you if you think that's what you need to do. But I want you to really think about it first, okay?"

Luna sniffled and wiped her face with the back of her sleeve. "I know." But he was right. Without evidence, there was no case. Things would only get worse for her, and she risked the possibility of Chance turning on her the way he had Kate and Susan. Grudgingly, she said, "Take me home, please."

"Are you sure?" Nazir asked, brow furrowed with

concern.

It felt as if he were the only one who truly understood her. And if she couldn't tell *him* everything she knew, she wouldn't be able to tell a complete stranger.

"Yeah."

"Okay," Nazir said, shifting his car into drive.

Chapter Forty

NAZIR DROPPED LUNA off at the end of her block, and she snuck back into the house the same way she'd snuck out, her father none the wiser. She cried herself to sleep, and when she woke in the morning, the red numbers on her clock were the first thing she saw. In ten minutes, the alarm would go off, and she would have to get ready for school. In ten minutes, she'd have to face the full unpleasantness of the day.

She'd been fortunate in the fact that she'd had no bad dreams during the night. Her problem now was flashbacks of her reality.

How could Nazir not believe me? she wondered, but deep down, she knew why. *She* hardly believed it, and she'd been there to see all the things others would call crazy. She felt like she'd let Susan and Kate down by not following through with her plan.

I can still try; I just need to find evidence first, she reasoned.

Luna didn't think there was much to go on, but she would work with what she could. Primarily, she needed to make a timeline to figure out where the girls had been before they disappeared. And she'd need to do it without Chance finding out. Reaching up, she touched her throat tenderly in the spot his fingers had bruised. There was no telling what he would do if he found her meddling in his business.

Susan and Kate ran in the same circles as him so asking their friends meant word would get back to Chance, and he'd come for her. It might be worth trying to talk to Susan or Kate's parents, except she didn't know them. If she went to their house, they might try to contact her father, and she didn't want to risk that either.

Like a bolt from the blue, it hit her—Sarah, Susan's sister. She'd been quiet, blending into the background like Luna herself. They'd shared that moment the night of Prom where they made their mutual dislike of Chance known. Luna would ask her about it.

Hopeful, she sat up, then frowned as she tried to think of how she could possibly get away from Chance long enough to ask her anything without him overhearing. They didn't have all their classes together, and his brownnosing act for the teachers meant he wouldn't make a habit of skipping. For once, his lying might actually benefit her.

As Luna got up, she brainstormed how her morning would go. If everything went according to plan, she could find Sarah in the hall before first bell and hopefully get her to stop long enough to answer her questions. If it worked, she would have herself a new ally.

Luna hopped into the shower, drying off with a fluffy towel when she was done. After throwing on a blue T-shirt and baggy black pants, she looked in the mirror. Her appearance reminded her of the last time she'd seen Susan.

I hope she's alive, she thought.

She grabbed an apple off the table and her backpack from

the chair, then went out the door. On the walk to school, she didn't see Violet and wasn't in the mood to wait for her. When she arrived, she saw Chance's truck parked at the back of the lot in the usual place. She hurried past it, keeping her eyes peeled for signs of him.

Coast clear, she hurried up the stairs and into the building, continuing down the corridor. She made it all the way to study hall without seeing Sarah. Amy was seated at their usual table toward the back of the room, and Luna made her way over to her, sliding into the open seat. Amy had always had a calming aura. After the chaos of the last few days, it felt good to be next to someone normal.

"Hi."

Amy glanced up from her textbook. "Hello."

"How are you doing today?" Luna asked.

"Can't complain," Amy answered. "And you?"

"I'm good," Luna replied automatically. It was a lie. Had been for some time.

"Have you heard about Susan?" Amy prompted.

A sardonic voice in Luna's head mocked Amy's words. How could she not have? The town had turned into a macabre circus of dead girls and magic. Luna nodded anyway, trying to act like a normal high school student . . . at least for a little while. "Yes. I hope she's okay," she managed to say, doubting her words.

"It's like Kate all over again. I can't believe this is the second time, and the police haven't figured anything out." Amy continued. "Third time if it really is the same guy who killed Dahlia Moore."

Luna tried to ignore the lump in her throat. "I hope they catch the person responsible," she said, wishing more than anything that they would take Chance away in shiny silver handcuffs.

She would take pictures.

"They'll figure it out," Amy assured her, giving her forearm a gentle squeeze before she went back to reading her textbook.

"Yeah," Luna murmured, unconvinced. If Chance used his dreams to do his dirty work, they would never connect him to any of it.

Amy paused her reading and said, "Are you okay, Luna? Like . . . truly okay? You seem out of it."

Luna was a million miles away from okay, but there was no use in telling anyone. "Yeah. I'm fine. *Really*."

"Okay . . ." Amy said, sounding dejected. Uncertainly, she added, "If you need someone to talk to, I'm here."

Uncomfortable with the eye contact, Luna glanced up at the clock. She wished she could take Amy up on the offer, but there was no way to explain her problems to her.

"Can I . . . ask you a question?" Amy asked.

Luna swallowed but nodded. "Of course."

"What exactly is going on with you and Chance? You two seem . . . *close*."

"There's nothing," Luna said quickly, maybe too quickly because Amy pulled a face.

"If you insist," Amy said. "It's just . . . there's a rumor that you two are dating. Hard to tell what's fact from fiction anymore."

"If it's a rumor, it's usually fiction," Luna said flatly. She didn't know if she had prom to blame or if Chance himself had spread it. "Like in this case."

Amy nodded, but there was a pinched look to her expression that told Luna she didn't completely believe her. Luna looked past her to the clock again. She had less than five minutes to get to first hour before she'd be late, and there was no sign of Sarah.

Considering her mission a failure, Luna said goodbye to Amy and made her way across the room. When she hit the door, she almost crashed into someone. She looked up to apologize, stopping when she recognized Sarah's haunting ice-blue eyes. She gave Luna a once-over. Luna did the same, focusing on the swollen, puffy bags under her eyes. She'd tried to hide it under a layer of caked-on eyeliner that only made it more apparent that she'd been crying.

"Luna," Sarah said with a polite dip of her head.

"Hey, Sarah, it's been a while."

Sarah nodded in response and squeezed past Luna, walking deeper into the room. She watched the girl sit and rummage through her bag. No one joined her. Gathering her nerves, Luna walked over to Sarah's table, cautiously pulling out the chair across from her.

"So . . . Susan . . ." she whispered.

The light behind Sarah's eyes seemed to go out. "Yeah, I was the one who reported her missing."

"I'm sorry," Luna said.

Sarah shrugged. "Everyone in school is talking about it.

It's not like you're the first one to ask me questions."

"I was actually wondering if there's anything I can do to help," Luna said. "Pass out fliers or something? I heard you and Susan did a lot of that when Kate went missing."

"We did," Sarah said, spinning her chewed-up pencil. "And we all know how that turned out."

The news broadcast about Kate's discovery played through Luna's head.

"They think whoever did that took Susan as well," Sarah admitted. "My sister might already be dead."

"We don't know that," Luna offered, setting her hand on Sarah's shoulder in an attempt at comforting her. The movement came across as awkward, and Luna pulled her hand away.

"Susan had a lot of friends, but none of them seem too hopeful for how this will turn out," Sarah said, running her finger down the spine of her notebook.

Luna wanted to say something comforting, but the words wouldn't come.

"They're probably counting the days until she's found on the side of the road like Kate."

"I think she'll be okay. She's a strong girl," Luna said, running her nails along her thigh. The words burned her tongue.

Sarah sniffled but didn't say anything else. The bell announcing the start of first hour rang. Chance would have noticed her absence by now.

Now or never.

"Can I ask you something?"

"Might as well," Sarah said as she leafed through her

notebook.

"What happened to Susan before she disappeared?" Luna asked. "I uh . . . noticed she stopped coming to school."

"Ugh. You sound like the cops."

"I'm sorry," Luna apologized, staring down at the table with a fierce blush working its way into her cheeks. This wasn't going at all the way she'd hoped.

"You saw how she was. She stopped talking to anyone, and when I asked her what was wrong, she said it was about Kate, but I think it was something else. The last time I saw her was the morning of Skip Day. I went to school, and when I got home, she was gone and never came back."

Skip Day, Luna thought with a sinking feeling in her stomach. If Chance had also not bothered to go to school, then it would've given him plenty of time to harm Susan.

Luna kept the conversation going for another ten minutes, trying to make small talk so Sarah wouldn't see the horror in her eyes. When she politely excused herself, Sarah seemed more than glad for Luna to go. As she neared the door, Amy looked up from her book and cast a glance in Sarah's direction. There was a question in her eyes as she turned her attention back to her book, but Luna shoved off the curiosity as she continued her journey down the silent hall to her classroom.

It bustled with activity. Kids paced and chattered like a bunch of squirrels. Miss Kessler looked up from her desk, lips in a straight line in the middle of her blank face. "How nice of you to join us, Miss Ketz," she said. "We're in the middle of a group activity right now. Take your seat and find out from someone what you're supposed to be doing."

Different groups were spread around the room, and only one seat was left unoccupied in the middle of the space. As she walked toward it, her eyes drifted to the desk behind it, already knowing who would be there.

Chance.

One hand propped his face up as he leaned on his elbow. He was disconnected from the activity in the room, obviously waiting for her arrival. When she approached, his eyes flicked to her, burning cold blue fire.

Luna tossed her backpack beneath the desk and sat down in the chair, preparing herself for his barrage of questions. She sat sideways so she could see him from the corner of her eye while at the same time keeping tabs on her teacher's location at the front of the room.

"Where were you?" he demanded in a strained whisper, hand dropping off his face.

"I was in study hall and lost track of time," Luna said passively. "I got caught up on all the lies that have been going around school about us."

Chance laughed. "They believe it all too. That we've been dating. Some of them think we've got plans to move in together after graduation. People are so gullible."

Luna clenched her jaw. "If you want to play that game, I've got some rumors I can start too."

"Maybe, but who would listen to you?" he asked with mock sympathy. "Little foul-mouthed weirdo like you? The rumor wouldn't spread far coming from your lips. People would laugh it off, baby."

Luna seethed. "We'll certainly see."

"We're not gonna see shit. Why were you late?" Chance demanded.

"I'm not that late."

"You're *never* late is the point. Last time I checked, your grades and attendance were your life. What were you up to?"

Luna looked down at her hands, twining her fingers together. She hadn't settled on an answer.

His desk creaked as he leaned toward her. "Your lies are going to make things so much worse for you," he whispered in her ear.

She whipped her head in his direction, locking her gaze with his. "I'm not lying. I *was* in study hall, and I got caught up talking to Sarah."

Chance furrowed his brow. "Sarah Cross?"

"Yeah. We haven't talked since prom so I wanted to say hi."

"I guess I can understand that," he said, twisting his pencil between his fingers. "But this is why I don't leave your side. Without me, there's no one to keep you in line. I leave you alone *one time*, and you manage to be twenty minutes late to class. And you wonder why people believe the rumors about you."

"They'd believe things about you, too, if enough people circulated it."

The sharp point of his pencil jabbed into the middle of her back. When she turned to look at him, his teeth were clenched, cheeks flushed different shades of red. Luna stood up, glad to get the sharp tip out of her back, and approached a group on the other side of the room.

LUNA WAS QUICK to discover that crossing the room in first hour was a mistake. When Chance was mad, he was more likely to act out. She patiently waited for the bell to ring and lunch to come, but it tested her patience. Staring at the clock, she nearly *willed* time to move, but it never seemed to when Chance lurked nearby.

One more minute. Luna squeezed her eyes shut.

Chance tapped his pencil incessantly on his desk, trying to get her to turn around.

Then the bell. She grabbed her books and hurried out of the room with Chance right behind her. No matter what she did, she couldn't shake him. Luna got her lunch, and Chance copied the action. She searched for Violet, but her friend wasn't there. Crestfallen, Luna sat down at the nearest table, picking despondently at her food with plastic utensils.

Apparently, Chance sensed the mood change. "Are you okay?"

She ignored him, chewing a small bite as she stared at the lines in the white brick wall. What was the point of answering?

They were alone like he wanted.

Chapter Forty-One

WHEN VIOLET FINALLY made it to lunch, it was way after everyone else had arrived. She had Ms. Sable to thank for that. Her teacher had insisted on holding her after class to yell at her for her less-than-average grades which Violet had argued were the best she could do under her guise of permanent exhaustion. When she at last stepped into the cafeteria, she saw Luna and Chance at a table by themselves.

Luna picked at her food, not bothering to look up from her tray. Chance was close beside her, watching her. He had a tray in front of him as well, but for the time that Violet watched, he didn't eat. It was creepy, the way he shadowed her. Violet wanted to go over there, to talk to her best friend and help her get away from that mental freak.

She'd heard the rumor about them—that they were dating now—but she didn't believe it. *Couldn't* believe it. When she saw them together, it was understandable why everyone else fell for it hook, line, and sinker. The way he watched her would seem doting, adoring. The scabbed cut on Violet's arm burned at the memory of his threats, and she had to remind herself that they were real.

She hadn't heard anything back from the officer she'd talked to, and it didn't seem as if anything had happened to

Chance either. *The police don't care*, she told herself.

It was hard to come to terms with.

Violet contemplated between sitting with Luna or sitting at a table on the other side of the room in a spot where she knew she'd be safe. She took a step toward her friend's table but stopped when Chance's gaze slid up over Luna's head to meet her. Violet retracted that step. Besides appearing depressed, her friend seemed otherwise okay. Violet gave her one last look before she turned to head to a different table, cheeks burning in shame.

Chapter Forty-Two

LUNA'S WALK HOME was spent mulling over all she'd learned from Sarah that morning. Without Chance by her side, she felt as if she could breathe. She stopped by the smoothie shop and got herself a treat, using the time to calm her nerves. On her way out, she spotted a familiar vehicle in the parking lot.

It's not him, she told herself but started to walk faster, the hairs on the back of her neck standing on end.

As she crossed the street, the truck's engine started, finding its way out of the parking lot, and a sickening sense of fear blossomed in Luna's stomach. The truck crept along a few paces behind her. She started to run, heart hammering. She rounded the block, relieved when her house came into view.

Almost there. She risked a glance over her shoulder.

He was closer.

She pushed everything she had into moving faster, dashing up the path to the door.

"Hey, wait for me!" he called out the window.

She didn't listen as she ran toward the house, hoping her father would already be home so Chance would have to keep his distance. She ran into the kitchen, disappointed when she saw the note taped to the fridge.

Luna,
At Henderson's again. Don't know when I'll be home.
Love,
Dad.

"Shit!" she cursed.

Luna threw her backpack onto the nearby chair, letting the note slip to the floor. Glancing out the window, she watched Chance get out of his truck. He seemed to be taking his time, and Luna considered her options. She hurried to the door and turned the lock before she grabbed the phone, dialing Max's number. She held it to her ear, desperate to hear his voice.

"Hello?" Max said at last.

"Max!" Luna said, shoulders slumping in relief. "I need to tell you—"

The phone was ripped from her hand before she could finish her sentence. Wide-eyed, she spun around to see Chance glaring at her, phone to his ear. "Luna can't come to the phone right now," he said and slammed the phone down.

Luna jutted out her chin. "How did you get in here? I locked the door."

"Not much of a security system when it can be opened with a bobby pin," he said, rolling his eyes.

"Get out of my house before I call the police!"

"And tell them what, exactly?" he asked, tipping his head to the side. "I haven't hurt you. And I would tell them that you let me in here."

Luna's heart pounded so hard against her ribs she wondered if he could hear it. Being alone with him was the one thing she vowed she wouldn't let happen again, but somehow, it had. "What do you want from me?" she asked, barely able to hold back her tears. Last time he'd been here, she at least had Violet to help. Now, she felt utterly alone.

"You're not supposed to be on the phone when you're grounded . . . especially with *him*," Chance spat as if Max were a disease.

A thousand things flared up at the same time, the primary one being anger. How did he have the audacity to continue to insert himself into her life? And how did he know she was grounded? Luna's stomach flipped with uneasiness. "What do you have against Max? You don't even know him."

"I know more than you think," he stated matter-of-factly. "He's no good. And I don't want you around him anymore."

Luna snorted. "You can't tell me what to do."

"No, but your *father* can. All I have to do to get Max permanently cut from your life is somehow get him to believe Max is the reason you started drinking."

"You wouldn't dare."

"I would," he said, glaring down at her. "I know exactly how I'd pull that off."

Luna stared back, clenching her jaw. She didn't doubt him.

"Don't get your panties in a bunch," he added, then his voice softened. "You can talk to me about anything. You don't need him."

His words were meant to be kind, but they only filled her

with rage. All she could think about was what had happened the previous morning. The wound Max had shown her. Did Chance want her to stay away from Max so his dogs could kill him?

"I don't want you," she said.

Chance's icy expression said more than words ever could. Before he could speak, tires on the stone driveway announced her father's return home. Chance stared into her eyes a moment longer before retreating down the hall and slipping out the back door.

Chapter Forty-Three

AMY'S HEART HURT when she opened her eyes that morning. She'd spent the night tossing and turning, suffering through images of violent dogs and a fear-filled run through the woods. It was her partner trying to tell her something, but other than the stark terror, nothing else really came across.

Groaning, she held a hand to her chest, trying to ease the sporadic beats of her heart, when a voice flooded her mind. *I need to show you something. Usual meeting place?* her partner asked.

I'll be there soon, she replied and in a flash of frantic movement, threw on the nearest outfit and sought out her masquerade mask. Meeting her partner once in a while on this side of the realm wasn't unusual. Twice in as many weeks? It couldn't be good. *It must be related to the cycle.* She scooped the mask up off the floor. *Maybe it ties to the dogs too.*

She stood in the doorframe, listening for the sounds of her sister moving around in the house. When no noise came, she slipped down the stairs and out the front door, heading straight for the car. The meeting place this time wasn't the woods. It was a library. A midway point between the two of them. When she arrived, her partner was already there in the shadows by the library door.

"What is it? What's happened?" she asked.

Her partner didn't speak. He set his hand on her shoulder, leading her to the side of the building before he pulled down the collar of his shirt, exposing a purple wound on his shoulder.

She gasped. "The dream cycle?"

He let the fabric snap back into place. "It's violent, and it's the reason behind the cabin."

"This all has to do with dogs too?"

"I escaped, but not without bringing one of those hellhounds through with me," Max said. "We'll have to be extra careful."

"Who's responsible for the cycle?" Amy asked.

"His name is Chance."

Amy perked up. "Welfrey?"

"You know him?"

"I know *of* him," she clarified and frowned at the part of his shirt that concealed the grotesque wound. "Do you want me to take over the assignment?"

"No," he said. "Let me handle him, and you continue keeping your eye on Luna."

"There's rumors about her at school," Amy said.

Her partner shrugged. "And? High schools are like that."

"I've heard things about her and Chance. That they're . . . *sleeping* together. If that's true, it must mean they're working together, too, which would make our jobs a lot more complicated."

Her partner froze. "Have you spoken to her recently? Asked her about any of this?"

"Yes, of course. She denied it all. Said Chance was behind

it, but then I saw her talk to Sarah Cross, of all people. They've never run in the same circles but since the rumors began, her friendships changed, and I have to wonder. I mean, that's not something you do for someone you hate."

"That *is* odd," her partner agreed in a strained whisper.

Amy liked Luna. She didn't want to believe the girl was plotting *anything,* but she and her partner knew that believing everyone was innocent was choosing to be ignorant. No matter how big or small, everyone had *something* to hide.

"I think it's time Luna learns the truth," her partner said. "Things are escalating, and she could help us more if she knew what to expect."

"Is that the best idea?" Amy asked. "She could turn reckless. That would interfere with the entire investigation."

Her partner was silent, face drawn tight as if he'd tasted something sour.

"I'm not saying *no,*" she clarified. "I just think it's best to tell her things on a *need-to-know* basis right now. Until we know what Chance is planning. If they *are* working together, too much information in the wrong hands could be our downfall."

***

MAX WAS THE one to end their conversation on the premise of going home. As soon as his partner couldn't see him, he started to run down the road but not in the direction of the bus stop. He ran toward Luna's house. Anger and fear pulsed through him in rhythm to his partner's words. He didn't want to think Luna could be working with Chance on any aspect, but that phone call and Chance's icy threat didn't point to good things.

Luna would never take his side. And I'm going to prove it.

So far, Max's journey had been easy, but he wasn't a fool. The dream Rottweiler lurked somewhere. At night, he could hear its blood-chilling howls and knew it was waiting for the perfect moment to strike. He'd been able to keep away from it so far. If he couldn't beat *Cujo,* then he had no business being a Keeper.

About a half mile from Luna's house, he heard it—the deathly, haunting howl of the dream dog. It sounded far away, but that didn't matter. He was vulnerable, and it was coming for him. Max started to look for shelter, but where he was didn't offer any. There was forest on one side of the street and a looming cemetery on the other.

The eerie howl came again, accompanied by a bush rustling nearby. Max pushed himself to run faster as a large mangy dog flew out of the undergrowth, rushing across the road toward him. From the time the Rottweiler had seen him in Dreamworld, it wanted nothing more than to tear his flesh right off his bones as Chance had ordered it to do.

Max tried speeding up, but the dog already nipped at his heels. It lunged, clamping onto the back of his thigh to injure the leg he depended on. Max screamed, angry at himself for allowing the canine to bite him a second time as he went flying, the weight of the unrelenting hound knocking him forward. He rolled onto his side in the grass. The dog let go. It sniffed him, lip pulling back into a snarl as it stood above him, searching for the best place to sink its teeth.

Max snarled right back. After everything he'd been through, he wouldn't let things end now. Not like this. Heart pounding, he swung out, hand close enough to strike the dog's nose. What should have felt like warm, furry flesh turned into nothing. He watched in stupefied silence as his fingers swung *through* its snout, and the dog's face shifted as if it were made out of mist.

Max's knowledge of DreamWorld hadn't prepared him for something like *this*. When the mangy black fur realigned, that murderous gleam was still there. The one so much like its master. The dog lunged, and Max lifted his arms in a futile attempt to protect himself from its razor-sharp teeth.

Chapter Forty-Four

LUNA SAT ON her bed, untangling her wet hair with her fingers as she decided what to wear. A week of being grounded had passed, and it was Saturday morning once again. Pawing through the clothes hanging in her closet, Luna settled on a dark blue long-sleeved blouse and light gray pants. She pulled them on and let the towel she'd been wrapped in drop to the floor.

"Luna!" her father called from the other room.

She eyed her open window, thinking of the night she'd snuck out and wanted to do it again, but she had nowhere to go. Nowhere was better than being near her father when he yelled like that.

Nerves braced, she wandered out of the safety of her room. She found Abrahim waiting for her in the kitchen. Not meeting his gaze, she answered, "Yeah, Dad?"

"I've decided you've been grounded long enough," he said, the furrow between his brows showing a lingering touch of concern.

Momentarily, her face brightened. "Really?"

Her father nodded. "Your mother convinced me that I may have been a bit too overbearing lately, so this one time, I'll look the other way, but if I ever catch you with alcohol again, you'll be on a one-way flight to your mother's doorstep. Do you understand?"

Luna's nostrils flared. She wanted to be understanding, to see the situation from his point of view, but she was hurt. In spite of her thoughts, she managed to flash a fake grin anyway. She didn't want to say anything that might make him change his mind. "Of course, Dad."

"Good," he said.

"Is that all?" Luna asked, eyeing the phone behind him.

Her father's voice brought her back to the present. "Remember, Luna. Last chance."

Her skin crawled at the finality of his tone. "Yes, sir."

Abrahim gave her a curt nod and made his way to the living room. Luna's shoulders slumped, and she scooped up the handset, dialing Max.

The last thing Chance had said to him rang in her head. *What does he think of me?* she wondered over and over again.

The phone rang twice before Max's mother's voice answered.

"Hi, it's Luna. Is Max home? I need to talk to him."

"I'm afraid he's not," she said.

"Can you tell him I called?" Luna asked, put out. It almost sounded as if she were tired or simply didn't want to talk. "It's kind of important that I talk to him as soon as I can."

"He won't be home for a while," she said, and Luna understood her tone was grief, not disinterest. "He's in the hospital right now."

"What . . . what happened?" Luna asked, barely managing

not to drop the phone.

"He was attacked by a dog the other day," his mother said. "It didn't break his windpipe, thankfully, but he had some pretty heavy damage to his neck and chest. Doctors are keeping an eye on the wound in case there are complications. If you want to talk to him, I can give you the number for his hospital room. He'd be happy to hear from you."

Everywhere I go, hellhounds are trying to kill me! I barely escaped that dream alive. The dream dog had gotten too close to succeeding in its mission. "Of course," Luna said, pulling a notepad and pen out of the nearby junk drawer. "What's the number?"

She repeated it twice and Luna wrote it down, double-checking each number. Seemed as though they both had a lot to discuss about the week since they'd last seen each other, and she was eager to hear all that Max had to say.

"Thanks," Luna said.

"Of course, sweetheart," she replied and hung up.

Luna punched the new number into the phone. As she did so, she thought of Chance. How calculating he was to be able to almost rip the life out of her friend while being nowhere near him. *Wicked bastard.* It left her wondering what he had planned for her. At school, he'd been oddly distant, giving her space and hardly saying more than two words in the classes they shared, yet she always caught him watching her from the corner of her eye.

"Hello," Max answered, voice surprisingly frail.

"Max, are you okay?" Luna asked immediately.

"Luna," he breathed. "I take it Mom told you what happened.

"Yeah, she did," Luna said. "It wasn't a real dog, was it?"

"No," he said, and his voice grew weaker. "When I tried to hit it, my hand went through it. The first time, I could fight it. This time, it was like it was made of smoke. I don't know how I got away."

As much as Luna didn't want to admit it, it sounded as if he'd survived on pure luck. Did the dog know that it failed? With Max in the hospital, where would it go? Would it hide somewhere, waiting for him to recover so it could attack again? Or had it disappeared back to the impossible place it had come from?

"Enough about that," he added. "Let's talk about why in the world *Chance* cut off our phone call, and I went a week without hearing from you. I thought something bad happened to you. Or, you know, you switched teams."

"Ugh, don't even joke," Luna said. "He got me grounded, and my father wouldn't let me anywhere near the phone. Remember that stunt with the alcohol? After we left, he planted the bottle of whiskey in the house so my dad would find it."

"He did this to keep us apart. He's getting scared."

"He has to be. I haven't had any new dreams this week."

"I'd say that was a good thing, but it's most likely not. Probably means he's planning something else. He assumes I'm out of the picture, so his new plan won't be so much about me."

Dread crawled down Luna's spine. Why, out of everyone in Lima, was she the one Chance was focused on?

WITH A WEEK of no nightmares, Luna had built up a false

confidence when it came to going to sleep. She'd been so exhausted that she would fall into a dreamless slumber, black and deep, and would wake fully refreshed. So when she dozed off that night and opened her eyes to the dreaded dream cabin, she felt sick all over.

He assumes I'm out of the picture, so his new plan won't be so much about me. Max's words rumbled through her brain again.

Right away, she noticed the body slumped in the corner where Max had been the last time she'd had this dream. It was a woman this time. A slight rise and fall of her chest told Luna she wasn't dead . . . yet. The breaths were erratic, coming in such an odd pattern that Luna guessed in ten minutes they would stop altogether. Luna didn't recognize her. Was she significant to Chance or just unfortunate enough to be in the wrong place at the wrong time?

Chance leaned against the table, a long shining blade in his hand. It was different from the knife she'd seen before. More like a sword. He caught her eye before taking a few steps forward, situating himself next to the body. Both hands clasped the handle, the tip of the blade hanging above the woman's chest.

"No," Luna whispered.

Chance arched the sword over his head and back down into the woman with one solid *thwack*. The cabin echoed with the horrible sound of ripping flesh. Blood splattered the walls and ran down the silver blade, dripping onto the floor and merging into the pool that surrounded the woman.

A rush of nausea claimed Luna's stomach. In her panic, she made the mistake of looking at Chance's face, at the slow grin crinkling the blood on his cheeks. "It's beautiful, isn't it? The stillness of death. The blackness when the light leaves their eyes. You'll come to enjoy it too."

"No," she spat with much more ferocity than the first time the word had left her lips.

Chance turned toward her, taking one slow step after another until the tip of the bloody sword pressed into her chest. Her heart fluttered with new panic as a single drop of blood landed on her shirt. She wanted to be brave, but she was too aware of her situation. How quickly it could end. Violently too.

"Come on, kitten, that's not what I want to hear," he said.

"I am not like you, and I never will be. Don't you get that?"

"You're breaking my heart," he said. The sword dug into her skin, and she winced. "There are only two possible outcomes to this situation."

"Bonnie and Clyde or death?" Luna guessed, copying one of Max's humorless chuckles.

Chance's eyebrows shot upward. "Correct, sweetheart. Now, what's your choice? You know too much to leave you alive if you decide you simply can't be bothered to work with me." He locked her in his gaze, his cold blue eyes reminding her of an icy winter day. There was no warmth, no remorse. Only death.

"I . . . I . . ." she began, unsure how to respond. Of course she didn't want to *help* Chance, but she certainly didn't want to die at his cruel hands either. If she was going to go down, she wanted to die fighting. There was no glory in a death like this. The blade dug in deeper, a thin trickle of blood making its way free. "Okay,

okay," she said as the pain flooded through her. She wanted to look at the wound but didn't want to give him the satisfaction of knowing how badly it hurt. "Please stop. I-I'll help you."

Chance smirked, shoulders straightening as he pulled the sword back. "I'm so glad you agree. It would have been such a pity to kill you when you have such a marvelous ability."

"Ability?" she asked, glancing up at him wide-eyed. *Some people are stronger than others. To the point where what they do can have effects in this world too.* Max's words bounced around inside her head. If she had something special about her, it would explain why Chance had sought her out, targeted her. Why he was so desperate for her help.

If I can do something important, why wouldn't Max tell me?

"Oh, it's nothing, really," he said with the tiniest hint of a smirk that told her he would do no further explaining.

Luna was angry despite the fear that overwhelmed her. Was he playing with her? "Is that why I'm here?"

"Why are any of us here?" Chance scoffed and dropped the sword. It landed next to her with a metallic *clang* that hurt her ears.

"That's not what I meant."

"I'll be straight with you," Chance replied, crouching down to her level. He rested his bloody hand on her shoulder, cold winter eyes boring into hers as he said, "I need a queen."

She screamed as loud as she could, thankful to sit up within her own four walls again. *What a nightmare,* she thought, the echo of the sword slicing through the woman's body playing on a loop in her mind. Luna took a deep breath to try and calm herself down, wincing at the pain in her chest.

There was the smallest puncture where Chance's sword had been.

***

CHANCE HADN'T ASSUMED anything would come out of the gentle contact between his hand and Luna's shoulder. Then she had woken, and he could feel himself being ripped right out of DreamWorld. When he came to in the Real World, he was in terrible pain. His skin radiated with it as if he'd been lit on fire. He struggled to breathe, his chest caved under the invisible force being placed on it. Pain ripped through him, wave after wave, and he would've been terrified that he was about to die if he didn't know what this all meant.

With the agony at its peak, Chance teetered on the edge of passing out. Then it subsided. He buzzed with energy. No more smoke and mirrors—this was the real thing.

Chapter Forty-Five

WHEN LUNA FINALLY convinced herself to get out of bed, she made her way to the bathroom and winced at her reflection in the mirror as she brushed her hair. There were deep circles under her eyes as if all the stress of the past few weeks was enough to age her prematurely. Stomach rumbling, she set the brush down and left the bathroom, ready for breakfast.

Luna made her way to the kitchen, rummaging through the cabinet for anything quick and easy. Her father sat at the table, reading a newspaper. His presence startled her. She'd gotten used to him being gone first thing in the morning. Luna moved her search to the fridge, listening to the rustle of the paper as her father spread it out on the table to watch her.

"Any plans for today?" he asked.

"Not really. I was gonna go for a walk in the park, but that's about it."

"Alone?"

That wasn't the usual response she got about leaving the house. Luna squinted at him over her shoulder. "Of course, why?"

"This town isn't safe anymore. There's another missing girl, you know," he said matter-of-factly.

"I'll be fine, Dad," Luna replied, losing interest in the conversation when she realized it was steadily sliding into lecture territory. She plucked out the gallon of milk and grabbed a box of cereal off the counter.

"I bet those girls thought the same," he said as she prepared her meager breakfast.

"Now you're concerned?" Luna asked and set her bowl on the table, settling in to eat.

"I am your father. I'm always concerned."

Luna rolled her eyes and took a bite, sloshing the sugary flakes around inside her mouth.

"I don't care for the attitude, young lady."

Luna's skin vibrated with frustration. Would she ever be enough for her father or would he always find something to criticize about her? "You don't care for anything about me," she said, throwing the spoon down with a *clang*. "I mean, honestly, Dad, you've always looked out for yourself first. I come second. Always have."

"Your mother and I work hard for you every day."

"Mom does," Luna agreed, chair screeching as she stood up.

"How can you say that?"

"Why is your first instinct to get rid of me anytime anything goes even *slightly* wrong?"

He floundered for a response, and Luna decided she didn't want to hear what he had to say.

The bite she'd taken soured in her stomach, and she left her bowl on the table, walking out of the kitchen without cleaning it first.

"Where do you think you're going?" her father demanded,

slamming his hands on the table for effect.

Luna slid her shoes on and pulled the door open. "Mind your own damn business for once," she retorted and stepped into the warm afternoon air. She let the door slam shut behind her before her father could say anything else.

Graduation is two weeks away, she told herself, imagining packing all her things in boxes and moving away for good. *I have to make it until then.*

Clenching her jaw, Luna began to walk down the street, skin prickling with lasting anger. A walk around the park had sounded like a good idea when she was in a serene mood, but now? It seemed like a chore. She wanted to run far away. Except she didn't have a place to go. Max was in the hospital, Violet had made a habit of avoiding her, and Nazir was permanently away on his bigger and better life.

At the park, Luna ambled through the shaggy grass to the swing set. She sat on one of the swings, staring up at the sky. There was something about the vast expanse of space that made her feel so small, her problems insignificant.

A loud laugh alerted her to a new presence in the park. A group of teenagers entered the other side of the playground. Chance was in the centermost of the group, the rest of them appearing to be cheerleaders. He had his arm over a girl's shoulders, looking like an ordinary teenager.

He hid his true self well so Luna could understand why no one believed her. A loud giggle from one of the girls carried on the wind, and Luna almost felt sorry for them. Chance had sucked them all under his spell, and they had no idea they were in danger.

Luna's stomach knotted, and she got up, sitting the opposite way on the swing so that her back was to Chance and his group. With witnesses around, she didn't worry about him so much. He would keep himself in check.

Kicking her feet, she moved the swing, resuming her watch on the clouds. Time passed, the sun high in the sky when she finally started thinking about going home. What was her father doing right now? Would he call her mother again or simply forget about the argument?

He'll wait to keep it going.

A fresh series of giggles made Luna grimace as three girls passed her, the same ones who'd been flocked around Chance. One of them openly glared at Luna, whispering something to the girl beside her as she did so. She laughed then the other two joined in.

"Problem?" Luna called to them.

The leader's eyes went wide with surprise that Luna was so direct, before she lifted her hand and coughed into it. "Slut!" she said, causing the trio to burst into another fit of giggles.

Luna rolled her eyes as they walked away, then called, "It takes one to know one!" after them.

The brunette huffed before they stormed off. They could think what they wanted about her, it would change nothing in her life. At least she saw Chance for what he was.

"Girls like that don't make you lean toward the idea of murder?" Chance's silky voice purred from behind her.

She flinched and stood up off the swing, using it as a barrier between them. "No, they don't. They're awful, but I would never hurt them."

Chance pushed the swing out of the way to leave only a few inches between them. "Aren't we supposed to be a team now?" he asked, voice stiff as he hooked the collar of her shirt open to peer at the purple scar by her collarbone. "That *was* your choice last night."

Luna smacked his hand away. "Murder isn't something I can ever condone, but lying is something I can get behind. The fact you would even *ask* says so much about you."

"And what's it tell you, exactly?" he asked, tone even.

Luna didn't like it. It was *too* calm. Averting her eyes, she scanned the deserted park around them, aware of the fact that now that they were alone he could—and would—turn into the monster she had grown so used to seeing. The one who threatened to tear her to pieces. "That there are more than just a few screws loose in your head. There were never any to begin with."

He smirked and stepped closer. "The human psyche is a complex beast."

Luna took a measured step back. "Which is why you should focus on building the good parts in you, not the evil."

"There's good and evil inside everyone, kitten," he said softly. "And that's why we'd be so *perfect* together. No matter how much you want to believe in the good, you are just as prone to evil. More so than you allow yourself to believe."

"Maybe, except I don't want to *be* with you!" Luna screeched and shoved him.

Chance stumbled backward a step. While trying to catch

his balance, something tumbled from his pocket. She squinted, then her eyes went wide in recognition. It was the dagger. The same one from the dream. Dried blood covered the blade and next to it was a white ribbon splattered with dark brown spots. Susan's hair ribbon. Luna could guess the blood belonged to her as well. Knees buckling, Luna caught herself before she could full-on faint. Black spots clouded her vision as she knelt in the dirt, eyes on the bloody objects, the physical evidence she was after.

Chance picked them up, face solemn. "Sorry you had to see that," he said. His voice was cold, remorseless.

"Stay away from me!" she shouted and bolted.

Crunching grass from behind her meant he was right on her heels. "You can't leave me!"

Luna didn't stop, eyes on the fence and the highway beyond it. When she threw a glance over her shoulder, Chance wasn't too far behind. The dagger was gone, and she guessed it was back in his pocket along with Susan's hair ribbon. The fear made her run faster, and she moved like a bat out of hell, careful not to make the cliché horror movie mistake of tripping over nothing. She considered screaming but bit it back. Chance would deny everything the second someone came to her aid, and she'd look like the insane one.

She was on her own.

A dog howled in the distance, and a new wave of sickness washed over her. Chance's dream dog was coming to help him with the hunt.

Luna made it through the opening in the gate and kept running until the park was far behind her. She risked another glance over her shoulder, but Chance was no longer behind her. A shuddering breath of relief worked its way through her as she slowed down, feeling the strain from too much exercise. She slowed to a brisk walk as she caught her breath but kept moving.

She rounded a corner and peeked back, expecting Chance to appear, but he didn't. That should've made her feel better, but it didn't. He knew where she lived so it wouldn't be too much of a stretch to believe he'd come for her later.

Not much of a security system when it can be opened with a bobby pin.

I can't go home, she realized, skidding to a stop.

Problem was, she had nowhere else to go. Suddenly, she understood exactly what it felt like to be hunted. The panic, the desperate need to live sparking that fight-or-flight reaction. She laughed at the irony, heart pounding too hard as she watched a car the color of blood slow down beside her. She shifted her weight, unsure if she should run or stay and figure out who it was. The window rolled down, brown eyes peering at her, and Luna let herself breathe.

"Luna! Are you okay?" Amy asked.

How long has she been watching me? Luna wondered. *How much did she see?*

How could she explain herself? A rustle in the nearby bushes had the hair on the back of her neck standing on end. "I need help," she blurted out.

Amy popped open the passenger door and said, "Get in."

The authority in her voice temporarily shook Luna, and she obeyed, closing the door behind her. The locks clicked into place. As Amy began to drive, Luna leaned back against her seat, finally feeling safe. A glance in the side mirror showed Chance emerge into the place where she'd been standing a minute before.

Amy squinted at the rearview mirror. "Is that Chance?"

The angry expression on his face was all Luna could see as his figure grew rapidly smaller. She'd successfully escaped for now, but this wouldn't be the end of things.

Chapter Forty-Six

AMY DRAGGED HER eyes from the rearview mirror to the girl in the passenger seat. Anyone could see she was scared. That was what had drawn Amy's attention in the first place. She'd been out to get some groceries, but when she'd seen Luna bolting down the street, it was clear something had happened.

"What happened?" she asked at last.

Luna bit her lip, gaze angled out the window. "I . . . I got in a fight with my dad and kind of stormed out. I went to the park for some air, but Chance's dog was loose and chased me."

Amy noted the corners of her lips, how they were pulled down into the slightest hint of a frown. She was lying. *Why?* "Did you get bit?" Amy asked, deciding to play along. Flat-out arguing wouldn't make her tell the truth.

Luna stared down at her feet as she said, "I managed to outrun it, but that might not have been the case if you hadn't shown up."

By her tone, Amy guessed she wasn't talking about the dog anymore. "Happy to help."

Luna sniffled and wiped her face with the back of her hand.

"Do you have any particular place you were going?" Amy asked. "I imagine you don't want to go home right now if you're fighting with your parents."

Luna pursed her lips and said, "No, I don't."

"Well, you can stay with me until you feel things have cooled off at home if you want."

Luna perked up. "Your parents won't mind?"

"Nah. I live with my sister, and she's pretty rad. We've got a guest bedroom and stuff, so it'll be fine."

"I would appreciate that," Luna said, and Amy's heart ached. By the look on her face, she would guess it wasn't often that people showed her kindness.

"No trouble at all."

The conversation fell to silence again, and Amy wrapped her fingers tighter around the steering wheel. In her head, she tried to send a signal to her partner, waiting for the confirmation that he was paying attention to her.

I've got Luna with me, she informed him. *She's got nowhere to go.* As soon as the message was out, Amy felt uneasy. She didn't like communicating with her partner in this manner to begin with, but when it was in the presence of people who were sensitive to the Other Realm, the feeling was intensified. She worried it would be overheard. If Luna somehow tapped into the connection, Amy would have no way to explain herself, and the truth was something neither of them was ready to discuss yet. Amy glanced at Luna from the corner of her eye. The girl hadn't moved.

Learn what you can. I'm going to be out for a while, Amy's partner replied at last. *Be careful.*

Where are you?

The hospital. Beware the dogs, he communicated back.

Dogs. She sent another quick glance to Luna. It couldn't be a coincidence.

A loud unearthly howling sounded, and Amy tensed, peering into the rearview mirror. In the road far behind the car stood a huge mangy Rottweiler.

If Luna and Chance were close, his dog wouldn't want to hurt her, Amy told herself, then told her partner, *Luna and Chance aren't working together.*

How can you be sure?

The dog is here. And it tried to attack Luna not too long ago.

Interesting, he replied.

Amy couldn't have said it better herself.

Chapter Forty-Seven

WHEN LUNA AND Amy reached Amy's house, Luna was glad to see the normalcy of it. An unassuming little home with a red tile roof and tiny porch in the middle of a quiet neighborhood. Amy pulled into the driveway, and they climbed out of the car. Luna was hesitant to follow Amy up the path, but something about the flowers growing along both sides comforted her. It was the femininity, a woman's touch, that assured her she was safe here.

Amy went inside, but Luna stayed at the entrance, watching Amy disappear into an arch that separated the living room from the kitchen. Luna felt an odd sense of relief at the fully functional light fixtures and normal array of furniture clean of dust and cobwebs. It was a complete contrast to the place that Chance called his home.

Peeling off her muddy shoes, Luna set them beside the door and went inside. Amy reappeared with a much taller woman beside her. The woman resembled Amy with the same flowing brown hair and deep amber eyes, but Luna could tell she was older. If only by a few years.

"Luna, this is my sister, Michelle," Amy said.

Luna extended her hand. "Nice to meet you."

Michelle returned the gesture. "Same. Amy told me about

your situation and boy, do I remember being a teenager. I had problems with my parents all the time. It'll all blow over, but until then, you're welcome to stay with us as long as you need to."

Touched by her kindness, Luna said, "Thank you. That's very kind."

"It's no problem," she insisted. "We love the company. I'm making dinner, and you're more than welcome to join us."

"I would love to," Luna agreed.

Michelle disappeared back into the kitchen.

Amy glanced at Luna. "So what do you want to do until dinner's done."

"I don't know," Luna said. "What do you like to do?"

"Come on up to my room, and I'll show you."

Luna followed Amy up the stairs, thinking how easy it was to be around her. Even when she was with Violet, Luna didn't let her guard down this much. *Is this what true friendship feels like?* She was struck by a bout of sadness by the fact she couldn't answer her own question.

Amy opened the first door in a long hallway and flicked on the light. Luna was a second behind her, studying the room. There was a white bed with a light blue dresser. A white carpet covered the floor, and the walls were pink. Huge canvasses of white paper were stretched out over each wall with detailed cartoon drawings on them.

"Did you do these?" Luna inquired, running her finger along the edge of the nearest drawing.

"Mm-hmm. I love drawing."

"These are all really good," Luna murmured as she studied

the cartoon elephant on the next canvas.

"Thank you. Want me to show you how to draw one?" Amy asked, digging through her closet on the other side of the room. When she emerged, she had a box of colored pencils and a small sketch pad.

"Of course," Luna said.

They sat down on her bed, and Amy started to draw, explaining each step of the process. Luna listened in wonder. She hadn't truly known Amy before and had a second where she wondered if everyone was this different outside of school.

Chance is, that dark little voice in her head whispered.

Involuntarily, she found herself thinking of Kate and Susan. They'd probably had promising potential, too, which had been cruelly ripped away. Amy finished her drawing, having no idea about the direction Luna's thoughts had gone. She held up her picture of a smiling dog.

"Not bad for a quick drawing," she said.

Trying to bottle her darkness, Luna forced a smile and said, "I couldn't agree more."

"Amy! Luna! It's time for dinner!" Michelle called from downstairs.

Amy set the drawing down and looped her arm through Luna's. "We should get down there. If you wait too long, she gets anxious. She has this weird thing where she thinks people hate her cooking, but she's a professional chef."

"That is a bit strange," Luna agreed and followed Amy downstairs.

In the kitchen, Michelle placed three plates of Salisbury

steak on the table. The aroma was enticing, causing a stirring in Luna's stomach that made the bite of cereal she'd eaten that morning seem like a million days before. Luna sat down to eat with Amy right beside her. Michelle sat down, too, but didn't touch her food until both of the younger girls had their mouths full, as if waiting for approval.

"This is really good, Sis," Amy said.

Luna's mouth was too full to say the same. Amy's comment said it all. It *was* good.

Michelle beamed. "Thanks. Made it all from scratch. What do you think, Luna?"

"It's amazing, thanks for letting me have some," Luna said when she at last managed to swallow the large bite she'd taken.

Michelle started to eat when a knock sounded from the front door. "Mmm," she said and wiped her mouth with her napkin as she rose from her seat. "I'll get it."

Luna took another bite, enjoying the meal. When Michelle came back, she was alone.

Amy raised an eyebrow. "Who was it?"

"Dunno," Michelle said. "But they left this for you."

Luna looked up and realized that Michelle was holding an envelope out to her. On the front, her name had been scrawled in fancy handwriting. Luna's blood turned to ice as she flipped it over and untucked the flap. Michelle and Amy resumed their meal a few feet away, but Luna felt as if she were isolated in her fear. Inside the envelope was a single piece of paper that had been folded over.

Meet me on the bike path by the bridge tonight unless you want to see another girl on the news.

"What's it say?" Amy asked.

Luna jumped and hurried to close the paper so the words weren't visible. It was a clear threat against Amy. She was the only friend Luna had left, and it wasn't a coincidence that Chance had decided to leave the note here.

No matter where I go, he'll find me, she realized, cold.

"I-I have to go," Luna said, rising from her seat so quickly the wooden legs screeched across the floor.

"So soon?" Michelle asked in wide-eyed surprise.

"Yeah, I just remembered I have something I gotta do," Luna said, hurrying to the door. She slipped her shoes on, purposefully avoiding making eye contact with either of the sisters.

"Want me to give you a ride home?" Amy offered, peeking at her around the arch.

Luna's heart ached. She wished she could say yes, but the last thing she wanted to do was endanger them both. Especially since Amy had already swooped in to save her once.

"I'll be okay," Luna said.

"Okay, well, you're welcome here anytime," Michelle said. "Don't be a stranger."

"Thank you both for your hospitality," Luna said and slipped outside into the darkness.

***

THE BIKE PATHS of Lima were beautiful for the most part, but there were sections that gave Luna the chills—dark stone walkways under bridges and roads lined with nothing but trees for miles. They provided the kind of cover someone like Chance would relish. The section of the path he wanted to meet her at was one such part. It was far enough away from the road that no one passing by would be able to see her. Beside the path ran a canal of questionable depth filled with murky brown water. There was a road bridge over the path, but at this time of night, it'd be next to impossible to see beneath it.

Skin crawling, she hugged herself tighter as the shadows engulfed her. Her instincts told her to run away, but she wanted to be brave. The words on the note swam around the front of her brain again and again. It was one thing to threaten her, but she wouldn't stand by and watch another friend disappear like Susan had.

Probably safe to say he's not going to kill you if he's keeping you hostage. Max's words butted into her head, and she focused on that, drawing what comfort she could from them until her shirt shifted and rubbed across the wound on her chest.

If Chance had no immediate plans to kill her, she would use that to her advantage. Or at least that was what she'd been thinking when she stopped at the general store on the way to buy a tiny tape recorder. She might be showing up to *his* meeting, but it would be on her terms. She'd get the evidence she needed to at least get Chance put in prison. From there, she'd figure out how to wrangle him on the Other Side.

As Luna approached the meeting spot, she eyed the thin black railing that separated the path and the water. How easy it would be to push someone over it. The water on the other side churned past, an unforgiving black abyss in the darkness. She imagined sinking into the depths.

"Luna, sweetheart! You got my note," Chance's lilting voice drifted through the shadows of the tunnel.

She jumped and stumbled, the back of her heel catching on the railing. Heart plummeting, her body leaned dangerously against the guard. Before gravity could decide her fate one way or the other, Chance grabbed her, securing her body against his own.

"Right now, I have two choices. I save you or push you over," he said, cold and calculating. "Why don't you take a guess which one I prefer?"

"Chance, please don't do this," she said, holding onto him. She was uncomfortable with his proximity, but the idea of falling into the water was worse. She hadn't expected the meeting to go well but hadn't thought her own clumsiness would be her downfall.

He peered into her eyes as if he considered throwing her over. "Only if you promise to hear me out before you run off."

"Deal," she said quickly.

He pulled her away from danger and let go of her, one finger at a time. "Thank you," he said, clasping his hands behind his back. "We have quite a few things to discuss."

She peered up at him through her lashes. In the darkness, his hair cast such thick shadows over his forehead and eyes that she could only make out a slight gleam. The thought that his face could be the last she ever saw brought real fear to the front of her psyche. Slowly, she slid her hand into her pocket, clicking the button of her little device *on.* "I agree. Why don't you start by telling me how the hell you found me at Amy's, of all places."

"It wasn't that hard. You talk to maybe three people in the entire school. How about we get to the *real* business?"

"Which is?"

"Susan. I can't have you going around town telling people what you saw this morning."

"You mean your bloody knife?"

Chance smirked and held his hands out in a way that said, "Obviously."

"That *was* her blood, wasn't it?" she asked, hoping she was speaking loud enough for the recorder to pick up.

"Don't ask questions you don't want the answers to, kitten. Keep your mouth shut, and we'll be okay."

Luna tried to think of a way to keep the conversation going, but this had been a bad idea. He wasn't going to confess. Her skin crawled with danger, and she wanted to leave, to get to safety.

How do I get out of here? she wondered, eyeing him. She remembered the run through the park earlier, how quickly he'd nearly caught up to her.

"Don't look so frightened, Luna," he said softly, reaching toward her. He stroked her hair, pausing to cup her cheek before he dropped his hand away. "Though I must admit, it's a good look on you."

No one knew the depths of his depravity like she did. There was no telling how far his act could get him, how many *years* it could hide his nasty crimes from surfacing if she couldn't put a stop to him.

It's a shame. She eyed the pocket the ribbon had fallen from. If she could get her hands on it . . . that, coupled with the recording, would be it—indisputable proof of his connection to Susan's death.

Chance watched her through unreadable blue eyes. An idea crossed her mind, one that made her stomach flop. If he wanted an actress, she could be one. "You think so?" she asked, voice softening in her attempt to sound flirty. Her throat was so dry, she had to force the words out.

He watched her take a small step toward him, obviously suspicious, but he didn't say anything. Without much confidence, she set her hand on his chest. He didn't stop her as she brought her body against his, eliciting a soft groan. She didn't speak. She *couldn't.* If she did, he'd hear the repulsion and the fear and know she was up to *something.* For once, she wanted him to think she was compliant. His little Bonnie.

She met his gaze and pressed her lips to his. He was rigid at first, but it wasn't long before he was kissing her back, one arm wrapped tight around her waist to hold her against him. Luna's heart hurt from the strain of its work as she deepened the kiss, and when he broke away to breathe heavily into her ear, she knew she was doing a good job of distracting him. She caught his lips again and let her fingers move closer to the pocket, working against herself to not glance down. The sharp edge of his hip bone through his black pants was a guiding point she used to inch closer to the pocket. Her finger dipped into it, and the cold metal of the knife stung her skin.

There was no sign of the ribbon.

It was gone.

Chance pulled away and chuckled in her ear, catching her wrist with the hand he'd had snaked around her waist. "That was a nice try, baby doll. You really think I'd keep evidence on me after you saw it?"

The color drained from her cheeks.

Chance smirked and held up his other hand to show off her recorder. Lazily, he glanced at it before looking back at her. "Hey, you tried, right?" He laughed and tossed it into the canal.

She blinked, both humiliated and ashamed. *He's always one step ahead.*

He watched the recorder disappear with a *blurp* before he turned back to her. "That's what I like about you. You keep fighting. No matter what happens, you don't give up."

Luna glowered, subconsciously balling her hands into fists, and thought once again about making a run for it.

"Come on. I'll give you a ride home," he said.

Luna shook her head from side to side. The last thing she wanted to do was willingly climb into his truck of death. He would take her back to his house again, and she had a feeling that this time, she wouldn't be so lucky. "If it's all right with you, I'll walk home. Thanks."

"I don't think I asked," he said and grabbed her arm.

"I said *no, thank you.*" She shoved against his chest so hard that she temporarily broke free.

"Stop being stubborn," he said and made a move to grab her again.

Luna dodged, and when he tried to lunge for her, she elbowed him in the diaphragm before she took off running into the night.

THE RELIEF OF making it to the safety of her home didn't last long. As soon as Luna stepped through the door, she could hear her father's angry voice from the kitchen. She winced, at first assuming he was yelling at her, then she realized that he was on the phone. She'd been so wrapped up in the situation with Chance that she had completely forgotten about the fight with her father.

"This is unacceptable!" he was saying.

In spite of everything, Luna managed to find a bit of anger deep inside herself. She slammed the door loud enough that he would be able to hear it over his yelling.

"Luna?" he called and appeared around the divide. "Where have you been all day, young lady?"

"I was *away*. What does it matter? I'm back now," she said, walking into the kitchen to snag a can of pop out of the fridge.

"Don't walk away from me, young lady," he said, right behind her. He almost tangled himself in the phone cord trying to stay in pursuit.

Luna couldn't help but laugh and slammed the can down to face him. "That's just it, Dad. I have less than two weeks until I graduate. *Two*. I am not your little girl anymore."

"You see what you left me with?" Abrahim asked into the phone.

Luna lunged for it, wrestling it out of his hands before she held it to her ear. "Mom?"

"Yes?" Rose said, sounding exceptionally tired.

Luna tried not to focus on that. "Tell Dad he's overreacting like he *always* does."

"That's en—"

"She's right, Abrahim," Rose said.

Her father stopped at once. "She is out of control!"

"You're smothering her, sweetheart," Rose continued. "Luna is right in saying she's growing up. You promised that if she got to graduation with good grades, this would stop. And she has. Let her breathe. Let her *live*. As much as you don't want to admit it, you can't control her forever."

Red flushed up her father's face, and he snatched the phone from Luna, slamming the handset to hang up on Rose. Luna stood her ground, glaring at him with the expectation that his outburst would turn to her, but he turned away to go to his bedroom.

Thank you, Mom.

She stared at the phone, waiting to see if her mother would call back. When the phone didn't ring, she called Max, collapsing into her seat as she did so.

"Hello?" he said.

"You would not believe the day I had," Luna said.

"That's . . . mysterious. What the hell happened to you?"

"I saw Chance at the park this morning. He had a bloody knife and Susan's hair ribbon."

"We knew he killed her, this is proof."

"Yeah," Luna said, disappointed. "And I tried to get that

proof, but it didn't go the way I'd hoped."

"Did he hurt you?" Max asked, voice sharpening with anger.

"No. He wanted me to get in his truck, but I ended up fighting him and getting away." She shivered, feeling the places where his hands had lingered during the kiss.

"That's alarming."

"Tell me about it." If he had been that determined to take her somewhere, this wouldn't be his last attempt. He would try again. "I don't think this is going to be an isolated incident. He knows where I live, the route I walk to school, *everything* about me. I can't avoid him forever."

"Have you told your dad what's going on? He could drive you," Max suggested.

Luna's shoulders slumped. "He doesn't know anything about Chance. You know how he is. I can't . . . *tell* him things."

Max sighed. "Watch your back at school, and once they let me out of here, I can start walking you home. We graduate a week before you guys do, so I'll have the time. He won't do anything with witnesses around."

That was the start of a plan, but it meant she would have to fend for herself until then. *I need to talk to Violet.* If they could go back to walking together like they used to, it would keep them both safe.

"It's getting late," Max said. "Try to get some sleep. We need to be at our best for whatever comes next."

He was right, but she couldn't imagine that Chance wouldn't try to bother her on the Other Side. Rather than argue, she said, "Okay."

"I'll call you tomorrow."

Luna hung up without saying goodbye. What horrors would tomorrow bring?

Chapter Forty-Eight

LUNA STRUGGLED TO fall asleep, confident that she would wake in a new horrific nightmare. When she finally slipped into unconsciousness, it was to a deep black rest devoid of dreams, and she woke more exhausted than she'd been when she'd gone to sleep. The idea of her walk to school filled her with dread, and she turned over in bed, considering going back to sleep but forced herself up, knowing her dad wouldn't allow it. She almost asked him to drive her, but when she remembered their argument the night before, she decided against it. There was no telling what mood he would be in today.

Her walk to school was plagued with images of Chance on the bike path. His words blazed through her mind over and over again, the blatant dismissal of Susan's death and his involvement in it. If he hadn't caught on to her plan, she would've had everything she needed to get him arrested. *He probably realized I had the recorder when he stopped me from falling,* she thought, remembering the way his hands had trailed her hips long after she was situated. *He knew the whole time what I was doing.*

The exhaustion was catching up with her. Both feet felt like lead weights. She'd never been so emotionally, physically, and mentally drained in her entire life. She glanced up at the sky, at the sun covered over in a layer of clouds. An omen.

Moving away isn't going to solve my problems, she realized. Dreams could follow her anywhere.

When Luna rounded the block and approached the place she used to meet up with Violet, she didn't expect to see her. It had been two weeks since they'd last walked together. *Does Violet even want to be my friend anymore?* She couldn't help but wonder.

Then she saw her. "Oh, Luna."

Luna deciphered her friend's emotion the best she could. Fake enthusiasm. "You sound like you were hoping not to see me."

"It's . . . " Violet looked out toward the road as if she were searching for someone to come finish her sentence for her. "I can't . . . do this anymore.

Luna paused, caught off guard by the statement. "What? You're getting rid of me soon. Why cut me off now?"

Violet shifted uncomfortably, taking a few steps to increase the distance between them. "You've gotten . . . weird."

Luna scoffed. "I wonder why that could be."

"Look, I don't want to hurt your feelings or anything, but I think it's for the best that we don't talk anymore."

"Is that right? What happened to wanting to right your wrongs because I'm your best friend?"

"Sometimes, it's not possible," Violet said and turned away.

***

VIOLET'S WORDS STAYED with Luna throughout the day.

Everything else was background noise. The end of high school and the transition into her adult life was turning into a complete and utter nightmare. It felt as if Chance had shoved her into a box and closed the lid. Now the air was starting to run out.

When lunch came, Luna got her food and sat down at the table nearest to the window. She set her elbows on the table, staring at the birds beyond the glass. The seat next to her creaked as someone sat down. She turned, on instinct, hoping it was Violet coming to apologize.

"There you are," Chance said.

Luna turned her gaze back to the window, pretending he wasn't there. A second later, he set his hand on hers. The gesture was probably meant to be kind, but there was something about physical contact that made everything more concrete.

"Tell me, any more escape plans up your sleeve?" he asked, bowing his face close to hers. "Last night was awfully fun."

Luna shifted in her seat, pushing her tray aside. When her gaze dropped to it, her stomach rumbled. If she'd eaten any of the food, it would've come back up. "No."

"Now that doesn't sound like you," he said, looping his fingers through hers to heighten the unpleasant sensation of skin-on-skin contact.

Luna brought herself to look him in the eye. "What do you want me to say? I've got nothing . . . no one. Even Violet thinks I'm not worth her time anymore."

"What do you care? She's a shitty friend anyway."

"It wasn't always that way. I used to be closer to her than I was to anyone else."

"Don't blame *me* for your falling out. It's high school. Friendships here aren't meant to last forever."

Luna ripped her hand from his. "Don't give me that. You knew what you were doing when you started talking to her. You knew how she felt about you, and you used that to turn her against me."

"I protect myself however I see fit," he replied, curling his fingers into a fist. "Might I remind you that you do the exact same thing?"

"Protect yourself from what?" she demanded. "You're the one causing issues. Everywhere you go, you leave a trail of destruction behind."

"Without chaos, there is no order. It's the sad truth of the world. My role in it is as necessary as yours."

Luna had heard enough. She rose from her seat and stormed across the cafeteria. She could guess his plan. He had the assumption that if she was alone, she'd be weak and more inclined to listen to him. That would never be her. He could take all her friends and her family, and she would never willingly be his Bonnie.

"You'll always have me!" he called after her.

She shuddered as she left the cafeteria.

LUNA MADE IT through the rest of the day, surprised that Chance seemed to have left after lunch. Normally, she would've been relieved, but the timing of it all had her suspicious. Why would he avoid her now?

It would have been such a pity to kill you when you have such a marvelous ability, he had said. Whatever that ability was, could it be possible that she was somehow using it to keep him from going to the next step of his plan . . . whatever that may be?

On the walk home, the sun was out, and Luna felt a little more hopeful with it beating on her skin. Then she saw Max leaning against a tree trunk, and her heart soared. "You're okay!" she said, weak with relief. He didn't look great. There were heavy dark marks under his eyes and a giant swathe of bandages around his throat, but he was alive. Hesitantly, she reached up to point at the bandages. "Does it hurt?"

"A little, but the worst of it's healed," he said and stuck his hands in the pocket of his hoodie. "How have things been here?"

"It's been . . . odd," she said at last, mind volleying between the confrontation with Violet and Chance's strange withdrawn behavior. "Everyone is on edge."

"Sounds about right. Have any more dreams lately?"

Luna shook her head, her earlier question burning the tip of her tongue. "In the . . . Other Realm . . . is it possible to have an ability?" she asked, peering up at him through her lashes.

"An ability?"

Luna clenched her teeth, remembering what Chance had said. "The last dream I had . . . Chance said I had one. A . . . gift of sorts."

"What kind of gift?"

"He wouldn't say," Luna replied, the haunting scene from her dream replaying in her head.

A creak sounded from the street as Chance's black truck drove by slowly. Luna glanced up into his eyes. He looked from her to Max, then turned his attention back to the road and sped away. Whatever had been on his mind vanished when he saw she wasn't alone. Like the previous two days, Chance had made it a point to leave school early, so the fact that he had come back left her uneasy.

Had he come back for her?

A tear dripped from her eye, and she wiped it away.

Max watched the action. "Are you sad he drove off?"

"No, I told you before: my eye does that sometimes."

Max stopped walking. "I think I figured out what your ability is."

Luna stopped, too, eyes wide. "What is it?"

"Your ability . . . it lets you subconsciously connect to DreamWorld when you're awake. The tear means you're sensing something in the Other Realm that has the potential to affect you," Max said. "Come to think of it, your ability might actually be the reason why Violet wasn't harmed."

"I kept her safe?" Luna asked.

"Possibly."

"Interesting," Luna mused. "But how is that helpful to Chance?"

"There are a lot of perks that come with a gift like that. Advanced healing, for one. Dimensional Theft is also easier. That's probably what Chance wants, but for what, I have no idea."

"What the hell is Dimensional Theft?" Luna asked.

"When something is pulled from that realm into this one."

"So, the thing that happened with Chance's dog?"

Max nodded. "Your ability makes it easier to do it."

Luna had never particularly believed herself to be strong or weak, so having an ability with significant magnitude gave her hope.

Maybe I have a fighting chance after all.

***

ANGER OVERWHELMED CHANCE when he opened his eyes that morning. Ever since the contact with Luna in DreamWorld, it had been hard to keep his emotions under wraps. It was part of the reason he'd gone out of his way to avoid her. The last thing he needed to do was cause another confrontation and risk ruining everything.

Get out of my house before I call the police! she'd said. Based on the look in her eyes, he had believed her. Not that the police would do much, but it was attention he didn't need.

Chance punched his lumpy mattress, trying to distill his unadulterated rage. He was glad his knife lay across the room so he wouldn't be tempted to stab it. It was uncomfortable enough without doing anything to intentionally make it worse.

I didn't know it would feel like this.

He jumped up out of bed and made his way to the bathroom, standing in the dark as he stared at his reflection in the cracked mirror. A flash of green shot through his blue eyes, spiraling carefully like ivy before disappearing again. His fusion was almost complete.

Chapter Forty-Nine

TWO DAYS PASSED, and Luna's life didn't get any better. The tension between her and her father lessened only because he spent more and more time outside, away from her. It probably wasn't all work-related, but she knew better than to ask. She used what time she could to focus on the road ahead. Her graduation gown was picked up, and she studied the details of the upcoming ceremony, trying to revive some kind of hope. But the nights were increasingly harder. Sleep simply refused to come, and if she was lucky enough to drift off for brief moments, she'd wake up somehow feeling worse.

Luna gave up on her attempt to sleep two hours before her alarm was set to go off. As she sat in her dark room, she held herself. A few days ago, she'd believed the nightmares were the worst thing she could experience, but not being able to sleep at all was *worse*.

No wonder Violet's changed. Days of this was unthinkable. Weeks? It was torture.

As Luna crept to the bathroom, she had a flashback to the last dream she'd had. When Chance had put his hand on her shoulder and she'd promptly woken.

Maybe it's connected, she thought as she finished her business and went back to her room.

She threw on a clean outfit and went through her morning prayers, the entire time sorting through everything Max had told her.

Max pulled a dog out of the dreams when it touched him. It wasn't possible to do the same with people, was it? *Max didn't touch the dog. The dog touched him, and it came through.* She tried to reason, but it didn't make her feel better. *I have to tell him. He'll know one way or the other.*

She tiptoed into the kitchen. It was quiet and dark. Her father was most likely asleep. Carefully, she raised the handset and dialed Max's number.

When he answered, he sounded more annoyed than anything. "Hello?"

"Max," she began, words rattling around the inside of her head that she didn't want to say.

"Luna?" he asked, then paused. "It's early. What's happened?"

"I couldn't sleep," she admitted.

"Yeah, me neither."

"I've been thinking about what you told me," she said. "Dimensional Theft. How . . . exactly does that work?"

Silence lingered on the other end of the line before Max asked, "Why?"

Luna didn't know how to answer.

"What did you do, Luna?" Max prompted. His words were clipped, edgy.

"Promise me you won't get angry."

"I promise not to wring your neck the next time I see you.

Now tell me what the hell you did."

"I might have . . . done the Dimensional Theft thingie by accident."

Silence again, followed by a stream of curses. "Did you bring through your shackles or something?"

"I . . . it's worse than that," Luna said, rolling her lip between her teeth.

"Worse how?"

"You pulled the dog through," she started, meaning for her voice to stay calm, but it wavered. "Is it . . . is it possible to pull bigger things through?"

"Bigger things?"

"People."

"What?"

"Can people come out of the dream?"

"What. Did. You. Do?"

"Four nights ago, I had this dream where Chance touched my shoulder, and I . . . I woke up before he let go. I haven't . . . been able to sleep since."

"*Four* nights ago? Why didn't you tell me sooner?"

"It slipped my mind. I'm sorry! I didn't think it was that important," she said, pacing across the kitchen as much as the phone cord would allow. "What does it mean?"

"You didn't pull *him* through, but you may have linked his DreamWorld abilities to the real world."

"So he has . . . powers?"

"Essentially," Max said, sounding defeated. "If he fuses, it's bad news for us. Chance is scary enough on his own, but with powers? We might as well put ourselves in the guillotine."

"You said I have a power, too," Luna reminded him.

"I don't know if that'll be enough to stop this."

"What does this fusion do?"

"Exactly what you think. Whatever he can do over there, he can do over here. Most likely he'll do everything he did in the dream to tie up loose ends. That means Violet will die."

Luna's stomach twisted. "I think she's been on his list either way. But it doesn't matter because there has to be a way to stop this, right?"

On the other end of the line, Max was silent.

"Right?" she insisted.

"At this point, it might be too late."

AT SCHOOL, LUNA hoped Chance would cling to his routine of checking in at the beginning of first hour and dipping out at the end, but he stayed the entire day, making his presence known in each class they shared. Luna did her best to study him without seeming as if she were. Max might be ready to give up, but Luna wasn't. Every problem had a solution. She wanted to believe that whatever Chance was experiencing could be stopped.

When the end of the day came, Luna kept an eye out for Chance, but in the crowd, it was hard to tell if he was around. Luna also did a scan for Violet. Their friendship was DOA at this point, but habit had her longing for her old friendship. She'd hoped to see Max waiting for her on the way home, but when she passed their meeting place, no one was there. Sighing, she continued home, running a list of math problems through her head to pass the time. The solitude of walks home was lonely.

A screech sounded as a black truck slowed beside her. Luna paused, not looking up from the tires as Chance rolled down his window. Heavy black sunglasses covered his eyes.

"Need a ride?" he asked.

"No thanks," she said and gripped the strap of her backpack, walking faster. She thought of how much farther she had to go and considered possible places she could duck into for safety. She'd already passed the café.

Chance crept the trunk along beside her. "It's no trouble, really."

"I said *no, thank you*," she said, squinting at him. "And the glasses make you look ridiculous."

He shrugged nonchalantly. "It's bright out."

She glanced up at the glowing, cloud-covered sky, unconvinced.

Chance's truck continued to idle beside her. Nervousness overcame her, and Luna started to walk faster, crossing to the other side. She looked up and down the street, wondering where everyone else was and how she continued to find herself in these situations.

Overhead, the first drops of water fell from the sky. On instinct, Luna started to run. Chance pulled his truck in front of her, screeching to a halt. The door popped open, and Chance rushed at her. Luna screeched as he grabbed her, trying to pull her closer to the truck.

The sky opened up, the rain falling harder and faster,

soaking through her clothes. "Let go of me," she said, trying not to let her panic overcome her, but her nose and mouth were full of the overpowering smell of his cologne, as if he were invading all her senses.

"Nah. Let's go for a little drive through the woods. Spend some quality time together and see what happens." His long bony fingers dug into her skin, refusing to let go.

Fuck! She ran a list of her current belongings through her mind. She had nothing she would consider a weapon. There were two textbooks in her backpack, but getting them out would take time she didn't have. Going slack, she waited for him to change his grip, then snapped to action, pulling out of the straps of her backpack and thrusting it at his face.

He scrambled to keep the bag from colliding with his nose, knocking his sunglasses to the concrete in the process. When he caught it, he watched her through pale green eyes. Luna couldn't tear her gaze away. She took one step behind her, desperate to get away before she *couldn't*. With a growl, he threw the backpack aside and lunged, grabbing her arm. The rain made it easy to pull free, and she raised a fist, prepared to strike.

He wasn't deterred. "Don't go, kitten. You aren't home yet."

"You weren't going to take me home," she said.

"Sure, I was," he said softly.

"As certain as green is your natural eye color," she snarled.

Chance was unfazed. "These are contacts."

"No, they're not!" She turned to run, but he grabbed the back of her shirt and choked her with her own collar.

"Get your ass in the truck!"

"No!" she cried and pulled so hard that her shirt ripped at the back. He lost his grip, and Luna ran to the edge of a nearby lawn. On the porch, an elderly man opened his screen door to peek outside. She glanced over her shoulder to see if Chance had followed her, but he'd climbed back into his truck, speeding away down the road.

"You okay, miss?" the elderly man called.

Trembling, Luna managed a nod but didn't speak as she started to run down the sidewalk.

"Do you need me to call 911?" the old man yelled after her.

Luna didn't stop or let herself feel anything close to relief until she was closing in on her own home. She ran up the path, onto the porch, and into the house, closing the door behind her. Only when the lock was in place did she let herself contemplate the word *safe*.

In shock, she leaned against the door, thinking, *He tried to kidnap me.*

Chapter Fifty

THE FAILED INTERACTION with Luna spiked Chance's adrenaline so much that his heart pounded the entire drive home. He couldn't help but wonder if the old man had seen his license plate. If he would call the police. Then he wondered what he was worried about. *The police in this town are a joke.*

At home, he crossed through the dark living room and into the bathroom, ready to see what it was that had startled Luna. His eyes were solid green. Fusion was complete. His attempts to get his hands on Luna had failed, but other opportunities would arise. And next time, he'd have a plan. It wouldn't be a spur-of-the-moment decision.

As Chance slipped out of his house, his brain went to work on his next steps. He needed to pay Violet another visit. It wasn't time to kill her. Not yet. He needed to use her one more time. He parked outside of her house and strolled up the path, pounding on the front door as he had done before. Unlike last time, a scraggly middle-aged man answered.

"What you want?" he demanded.

Chance flinched from the smell of him. BO and stale whiskey. "I'm looking for Violet."

"She ain't here," the man said and slammed the door in

his face.

Trying to process the interaction, he got back in his truck, glaring at the house. Violet was most likely at work, but Chance's palms itched with the desire to break into her house and sink his dagger into the man's neck.

That would be doing her a favor, he reminded himself, and it was what he needed to encourage himself to drive away.

He made his way to the grocery store, parking in a place where his vehicle wouldn't be noticeable from the inside. Shaking off the clinging unpleasantness of the meeting with Violet's father, Chance went into the store, browsing through one of the coolers at the front as he checked each register. Violet wasn't at any of them. He peeked down an aisle and spotted her surrounded by boxes. Engrossed in shoving cans of soup on the shelf, she didn't notice him.

"Hello there, Violet," he purred, much the way he had the first time he'd approached her.

Violet flinched, glancing at him from the corner of her eye as she asked, "What do you want now? I've been staying away from Luna like you said."

"Yes, she told me you've been cold. Proud of you for that," he said, crouching to get on her level. "This isn't about that. I have a . . . favor I need from you."

Violet shuffled backward, uncomfortable with the proximity. "What kind of favor?"

"Meet me in the woods outside town tomorrow."

Her face scrunched in clear disgust. "What? Why?"

Chance patted his pocket. "Do you need to ask?"

Violet bit her lip, then undid it. "Yeah, I do. I lost my best friend, haven't had a decent night's sleep in weeks, and you're threatening to kill me. My guess is that, what . . . I go out there so you can finally make good on your threats? Luna doesn't want to be alone with you for good reason, so why would I be dumb enough to do it?"

Chance would've been taken aback by her attitude if the man at her house hadn't already rattled him. "It'd be better for everyone if you helped me out."

"In what way?" she asked, shoving a can into place.

"Just do it, okay?" Chance growled, grabbing the top of the open box beside him with such force that the cardboard groaned. "Do it, or I'll kill you and your friends. How's that for motivation?"

"I don't have any friends left," she said.

"You have a brother, don't you? I would enjoy every *second* I'd spend with him," he hissed, forcing himself to let go of the box.

She caught his eye, expression morphing from annoyance to bewilderment. "What's . . . what's wrong with your eyes?"

"It'd take too long to explain," he said, waving a dismissive hand, "but here's what I *will* tell you. If you aren't in those woods by the time school starts tomorrow, you'll have more to worry about than my eyes. Are we clear?"

Violet swallowed, fear overriding her anger. "Crystal."

"Invite Luna," he commanded, and with that, left the store, leaving Violet to struggle for words behind him.

***

VIOLET MOCKED CHANCE'S voice in her mind as she shoved the rest of the cans onto the shelf. She already knew how this would go. If she set one foot in those woods, she'd die. He'd see to it.

The police aren't going to help me. She moved to open a new box. Her fingers brushed the fresh scab, the remains of the ugly wound he'd given her, and her mood darkened. She remembered everything he'd done to Luna and to *her.* He was a clinical psychopath. Nothing could put a stop to that but death.

Her father had a small silver pistol. She never did care for the man, but the one thing he'd done right by her was teach her how to use it. Of course she'd never shot at anything living before.

If the police weren't going to help her, she would help herself. She *would* meet Chance in the woods, but she would be prepared for whatever would come. Chance would never see it coming, and Luna would be her witness that she'd put Chance down in the name of self-defense.

***

AS CHANCE WAITED for it to get dark, he sat in his truck, taking a long draw of his cigarette. He buzzed with excitement. The only thing holding him back from achieving everything he wanted was himself. Whenever he decided to push that first domino, the rest would fall into place.

Tomorrow's going to be a big day.

Until then, he had things to do. Longing thoughts of Luna bloomed in his head, and he had to quell the urge to stop by her house and see her. If everything went according to plan, he would have her soon.

He stubbed out his cigarette, thinking of the red car that had taken Luna from the park. *A Keeper. Under my nose the entire time.*

The tiny frame and bushy brown hair? That matched the description of someone Luna knew.

Amy.

Chance pulled his lip back to bare his teeth. He hadn't put two and two together at first, but it made sense now. There were *two* Keepers watching him: one out to protect Luna and the other gauging him to see what would happen next.

No matter. He started to drive, confident in what would come next.

***

AS IF EVERYTHING about the Other Realm wasn't bad enough, Amy's discovery upon waking was worse. In the shadows of her room, it would've been easy to believe she was alone except for the animalistic breathing that warned her she was not. Amy's eyes opened wide, but before she could scream, a hand was on her mouth.

"Shut up!" a voice hissed, and she recognized it. Chance.

A thick piece of tape replaced his hand, and he hoisted her out of bed as if she weighed nothing. Desperate, she tried to scream for help, but the muffled sound died in her throat when his fist connected with her jaw.

"You best stop that, sweetheart," he hissed, pulling her onward. "I am in no mood, and I won't let a *Keeper* stop me. Not when I'm so close."

How does he know what I am? she wondered, growing rigid with uncertainty. She'd been nothing but careful, positive she covered her tracks and moved only when she wasn't being watched.

Chance dragged her through her own house, and only when they were outside in the inky blackness of night did she regain control of herself. Amy tried to dig her heels into the ground, pausing the so-far effortless walk. Chance turned to her, depraved smirk on his face.

"Girl, honestly. It's as if you *want* me to fuck you up."

"It'll be worse wherever you're taking me," she tried to say, but beyond the tape, not a single word was understood.

Chance rolled his eyes. "How'd you get to be a Keeper anyway? You have to be strong for that position."

Amy had no answer. It was a good question, one she had asked herself many times before. Why *was* she a Keeper? Why had the gods decided she'd be a good fit? She couldn't help anyone. She couldn't even save herself.

"Maybe you're crafty," he mused as he pulled open the door to his truck. "I sure as hell couldn't figure out what you were until you took Luna from me."

I wasn't investigating you, my partner was! She wanted to scream the words at him, but it wouldn't make a difference.

"Once you're out of the way, it'll be a simple matter of

completing the dream cycle and wiping out all the witnesses, including your partner."

"No!" she tried to yell.

"You only have yourself to blame, really. If you would've followed everyone's cues and left Luna alone, I would've let you live."

Amy's eyes filled with tears. Pieces started to fall into place—Luna's sleep troubles, the cabin in the woods, the wounds on her partner, and Chance. They were all connected, and now Amy would be another piece of the puzzle.

"Nighty night!" Chance said, smiling sweetly before he cocked his fist back and cut Amy's world to black.

Chapter Fifty-One

WHEN THE NEXT morning came, Luna wasn't ready for anything the day had to offer. Between the phone call she'd had with Max the previous morning and what Chance had tried to do, she felt heavy. Physically drained.

There's no way I can go to school today. And she wouldn't.

There was far too much at stake. Luna locked herself in the bathroom, running the shower. She sat in the steam for a few minutes, thinking of what she would do next, what she *could* do. She considered hopping a bus and ambushing Max at home, demanding they do something to put an end to this once and for all.

She turned off the water and switched on the blow-dryer. Warming the thermometer with it took far more time than she would've liked. When the reading was high enough, she picked it up and set the end under her tongue, wincing as it singed the inside of her mouth. She made her way to the kitchen with exaggerated slowness, hand held to her stomach to add to the effect. Her father sat at the table with a newspaper before him.

Luna took a deep breath and stepped into the kitchen. "Dad, I feel really sick," she said in a fake voice which sounded slurred thanks to the thermometer.

He looked up and frowned at her disheveled appearance.

"Let me see."

Luna pulled the thermometer out, showing it to him.

He studied the reading, eyes widening. "Looks like you *are* sick. Staying home today."

Luna sat down in the chair across from him, slumping her shoulders as she continued to clutch at her abdomen. She set the thermometer down and set her head on the table beside it. After their fight, this was the most they had spoken to one another in days. She was surprised that her father was giving in so easily.

Abrahim folded the newspaper and stood up, downing the rest of his coffee with one large swallow. He paused halfway across the room and turned to look at her. "I didn't get a chance to tell you, but Violet called last night. Said something about a trip, just you and her? This *illness* wouldn't have anything to do with that, would it?"

Luna tensed.

Look, I don't want to hurt your feelings or anything, but I think it's for the best that we don't talk anymore.

It was clear she no longer wanted to be Luna's friend. A phone call now made no sense.

Unless she had to make it. Luna imagined there was only one person who would require her to do that. Chance. *This is it. I'm out of time.*

"No, Dad. It's a coincidence, I promise."

Her father's face crumpled as if he were thinking of ways to poke holes in her story. Instead, he turned away as if the idea of another argument exhausted him as well. "I'm heading out, then. I'll try to be home in a few hours if you need anything."

Luna didn't move, wanting so badly to reach for the phone and dial Violet's number, but she'd have to wait until her father was gone. If he caught her, it would start a fight, and he would make her go to school.

"Okay!" Luna called back, trying hard to sound ill despite the anxiousness roiling around her stomach.

A minute later, the door closed, and Luna popped her head up. She stood, peeking out the window to watch her father disappear into his waiting car. He pulled away, and she counted to ten before she scooped up the handset and dialed Violet's number. It rang and rang, and Luna prayed that she hadn't already left the house.

"Hello?" Violet answered.

"Violet!" Luna exclaimed. "Whatever Chance told you to do, don't do it."

"How did you—"

"Doesn't matter, all right?" Luna interrupted. "You can't listen to him."

"You don't understand," Violet uttered softly, almost defeated. "I *have* to."

"No, you don't," Luna insisted, wondering what Chance had done or said to bring Violet to that conclusion. Luna remembered the conversation they'd had in her kitchen, where both of them had agreed being alone with him was a bad idea. *What changed her mind?*

"I'm going to the woods. And I'm going to end this," Violet explained.

"You can't go alone," Luna said, hoping she would be able

to stall her long enough to come up with a plan.

"Then come with me."

Luna's skin crawled at the idea, every part of her warning her that it was a bad idea. That *none* of them should go out there.

This is how the dream started, she thought, remembering Chance's masked figure putting a bullet between Violet's eyes. *He's going to do it for real.*

"If you won't come, that's fine," Violet said. "But I have to go."

"Violet! Don't—" The click of the phone cut her off mid-sentence.

Luna panicked. *What would Max do?* She had no clue. In a hurry, she redialed Violet's number. When she didn't pick up, Luna called Max instead.

As soon as the line clicked, Luna said, "Max, we have a problem! How soon can you get here?"

"Wh— I don't know," Max said, struggling for words. "Why? What's happened?"

"I got a phone call from Violet this morning. She wanted me to go to the woods with her. I told her not to, but she wouldn't listen."

"If she's that determined to go, what do you expect me to do to change her mind?"

Luna huffed, not amused by the response. "We're a team, Max. It's obvious she didn't wake up today and make this decision on her own. Chance is behind it, and if that's the case, he's making a move. Are you going to help me or not?"

Max let out a long, deep sigh. "Fine. I suppose there is *one* more thing we can try. I don't recommend getting into contact with Chance, but if he happens to find you before you find Violet, remember this tip: after fusion, for a small period of time, a person is weakened by their biggest fear. Enough exposure can cause them to split apart again."

"But Chance *has* no fear," Luna said. He *caused* fear, didn't feel it. Like he had done to her, to Max, to Susan, to Kate, and whoever else got in his way.

"Now you see why I say there's not much I can do."

"Just get here as soon as you can. I'll meet you in the woods," Luna said and slammed the handset down. His pessimism would only waste time she didn't have. As Luna slipped on her shoes, she prayed she wouldn't be too late to save Violet from whatever fate Chance had waiting for her.

Chapter Fifty-Two

Y THE TIME Luna made it to the woods, terrible wheezing sounds tore through her chest, and her vision started to blur. In her day-to-day life, she never got this much exercise. She'd never considered how weak her physical body might be. Time was precious, and every second she wasted fighting herself was a second Violet spent getting closer to death.

Luna burst through the thick overgrowth at the edge of the trees, carefully avoiding the mess of fallen twigs and pine cones. The last thing she needed was a twisted ankle. As Luna went deeper into the foliage, she realized how frighteningly familiar this place was. The bark, the sticks beneath her feet, and the sky high above produced a sinking feeling in her chest. She'd stepped into the first part of her nightmare.

Don't think about that, she chastised herself and kept running, more desperate to find Violet now than she'd been before entering the forest.

Luna pushed a low-hanging branch out of her face, but it didn't help clear the path ahead. Thick foliage was everywhere, and she had no idea if she was going in the right direction or not. Footsteps nearby had her freeze. She crept toward the sound, peeking through the undergrowth to see if she could catch a glimpse of who was responsible. In her mind, there were two options: Chance or Violet. In the clearing ahead was the familiar figure of her friend. One more step, and she saw that she wasn't alone. Chance was beside her, both of them wrestling for the weapon in Violet's hands.

"Violet!" Luna called.

She looked her way, and Chance seized control of the gun. In one swift motion, he held it up and pulled the trigger. The bullet punched a hole through Violet's forehead, and she crumpled to the grass, blood pouring from the wound. A sprinkle of crimson droplets covered Luna's face, and she fell to her knees. She'd failed. Her best efforts hadn't been enough to save her friend.

The sound of the gun cocking reminded her that the shooter was still there. She looked up through her raven hair and tears to see Chance pointing the revolver at her. "Glad you could join me, Luna," he said with a small smirk. "Nice of you to try and help your pathetic friend."

Luna's heart skipped a beat as she stood on shaking legs that didn't want to support her weight. "Why would you do this?"

"I needed you to come. Obviously, you wouldn't be here if *I* asked you so I had help. Honestly, I doubted the bait would work, but maybe I underestimated you. I mean, you've seen all this before. Why would you walk into a trap? To save her? She betrayed you!"

Luna ignored the sting of his comment. "Violet might have betrayed me, but she also came out here to put a stop to this. Me being here doesn't mean I'll help you."

"I think we've had this argument before, and I've always *won*," he said and stalked toward her, gun not faltering from its target.

Luna turned and ran, certain that staying put meant facing her own demise. She didn't know where she was going. All she knew was that Chance was right behind her. She cried out, afraid of what would happen when he caught her.

Up ahead, the clearing dropped off into a thick patch of forest. Luna couldn't turn to skirt along the edge or he would catch her. Holding her breath, she hoped for the best and let herself fall forward. Chance's weight slammed into her, the two of them rolling over and over as they plunged down the hill. Their bodies slammed together, leaving a trail of bruises on both of them.

Finally Luna's back hit the ground with such force that she struggled to breathe. Chance landed on top of her, straddling her as he pointed the gun at her forehead. Twin tears streaked her cheeks. "You thought you could run?" he panted. "*No one* runs from me."

"Except Max," she managed to hiss.

The frown on his face changed into an enraged snarl, and Luna closed her eyes, waiting for him to pull the trigger. It was too easy to imagine her brains covering the ground beneath her. Chance climbed off her. Slowly, she cracked open her eyes. "Get up," he told her, flicking the gun upward to exaggerate his command.

She stared blankly.

"Come on, kitten," he said, chiding her. "I don't want to hurt you, but it's always an option."

Luna whimpered but obeyed. Chance wrapped his arm

around her waist, body pressed to hers from behind. He held the gun to her temple like he feared she'd try to run again, then forced her up the rise like that, back to the clearing with Violet's dead body.

How did my life come to this? she wondered, feeling the revolver press harder into her scalp. She'd had such a bright future. Now she couldn't guarantee she would live to see tomorrow.

As they approached the top of the hill, Luna considered throwing herself backward into him. It might be enough to knock Chance off his feet, to stun him, so she could get away.

"Don't do it. Don't you fucking dare," he grumbled, and she guessed the tension in her shoulders had given away her plan.

Her feet hit the level ground at the top of the hill, and Luna pulled away slightly, testing her limits. Chance's fingers dug into her hip bone, and Luna glanced in his direction, but instead of seeing him, she was looking down the barrel of a gun. There was no escape. If his finger slipped and pulled that trigger, she would be dead.

A broken sound came from Luna, and she let herself drift closer to him. She wouldn't be able to beat him, and she wasn't foolish enough to continue thinking otherwise. "I surrender," she said, eyes trailing the ground to avoid seeing the expression on Chance's face. All she wanted to do was shoot *herself* for saying those words. Cooperating with the man who killed her best friend in cold blood was the coward's way out.

I'm better than this, she tried to convince herself before it fell away. *No, I'm not.*

"Good," he said, lifting his chin. His hand slipped from her waist, gun aimed at her temple. "Walk."

The bit of freedom he had reintroduced gave her the urge to try and run all over again.

"Luna!" Max's voice came from the depths of the woods, and she turned to see him. "Luna, Chance's biggest fear is being—"

Chance spun away from her, the gun going off before Max fell to the ground where he lay blocked by plants.

"Max!" she screeched, trying to break free to run to his side.

Chance stretched out his arm to clothesline her. Breath knocked from her lungs, he pulled her into his arms, the hand clutching the gun pressed to the side of her head. "*Shh . . . shh . .* ." Chance soothed, petting her hair as he tightened his grip. "It's all right."

"How could you?" she asked, voice barely above a whisper.

"You have no idea how long I've wanted to do that," he said, wrapping his fingers around a lock of her hair.

Anger rose in Luna's throat. She'd watched both of her friends die, and he was *happy*. Luna pulled one hand free long enough to slap him. Less than a second later, he had both her wrists in one hand, the gun held to her temple with the other. Cold metal burned her scalp, and she counted down, waiting for it to cut her world to black.

She dared to crack open an eye. Chance ran his tongue along his bottom lip. "Go."

He started walking, pushing her ahead of him. He let go of her wrists, but the gun was a reminder that she was a prisoner. A tear ran from her eye, but this time it wasn't her ability trying to connect her to the Other Side, it was sorrow for her lost friends. Sorrow for herself. She wouldn't be able to wake up and undo this.

What happened out here would be forever.

That's why you need to fight, a small voice in the back of her mind whispered. *If you're going to die, then you should do so swinging.*

Out of the corner of her eye, she glanced down at Chance's waist, examining both pockets. She couldn't see the handle of his dagger, but by the shape of the nearest pocket, she could tell it was there. Luna moved her hand, trying her best not to attract his attention. She flexed her fingers, mentally running through her plan, before she plunged her hand inside. In one swift motion, she grasped the handle of the dagger and pulled it out. He tilted his head down at the same time she sunk the knife into his stomach.

The world blurred as he shoved her to the ground, and she lay there, stunned. Chance aimed the gun at her, using his free hand to pull the dagger from his stomach. She expected him to faint or topple over. Rather, he slid it into the pocket farthest away from her and cocked his head, the hint of a smirk on his face.

Luna could only stare. "D-didn't that hurt?"

He snorted. "As if. Get real, Luna."

Lip trembling in quiet horror, she watched as he lifted his shirt to reveal the shining ivory skin on his stomach. She expected some kind of wound where she had pierced the knife into his body, but there was no sign he'd been injured at all.

"I don't see any blood," he said, gesturing to his stomach with the gun.

"H-how is that possible? I *stabbed* you. I felt the knife go into your skin," Luna murmured.

"I'll tell you right now that a knife is not going to harm me. I'm beyond that, but I give you an *A* for effort."

This was why Max had been so angry at what she'd done. Fusion made a person invincible. If she couldn't physically harm him, how could she escape? Chance's fear was his weakness. Max had been about to divulge his *fear*, but she couldn't figure out the end of his final sentence.

"All right, get up. I'm done playing around," Chance said, kicking toward her. She feared his boot would connect with her ribs, but he pulled it back at the last second.

Numb, Luna stood, wondering if Chance would really shoot her or if it was a fear tactic to get her to obey. She'd already run away and fought back, yet he hadn't been inclined to pull the trigger. How much more would she be able to get away with before he decided enough was enough?

Should I run again?

It was tempting, but she couldn't afford it. Another wrong move may be one too far. He might be invincible, but she wasn't. One gunshot and she would suffer the same fate Violet and Max had met. Chance's face didn't change as he reached his free hand toward her. Luna flinched, assuming he'd strike her. Rough fingers cupped her jaw, and he squeezed once before he let her go, turning her away from him. She recognized the feeling of cold metal to the back of her head as they resumed their walk through the trees.

Softly, Chance began to hum. In the otherwise silent forest, the happy sound was *loud*. Luna's silent sobbing halted as she listened. In the midst of every terrible thing he'd done over the past twenty minutes, he was *happy*.

Luna let that thought sink deep into her bones as they walked onward through the trees. The ground beneath them changed from grass to dirt to pine-needle-littered ground. The sky above was ominously gray, blocking out the warmth of the sun. Luna did her best to shut it all out, thinking again of Max and whatever it was he'd been about to say. She blinked her misty eyes, trying not to think of the immense sorrow building inside her.

"Where are we going?" she finally brought herself to ask.

"Home," Chance replied, free hand grasping the collar at the back of her shirt as if he assumed she would make another run for it.

Luna felt like an abused dog, humiliated and wary, but her fear kept her compliant. As they walked, the ground beneath their feet turned rocky, the trees around them thinning. Luna recognized the gravel path. In the dream, it had led to the cabin in the clearing. She took in a deep breath to calm herself, finding it difficult thanks to the swelling in her throat from her silent sobbing. In the distance, she spotted Chance's truck parked along the trees, and a brand new flicker of panic overtook her.

"Where are you taking me?" she demanded again, freezing a few feet away from the vehicle. *Never let them take you to a second location.* According to all the stories, a second location meant a higher likelihood of being murdered.

"I already answered that, kitten," he replied sweetly, tugging on the back of her shirt until the fabric pulled against her windpipe.

To relieve the pressure on her throat, Luna took a step backward. Chance wrapped an arm around her waist, holding her against him as he used the hand with the gun to open the door. He nearly crushed her to him as he leaned forward, grabbing the seat to pull it forward. There was a tiny row of seats behind them, caged in by the unmoving steel body of the truck. Once she was in there, the only way out would be through Chance's mercy.

Luna's fight-or-flight reaction kicked in, and she bucked against him in her effort to back away. He caught her easily. His lips brushed her ear as he whispered, "Don't make me tie you up. I might enjoy it a bit too much."

When she froze, he thrust her inside and moved the seats back into place. She tried to climb over them, but there wasn't enough room between them and the roof for her to be successful. Chance slid into the driver's seat, closing the door and sealing her tomb. As he turned the key in the ignition, he shot her a grin over his shoulder.

Luna couldn't stop the tears as he began to drive. She looked left and right, searching for anything she could use as a weapon, but he'd taken the time to clean everything out of his back seat.

"Don't cry, kitten," Chance said softly.

Luna sat back in the seat, sobs overtaking her. He floored it, the truck maneuvering left and right around trees. She almost accepted the idea of him plowing full speed into one. Out of nowhere, he took a violent left turn and Luna moved sideways with the force, head slamming against the window, taking her consciousness with it.

Chapter Fifty-Three

ONSCIOUSNESS CAME BACK to Luna violently and suddenly. Her eyes fluttered open to see Chance hovering above her. His long blond hair rolled down his face, hands resting on either side of her head as he watched her in rapt fascination.

The haze cleared, and she realized she was lying across the back seat. She pressed her cheek to the cold leather, inspecting his hands. They were empty. Taking the gun-less opportunity, she used the last of her strength to push him away, heart sinking when he didn't budge. He continued to smirk down at her, and she didn't want to know what that look meant.

Finally, he backed away, standing by the open door. He reached into his pocket, pulling out the gun. Luna froze, memories of the past hour of terror flooding her mind. "You'll do better if you don't push me again," he warned.

Luna sat up, backing against the far door. She couldn't get out that way, but she would use it to her advantage.

"I'll say this nicely," he said slowly, as if he were talking to a child, "get out of the truck."

She shook her head from side to side, feeling weirdly disconnected from her body and herself.

Red flushed up his neck as he bared his teeth. "Get. Out.

Of. The. Truck."

"No," she whispered.

Chance growled and tucked the gun away before lunging at her. He grabbed her legs, fingers meshing into her skin with such force that she'd be dotted with bruises later . . . if she lived long enough. She slid against the black leather seats, screaming and crying as she did her best to fight him off. For a few minutes, he used his natural strength and size to overpower her.

When she didn't show any signs of backing down, he crouched over her again, pinning her flat. "Don't say I didn't warn you."

He summoned his dagger, wielding the blade he'd hidden for so long. The tip of the knife hung precariously over her, and she jerked left and right, trying to dislodge him. It didn't work. Chance sunk the blade into her stomach. The pain was worse than anything she'd ever felt as it sank through her skin, ripping away her muscles and tendons. Fire spread through her midriff, and she screamed a bloodcurdling yelp. Breathing hurt, and she found herself without the strength to manage it as she stared up at him. The look he returned was cold.

He bent toward her. "It's not so fun, is it?" Gingerly, he pulled the blade free with a wet suction that made her want to hurl and held up the blade to observe the blood. He ran his fingers along it, staining his skin.

Luna clutched her wound, keeping as much pressure on it as she could. Her life fluid leaked through her fingers, and she couldn't imagine taking care of a wound of this magnitude herself. Chance put the dagger in his pocket and turned back to her. He sat her up with force, and she wailed miserably—every jostling movement sending rays of pain through her. Chance adjusted her, cradling her in his arms as he slipped out of the back seat and began to walk.

One hand on her wound, Luna's other smeared blood on her shirt in her weak efforts to break free. "Ch-Chance . . . please. I-I need to go to the h-hospital."

"No."

The ice in his tone was enough for Luna to feel positive she was going to die here. She clutched both hands to the wound, wondering how much longer it would take for her to bleed out. "Please," she whispered, hoping there was some small piece of humanity left in him that she could appeal to.

That caused the corner of his mouth to pull up into a smirk. "Come on, baby. Together we can paint the town red." He laughed and smeared a glob of Luna's own blood on her nose.

Luna was stunned into silence. If she'd had any control over herself, she would've balled her eyes out. Things started to spin, and Luna focused on the scenery around them, anything to take her mind off the fact that she was dying. She recognized the cabin at the edge of the clearing. It was small, and the dark brown walls had various plants growing through the cracks. She could only see one window, which looked as if it had been painted black, and the roof was badly damaged by the weather.

It matched the dream cabin exactly, and if she wasn't in so much pain, she would've assumed she was in the dream. The old building, even from halfway across the clearing, made her think bleeding out wasn't the worst thing that could happen. It would most likely be a gentler fate than whatever Chance had planned.

Chance's grip tightened, and he exhaled loudly. "Stop fighting me already. Don't you understand all that I'm doing for you?"

She tilted her head, not understanding much of anything as the world at her periphery started to go black. Luna said nothing as he stepped onto the rickety old porch. The door was already open, and Chance sidestepped through, careful not to hit her head or feet on the doorframe. The inside of the cabin was as dingy and dark as it was in her dreams. The air was musty, a single white candle on the table in the room casting enough light for her to see thin silvery cobwebs stretched across the walls like banners.

When Chance stopped walking, Luna was faced with a dark wall. The familiar silver dog-chain shackles were piled there. Gently, Chance set her on the ground, taking more care than he had in the truck. Each tremor made her scream, and she was so wrapped in pain that she didn't protest as he closed the shackles around her wrists. His green eyes looked almost black in the darkness when she dared a glance up at him.

Without warning, he leaned forward and pressed his lips to hers. Her first instinct was to push him away and spit rage, but he was armed, and she barely felt that she had control over her body. She'd lost a lot of blood already and expected she would slip into unconsciousness soon.

His face was emotionless when he pulled away. Bloody fingers reached out to cup her jaw and force her to continue looking at him. "You have no idea how much you mean to me."

Tears clung to her lashes, but she didn't bother to struggle out of his grasp. Her mind fogged, and she came up with no response.

"Come on, Luna, say something."

She stayed silent. Anything she was tempted to say would not help her.

"Don't look so glum. I thought you liked tragedies," he said, flashing his teeth. The candlelight reflected off the bright white, looking as if he had a Glasgow smile.

Another tear streaked her cheek, mixing with the blood Chance had smeared there. Desperate, she smooshed a fresh handful of her baggy shirt over the wound, desperate to soak up as much of her blood as she could.

Chance plopped down beside her, his long bony fingers caressing her knee as if they were on a date at the movies.

"Why are you doing this?" Luna managed to ask. "Killing Susan and Violet and Max? Kidnapping me? You're going to go to prison for this, and I don't understand why you did it."

"Kitten, do you realize how powerful DreamWorld is? How it *could* be if it weren't for the Keepers? That place . . ."—he paused to swipe a thumb across his lips—"it can make me a *god*. And you've been the key to unlocking it. I'm not worried about anything that can happen on this side of the realm. I can finally be *free*."

"But you're a *murderer*," Luna said. "All the magic in the world won't change that."

"Oh, sweetheart, you fight the good fight, but you're so naive." The candlelight flickered, and his eyes flashed. "This is the price I pay to do what I can do. But I'm not the monster here. There are worse people in the world than me. Hell, worse people in this *town*."

Luna digested his words before she asked, "You were responsible for Dahlia Moore, weren't you?"

Chance was quiet for a long minute before he said, "I was."

"Why?"

"Same reason for Susan and Kate, really."

"They were your friends. How could you do that to them?"

Chance rolled his eyes. "Don't act like Kate's death was some terrible tragedy. You hated her."

Luna grunted in pain as she shifted her position. "Doesn't mean I agree with what you did. No one deserves to be murdered."

"And here I was thinking you'd be overjoyed. Women are so hard to please!"

Luna's bottom lip trembled. "So what happens now that you've gotten what you needed? Are you going to let me bleed to death?"

"No." He rested his head against the wall beside her. His odd-colored eyes glowed in the firelight as he said, "You're the one person I want to keep alive."

Luna held up a bloody hand to emphasize her condition. In barely more than a whisper, she asked, "Why?"

Chance grabbed it and said, "When this started, I didn't *want* to feel this way. I honestly needed you only for what you could do. Then we started spending time together, and I realized that you weren't like everyone else. I'm drawn to you, in ways I can't explain. You infected me, and now I can't go back to who I used to be. And I don't have to. I came to the realization that this could work. That you could stay with me."

"You can't keep me here forever. People will look for me."

"Will they?" he asked, disinterested.

Luna thought of how strained the relationship with her father was. Nazir was out of town. Violet was dead and Sidra was too. Max was the only one who would search for her, and he was also dead, or dying.

Fresh tears welled in Luna's eyes.

Chance ruffled her hair and stood up. "Think about that for a little bit while you make yourself comfortable. I'm going for a walk."

"Wait! You can't leave me here!" she cried, desperately tugging against her chains. Fresh blood dripped onto floorboards she hadn't yet stained.

Chance pulled the door open, tossing a glance at her over his shoulder. "I can do whatever I want," he said as if the idea brought him nothing but pure joy. He crossed the threshold and closed the door behind him, leaving her in darkness.

Luna pulled her wrists against the binds again and again, hoping she'd get lucky and they would somehow open. *Fat chance.* If she hadn't been able to break them in her dreams, there was no way she'd break them now. Black spots across her vision grew in size and number, and she found herself slumping to the floor.

There was a considerable amount of dust and grime, but she rested her cheek on the floor, having no strength to keep herself propped up any longer.

I'm gonna die here, she thought. Part of her was ready to welcome it.

There are a lot of perks that come with a gift like that. Advanced healing, for one, Max had said.

Her body wasn't healing itself. It was shutting down. *You were wrong, Max,* she thought, then unconsciousness claimed her.

When she opened her eyes again, it was to cold liquid being forced down her throat. Her eyes shot open, locking with Chance's. Gingerly, he pulled the cup back but kept his firm grip on her jaw until she swallowed the mouthful of water.

"There she is," he whispered.

The sweet blackness of unconsciousness beckoned to her, and she found it nearly impossible to keep her eyes open. When he let her go, she slumped to the floor, studying him. There were thick trails of blood on his face and arms and fresher splatters across the white tank top he'd changed into. She pressed her shirt to her wound again, watching as he plopped down beside her. He plucked a rag from his pocket and handed it to her.

"Use this," he demanded.

Luna looked between him and the rag, wanting to do nothing more than throw it back at him. His dark eyes were cold, demanding, and she sensed he was waiting for her to argue. She took it from him with shaking fingers, wincing as she pressed it to her stomach.

"I got something I want to show you," he said, hopping

to his feet. He crossed the room to the corner. In the dark she could make out the shapes of various boxes and junk.

Luna tried her best to pull herself together, vaguely amping herself up for a fight. Whatever he wanted to show her would be anything but good. Chance tossed boxes to the side, moving farther back in the mess. He pulled back a white sheet, bending down to gather something in his arms. When he turned toward her, she realized in awestruck horror that he was holding the body of Susan Cross.

He came closer, dropping the corpse onto the grimy floorboards beside her. A tangled mess of hair covered part of her face, hiding one eye, and her bloody body was covered in a dirty white dress. Her flesh had turned gray with decomp. The eye that wasn't covered had white film over it, making her look eerier.

The smell of death had Luna retching, and she couldn't believe she'd caught no trace of it until then. She clamped her bloody hand to her mouth to try and block it out, then looked up at Chance, tears trickling from the corners of her eyes. How in the world could he do such horrible things to the people who trusted him? She had a flashback of their uncomfortable encounter at the restaurant, at the steak he had insisted stay bloody. How could he eat that without thinking of all the terrible things he had done?

Luna dropped her hand from her mouth as she asked, "How could you do this? Susan adored you. She would've . . . she would've done anything for you. You didn't need to kill her."

"If only things were that simple," he said and crouched beside Susan's body.

Luna didn't take her eyes off his. "I don't want to look at

her. Please take her away."

"I will, but look at this first. This is information you'll need," he said with barely concealed frustration.

His hand inched toward her. The thought of him touching her after holding Susan had her stomach roiling. She forced herself to study Susan again. Faintly, in the withered flesh, she could see the tiny sigils carved into her skin and wondered if those were the same ones that had been reported on Kate's body.

"Now that wasn't too hard, was it?" he asked and scooped Susan up, placing her back into the crate he'd taken her from.

Luna couldn't calm her brain enough to think of anything as he came back toward her. There was a look on his face that she didn't like. He was plotting again, and she wondered if he was considering carving sigils into *her* skin. He turned away, walking right out of the room and leaving her alone.

Except I'm not alone. She stared at the crate where Susan's body lay out of sight.

Luna shut her eyes until the sound of footsteps had her open them again. Chance leaned against the table in the center of the room. He'd set something down, but from her angle on the floor, she couldn't tell what it was. Chance took a breath and picked it up before he approached her. A bone entwined with a rose—the one she'd seen from her dream. He crouched beside her, holding it up, proud of it.

"This," he said finally, "is a very important object."

Luna didn't speak. Like everything else in this situation, she didn't understand enough to think of any questions.

"I call it the Rosebone," he said, looking down at it as if

he were holding palmfuls of precious gems. "I bet you recognize the rose."

Luna squinted, startled when she realized he was right. "That . . . that's the rose you gave me for prom."

The corner of his lip turned up slightly. "Correct."

"Wh-what—" she started and gathered herself before she finished. "What are you going to do with that?"

"With this, I'll give you some of my power. My plan won't work if something happens to you, so before anything, I need to give you this."

He held the item out to her, and she pursed her lips, not making any moves. If she accepted this *whatever it was,* what would it do to her? Would it brainwash her into following Chance's orders? Or would it put her out of her misery?

"Well?" Chance prompted, inching it closer. "Go on and take it."

"I-I can't," she said, dropping her hand.

"Why not?" The gentle tone vanished, the barely concealed anger shining behind his eyes.

"I'm scared," she said, pausing to take in another ragged breath of air. "I don't know what will happen."

Chance rolled his eyes. "Take it. You'll be fine."

Luna had the urge to smack it out of his hand. It looked old enough that any rough movements would shatter it. The menacing gleam lurked in Chance's eyes. She had to remind herself that being unable to see his weapons didn't mean they weren't nearby.

I have nothing left to lose. She held out her hands.

Smiling, Chance set the Rosebone in her palms, jerking his hands away. A sensation like an electric shock soaked her skin, paining the flesh on her hands before wiggling to her wrists. She tried to throw the object to the floor but found it wouldn't come off her fingers. It stuck to her as if it had been covered in crazy glue. As the panic grew, she squirmed, trying to pry it off inch by inch. A tightness in her chest changed to a sharp piercing pain that hurt almost as much as the gash in her stomach.

Chance watched her, green eyes narrowed slightly, but he said nothing.

In her head, Luna screamed, *I'm having a heart attack. I'm having a heart attack, and he's not going to help me.*

The pain radiated down to her legs and up to her head. Then, as suddenly as it had begun, it vanished in eerie respite. Luna's tense body went limp, the Rosebone falling from her open hands. Too weak to move, she couldn't so much as look at the smears of blood she left on the object as she slumped against the wall, panting.

Chance bent closer to try and catch her eyes. "Luna, talk to me. Are you okay?"

She didn't answer him. In no universe would any of this be *okay*. If she survived and got out of there, she wouldn't be okay ever again. Chance picked up one of her chained wrists, his fingers on her skin in search of a pulse. He must've found one because he let go, staring at her helplessly.

"What . . . did . . . you . . . do . . . to . . . me?" she finally managed to rasp.

"I've bonded us," he replied gently.

Each breath was a struggling wheeze, and the pain in her stomach was enough to consume her. Chance pulled a key from his pocket, undoing the locks on her wrists. They clattered to the floor, but she couldn't move. Some slight awareness in the back of her mind, beneath the pain, told her she was free, but she was too weak to flex her wrists, let alone escape.

Chance left the Rosebone on the floor, scooping her into his arms. When her head lolled at an uncomfortable angle, he shifted her so she rested on his shoulder with no choice but to look at him. His face was solemn.

Luna was on the verge of permanently passing into unconsciousness, but she was aware of the fact that they had ventured into a part of the cabin that she hadn't been in before. They passed a closet, and she wondered if that had been the one where Chance kept Max prisoner.

Chance carried her to the end of the hall and into the bedroom. In the middle of the room sat a queen-sized bed with a thick red comforter. He carried her past another window painted black and approached the bed. Balancing her on one arm, he lifted the covers and set her down. He straightened out her arms and legs, leaving her no choice but to watch him dole out these acts of kindness. He swept a lock of hair out of her eyes and pulled the comforter onto her.

Luna was almost grateful until she eyed the blood on his face. *Her* blood.

He did this to you, she reminded herself.

Chance's gaze ran over her before he turned and left the room. She heard a *click* as he closed the door behind him. She coughed, and the hitch in her breathing kept her wheezing. As blackness reached up to claim her again, she wondered if it would really be so bad to die.

Chapter Fifty-Four

WHEN LUNA CAME to, she was aware of the passage of time. The room around her seemed darker, and she guessed it was nighttime outside. She breathed in, glad to find it easier to do so. Movement beyond simple twitches was difficult, and she found herself thankful that Chance had tucked her under the covers with the violent shivering that racked her body.

Where was he? Maybe in the time she'd been unconscious, he went out. Perhaps if she could force her joints to work, she could get out. She struggled but only managed to turn her head. That's when she realized the blanket beside her was rounded in a lump. Chance's platinum hair was fanned on the pillow beside her. His eyes were closed, arm draped across her stomach in a way that left her wondering if he was really asleep or pretending.

"Chance . . ." she whispered.

His eyes popped open. "You're awake."

Luna swallowed, unable and unwilling to answer.

"How do you feel?" he asked, nearly whispering the question into her ear.

"Better," she forced herself to say. She didn't quite feel up to full health, but there was a strength in her that was absent after the stabbing.

"Good," he said, warm breath sinking into the side of her face as he nuzzled his forehead against her temple. "I was worried."

Uncomfortable, Luna tried to move again, finding it difficult. She would've wiggled enough to fall out of bed if it meant putting space between them.

Chance frowned at the silence, propping himself on his elbows. "Are the blankets comfortable?" he asked, searching her face for some sign of emotion.

Luna could've cried, though from frustration or confusion, she couldn't say. After everything he had done, he was worried about his *blankets?*

"Are you in a lot of pain?"

Where to begin with that question? Luna thought, dazed.

Chance's face crinkled with building frustration. She could guess what he wanted—he wanted her to talk, to pretend things were fine. She'd never felt so low in her life. Didn't think it was possible to lose all sense of hope.

"Doesn't matter," she said stiffly, resting her cheek on the pillow. And really, it didn't. If her life was bound to end in the next few hours anyway, nothing mattered.

"Does to me," he said and cupped her jaw in his fingers.

Luna managed to snarl.

"There's the fire," he said, and his grip tightened. "I'm yours, and you're mine. Say it."

Luna clenched her teeth. She'd rather choke on her own tongue than say anything of the sort.

Chance set his other hand on her stomach, dangerously

close to the wound he'd inflicted there, and she caught the implication as he leaned a bit closer to her. "*Say it.*"

For what felt like forever, she stared into his inhumanly green eyes, pouring all of her hate into them. If looks could kill, his heart would've exploded. Sadly, it did not. "I'm yours, and you're mine," she spat at last and wanted to rip her tongue straight out of her mouth. It would hurt less than this.

Chance gave her a soft kiss. "That's right, kitten," he said and crawled out of bed.

As he stretched, Luna realized he continued to wear the bloody tank top he had on before she'd passed out. His hair, which was usually so carefully managed, was a mess. The only thing that seemed different was that her blood had been cleaned from his face and arms. Her fingertips sunk into the covers on the edge of the bed as he leaned toward her. "Are you sure you're okay?"

Luna didn't know what the word meant anymore, let alone feel it. "I'm fine," she forced herself to say.

Chance nodded as if the answer pleased him before he turned away. "Be back soon," he said and disappeared into the hall, leaving the door open.

It was a beacon, summoning her. *Concentrate.* Closing her eyes, she tested which parts of her body hurt the worst. She could move her neck. Her toes and fingers worked as well. She twisted her left ankle and then her right, becoming confident enough to kick out. When she tried to move her arms to pull the comforter off, her wrists wouldn't move. She shimmied her shoulders until it fell away, then realized her wrists were handcuffed together.

Frustrated, she pulled, testing their strength as Chance reappeared in the doorframe.

He approached the bed, hair fixed. He'd changed out of the tank top and into a black button-down with long sleeves rolled up to his elbows.

Jerking her hands against the handcuffs, Luna thrust them in his face. "What did you do this for?"

"You're back to yourself," he said, ignoring her question. He pushed her wrists to the side, pulling up the bottom of her shirt to reveal her stomach. With an uncomfortable twinge, she realized she was dressed only in her panties and a dark-colored shirt she guessed was Chance's by the scent of cologne clinging to it.

"What are you doing?"

He didn't speak, fingers running over her stomach in the place where he'd stabbed her. A swathe of white fabric was taped over the laceration and all the blood had been mopped off her bronze skin. Chance's fingertips skirted lightly over the edge of the bandage.

"You're gonna live," he informed her, pulling his hand away.

"Yeah, but it doesn't change the fact that stabbing me was unnecessary," she stated, doing her best to pull her shirt back in place.

"It put you in your place," he said, running the edge of it between his fingers before finally letting go.

Luna covered herself the best she could. Chance watched with a smirk before reaching for her wrists. On instinct, she flinched.

"Stop it," he said, lips in a tight line.

Luna flared her nostrils. "Consider it a conditioned response."

With a quick flick of a key, he ripped open the handcuffs and put the keys back in his pocket. Gently, he grasped her arm, helping her sit up. She grimaced as the movements rippled her wound but did her best to hide the worst of her pain as he guided her off the bed. He let go and pulled open the top drawer of the dresser next to them, grabbing a white gown that he pulled over her head in a few quick movements.

Luna blanched. Susan had been wearing a dress exactly like it. She tried to push all that away, focusing on the fact that at least she was covered.

"I have something I need to do," he informed her, "and now that you're better, you're gonna help me."

"With what?" she asked, turning away slightly. Given his mood swings, she decided her best bet until she healed enough to fight would be to play along.

"If I told you, it would ruin the surprise, kitten."

If she didn't already know he was insane, Luna would have believed there were some good qualities to him based on his tone of voice when saying those words.

Snaking his fingers through hers, he started to walk her down the hall. Her eyes roamed every inch of the cabin, desperate for a weapon or some way out. Chance led her outside, pausing on the rickety porch. From the corner of her eye, she could see the massive temple with its ancient walls and ivy. In the clearing beyond the cabin door was a grave-like ditch.

"What's that?" she forced herself to ask, assuming it was her own grave.

"Final resting place for Susan."

Fresh pain stabbed through Luna, which was lost when Chance started to walk again, this time toward the temple. His grip tightened accordingly, forcing her onward. So she went, climbing up the rounded stone stairs and through an open gothic archway. The path inside sloped down into pitch-black air so dark it disoriented all her senses immediately.

"I don't want to go in here," she whispered, stopping.

Chance huffed in the darkness. He didn't have to say, "Too bad" for her to hear it anyway. The tunnel stretched on and on, and when she thought it wouldn't lead them anywhere at all, it emptied into a small smoky room, dimly lit by only a few sparse candles. With no ventilation, the smoke had formed a haze, making it hard to see.

In the middle of the room, Amy was on the floor. Beneath her, a red sigil had been painted on the stone floor. Her wrists were bound behind her back, as well as her ankles, with thick, white, lacy ties. A white dress like Luna's was draped over her, matching the gag shoved in her mouth. When Amy saw Luna, she started to mumble around it, excited groans that were indecipherable. Luna was more focused on the purple trail of bruises on her face.

"Chance, let her go," Luna pleaded, forcing herself to wrap her fingers around his forearm.

His eyes glinted in the low light as he said, "No, Luna.

You let her go." She took a step closer to Amy when his voice stopped her. "I don't mean untie her."

When Luna turned back to look at him, she realized he was holding a dagger out to her. Bile came up the back of her throat at the implication. "No," she said.

Chance sighed. "This is getting old."

There were a lot of things she couldn't guarantee. She didn't know if she'd get out of this cabin—hell, she didn't even know if she'd live to see tomorrow—but what she *did* know was that his knife would not taste Amy's blood. He could never force her to kill. She'd have to make the choice to comply on her own, and if he killed her for disobeying, at least she'd die a good person. Luna sent another glance in Amy's direction, thinking of the day they'd spent together. How Amy had saved her before.

A life for a life.

Chance shifted his grip on the blade slightly, a glint of candlelight bouncing off it. Luna slapped it out of his hand. The dagger skittered across the floor, and Chance watched it, his eyes pale green fire. "Pick it up," he said calmly but through clenched teeth. It was the same voice he'd used before stabbing her.

"No," Luna said, lifting her chin in defiance.

He pulled the gun from his pocket, cocking it with his thumb, the barrel pointed at the ground. "It's either you kill her, or I kill you. Make your choice."

"I already did." His hands shook as he lifted the weapon, and Luna zeroed in on it. "Is something the matter?" she prompted, eyes probing his face, ready to pick up any flicker of emotion.

"*You.* You're defying me. You can't do that! I'm all you have left," he spat, a sheen of sweat glistening across his forehead.

Luna took in his posture, the emotions behind his eyes, and everything clicked into place. "You mean, I'm all *you* have left," she said softly. "That's what you're scared of, right? Being alone?"

"No," he nearly yelled.

Luna flinched but didn't overlook the way his hand trembled again. She would pull that thread as long as she could. "That's why you took my friends from me . . . so . . . so I'd depend on you. That way I'd never leave," she said, eyebrows pulling downward as she gathered more evidence for her theory. "You stabbed me, but in a place you knew wouldn't kill me, so I wouldn't run. So I *couldn't* run. You don't want to be alone."

"I said I'm not scared of that!"

"Why is *that* your fear?" she asked, and this time, she wasn't jeering. She wanted answers. "People literally line up for you to give them the time of day."

He blinked, the green hue in his eyes flickering. "They're not interested in me for who I am as a person. They're interested in my reputation. Who they *think* I am. They wouldn't stay five seconds if they knew the real me. But you . . . you never cared about any of the fakeness. You saw me for me, and it made you *different.*"

Luna caught the brief change in color, and hope reignited in her stomach. "Of course I don't care about your popularity."

"You've always been no-nonsense, true to yourself. That's why I wanted you, fuck your ability," he admitted, switching the gun to his opposite hand. "Of course it's been helpful and all, but it wouldn't have been impossible to find someone else with it."

The nonchalance made Luna take a breath. He'd caused her actual trauma, but to him, it was an ordinary day. He'd chosen her as simply as someone chooses one beverage over another at the grocery store. "That's your reason for ruining my life?" Luna asked. "For ruining the lives of everyone around you?"

"Excuse me?"

"All the stuff you've done over the past few weeks? Isolating me from my friends, turning my dad against me, *killing* people." Luna scoffed, pressing her hand to her abdomen. "I have a hole in my stomach, thanks to you!"

"How *dare* you? I've done *everything* for you. For *us*," he spat. "It's not my fault you wouldn't listen. Things could be so much different if you would've *listened* to me."

"How about *you* listen to *me*? I've told you again and again that I'm not interested in you, but *you* won't accept that."

"Of course not," he spat. "Because I opened up to you, and you have no idea what that means for someone like me. You should be *thanking* me. I saved your life on the bike path when I could've thrown you into the canal and not had to worry about you ratting me out. Anyone else, I would've done just that."

"And that's on you," Luna hissed, trembling with actual rage. "I will *never* thank you. You murdered people, and you have the audacity to think I should *thank you*?"

"It's what needed to be done," he replied. "Don't you get that with me we can do absolutely *anything*?"

He doesn't understand the difference between right and wrong.

"What are you going to do about Max and Violet?" she asked softly. Then louder, exclaimed, "They're dead! You can't bring them back to life!"

"You're being emotional," he said. "I need you to see the big picture. This is the only way, or I'll never be free from that place. From them. They'll *kill* me."

Luna quirked her lip. Maybe being alone wasn't the *only* thing he was afraid of. *There are others,* she mused, remembering her conversation with Max. Chance wasn't the only one who had ever, or would ever, use the Other Realm for nefarious purposes. "That's what you deserve," she hissed. "For what you've done to Max, Violet, Susan, and everyone else."

"How about we both take some deep breaths and—"

"No, fuck that," Luna interrupted, catching a glimpse of Amy from the corner of her eye. The girl had gone silent, watching their exchange with wide doe eyes. It was a subtle reminder that Luna wasn't fighting this battle only for herself. "The truth hurts, and that's why I need you to listen when I say *I don't like you.* I never have. You might have fooled everyone around me, but I know the truth. There are many things wrong with you, and I doubt you'll ever be able to fix them. I can't wait for graduation because it means I'll never have to see you again. I was the only person you couldn't get under your little spell because I don't want to be around you. My one wish in life is for you to go away!"

"Th-that's not true," he said, taking a step closer before he halted, shifting back to his original place. "You need me."

Despite the gun aimed at her, Luna was utterly calm, determined. Chance's eyes flashed their normal blue again, this time the color staying.

"It *is* *true*. All the people at school? Your *friends*? They don't really like you. You are inherently unlovable."

He opened his mouth to say something when a scream of agony tore through his chest. Luna stumbled backward, watching his body emit a pale green glow—the same odd shade that had taken over his eyes. A deafening tearing noise filled the room, a streak of green rising to the ceiling in a way that reminded Luna of fire. It consumed Chance, and he screamed again, the gun firing as he clutched it in his fight.

The bullet sped past Luna, missing her ear by an inch, but she hardly noticed as she watched a purple mist seep out of Chance's body and up into the heart of the green flame. It hovered inside the emerald mist before the combination shot upward, through the ceiling, and vanished. Chance fell backward, slumping down the wall until he lay sprawled across the floor, gun clattering to the ground beside him. His eyes were closed, and Luna watched him in a horrified stupor.

He didn't move.

Is he dead? she wondered, hoping with all her might that the answer was yes.

Chapter Fifty-Five

LUNA CREPT OVER to Chance, counting her heartbeats. She was sure this would be like a horror movie, and he would rouse from his coma the second she strayed too close. She nudged him with the side of her bare foot. He didn't move, and the hope that he was dead blossomed in her chest. She brought herself to crouch beside him, holding her fingers to the side of his neck. There was a pulse, but it was faint.

On shaking legs, Luna turned back to Amy. The small girl was staring at Chance before she realized Luna was looking at her, and then they met gazes. Luna moved over to her on hands and knees and pulled the gag out of Amy's mouth before she went to work untying her binds.

As soon as she was free, Amy sat up, rubbing her sore wrists. "Are you okay?"

Luna paused. Of all the things Amy could've asked, she hadn't expected it to be concern for *her*. Luna decided to ignore the question. "Are *you* okay? Can you stand?" Luna eyed the trail of bruises on Amy's face again and wondered if she had a lot more in places Luna couldn't see.

"Yeah," Amy muttered and stood. She scooped up the discarded gun and glanced at Luna, looking as if she were considering repeating her question when she said, "Let's get out of here."

Luna glanced at Chance, eager to get away before he could regain consciousness. Amy was the one to lead the way down the long twisting corridor to the clearing outside. Neither of them spoke. In Luna's mind, she replayed the images of what had happened over and over again, hardly able to believe it. Outside, the sky was purple with the oncoming night.

Shivering, Luna asked, "What do we do now?"

"We need to get back to town and get the police," Amy said, eyes drifting to a patch of red on Luna's white gown. "Are you hurt?"

Luna grimaced and stared off into the trees, choosing to ignore the question. "Go on ahead. I'm going to hang back for a minute."

Amy eyeballed the side of Luna's face. "You can't expect me to leave you like this."

"I . . . need a minute," Luna said, voice breaking.

Amy pursed her lips as if she were ready to argue when she said, "Okay." She passed Luna the gun. "Take this, just in case. I'll be back with help as soon as I can."

Luna agreed and took the weapon. She watched Amy go, listening for the sound of cracking twigs as she disappeared through the trees. Gauging her location by sound, Luna started to walk through the woods in the opposite direction. She wanted to get as far away from Chance and the cabin as she could, but there was something she needed to do first. Fresh blood seeping through her gown from her reopened wound, she stumbled onward, weak from blood loss and pain.

Pine needles stabbed the soles of her feet, but over the rest of her hurt, she hardly felt it. She recognized the foliage ahead and remembered the way it had hidden Max from view when he'd fallen from Chance's bullet. She hurried forward, desperate to see him. Max lay on his back, blood soaking through his light shirt. His thigh was clamped in the metal teeth of a bear trap. She rushed over, falling to her knees beside him, and dropped the gun, hands hovering above the contraption. The spacer had been removed in what she guessed was another joke on Chance's part. She wouldn't be able to do a thing to spring it. When Luna finally brought herself to look at Max's face, she didn't see any movement. His eyes were closed, mouth barely parted.

She leaned forward, setting her fingers on his chest. "Max . . ." Luna whispered, grief welling inside her. Of all the ways this could've gone, she hadn't imagined Max would be the one to fall.

"Luna," a raspy voice responded.

She flinched and sat up, startled to find his eyes *open*. "Max! You're alive!"

"Barely," he said with wheezing laughter. "He knew I would come. He set a trap."

Luna swallowed, bile rising when she accidentally glanced at his mutilated leg again. The teeth had sliced right through the muscle and bone. If he lived, he'd have to get an artificial leg to replace it. The fact that Max hadn't bled out in the time she'd been in the cabin was nothing short of a miracle.

"Where is he?" Max rasped.

"He's in the temple, unconscious," Luna said, crinkling the corners of her eyes to keep herself from crying.

"What happened to you?" Max asked, spotting the red stain on her dirty white gown.

Ashamed, Luna stared down at her hands.

Max didn't take his eyes off her. "What happened to you, Luna?" he repeated. "With him?"

Luna needed to answer, but it was hard to find the words. "He was going to make me sacrifice Amy," she said, emotionless as she looked at clinging traces of Max's blood on her fingertips. "But I figured out what it was you wanted to tell me, and the fusion is over. Amy is fine. She left to go get help."

"That's something good that came out of this."

"Is it?" Luna asked. "The things we saw . . . that'll stick with me forever. I can't imagine how Amy will handle it."

"She's stronger than you think," Max said, and his eyes moved to the red spot again. "Who's blood is that?"

"It's mine," Luna admitted. "Chance stabbed me."

Max's eyes grew wide, and he sat up so fast he grimaced. "Are you all right?"

"I'll live," she muttered and winced as she remembered Chance uttering those same words to her. "I-I'll be fine." She tried to push the memory away before Max could notice the distant look in her eyes. "Your wound is worse."

"I don't think so," Max said. "I think you need to sit and wait with me for Amy to get back with the police."

Luna shook her head. "I'd rather not do that."

Baffled, Max asked, "Why not?"

"I need to go home." She didn't add that she had no idea how she would explain herself to the police if she stayed. Max nodded, eyebrows pinched in understanding, and Luna continued. "Before I go, what happens now? Is Chance going to die?"

"He'll live, but he'll be a totally new person when he recovers," Max said. "He'll have complete amnesia. He won't remember us or what happened today. Hell, he won't even remember his own name. We never have to worry about this happening again."

Instinctively, Luna looked in the direction of the temple. It was hard to believe everything someone knew could vanish so easily. "He's getting off light if you ask me," she said and rose to her feet.

"Don't go, Luna. Stay and wait for help," Max pleaded.

Luna gnawed her bottom lip. "I can't tell the police what happened. They'll never believe me."

"I understand, but we'll figure something out. You're in pain. Don't do this."

Luna stared at Max, touched by his concern. She didn't have a way to explain that the police weren't the only ones she feared telling the story to. Her parents would never look at her the same way again, especially her father, if they knew. Would he blame her for what happened? *He'll never understand,* she thought. "I'm sorry, but I need to get away from here."

"All right," Max said with a hefty sigh. "I guess I can't force you, but before you go, see Violet, okay?"

"Why? I watched Chance shoot her point-blank in the forehead," she said, replaying the horrible memory of Violet's death. For as long as she lived, she wouldn't be able to forget it, wouldn't be able to forget how she had let her down, had let her walk into the trap that had ultimately doomed her.

"You should say your goodbyes before they take her to the morgue," he said.

Luna dropped her chin to her chest and took in a deep breath. "You're right. Will you tell the police I was here?"

Max shook his head. "No. You've been through enough hell without me showering that kind of attention on you. Find Violet, then get some rest. You deserve it."

Luna nudged the gun closer to him. "Will you be okay here by yourself?"

Max stretched and groaned as his shoulder popped. He picked up the weapon and examined it. "Yeah, I'll manage."

"Okay." She gave him one last once-over before she started to walk in the direction of the clearing.

Retracing her path took her through the thick undergrowth that had been smashed by both her and Chance's footsteps. It didn't take her long to discover Violet's stiff body in the field. The smell of blood hung in the air like dozens of pennies.

"I'm sorry," Luna whispered, letting the words be carried away by the wind before she turned and started to walk away.

There was nothing more she could do.

You saved Amy, she reminded herself, but all she could see was the haunted look in the girl's eyes when she'd promised she would go get help. Luna pushed onward, leaves scraping her face and arms. Eventually she reached the road beyond. In uneven steps, she walked down the shoulder, tracing the white line on the asphalt as she followed it back into town. Torrents of tears ran down her cheeks as the events of the last twenty-four hours replayed in her head.

Everything that had started as a *nightmare*.

What would happen when the truth about Chance came out? When the town realized he was a cold-blooded monster responsible for a trail of heinous crimes?

Luna reached up to wipe the tears off her cheek and the loose sleeve of her dress drifted downward, giving her a clear view of her wrist. She turned it over, examining the skin in the fading light.

The ugly shackle marks were gone.

Epilogue

"LUNA KETZ!" PRINCIPAL Wilson called.

Her heart pounded in her throat as she crossed the stage. She didn't like the spotlight, so to be the focus of the thousand or so people in attendance made her skin crawl. It didn't help that her mother had picked out strappy little shoes with two-inch heels. Deep down, she thanked Susan for the practice.

Luna grabbed her diploma, listening to the screams and cheers from the audience as she left the stage and made her way back to her seat. She'd kept a smile on her face for the duration of the event, but something else loomed behind it.

The walk back to her chair forced her to acknowledge the five empty seats in the audience. The three at the front which were dedicated to the dead girls—Kate, Susan, and Violet—as well as the one that should've been Chance's and the other, Amy's. Thinking about any of them plunged her back to that day in the woods, though Chance lurked in her head without provocation. It was hard *not* to think about him. Especially when the slightest movement sent her into a spiral of pain.

The wound in her stomach had begun to heal, but it hadn't been an easy process. The first time she'd cleaned it, she had discovered the back-alley stitches Chance had used to close it up, which would only lead to a longer, more painful healing process.

According to Max's report, and what she'd seen on the news, Chance was in a coma and had been transported to a hospital out of town for treatment. In Luna's opinion, it wasn't far enough away. Amy must've felt the same way. Luna hadn't seen her since they'd wandered out of the temple together, and she imagined Amy was having as hard a time processing it all as she was, maybe more so.

Luna didn't ask Max what story he'd told the police when they eventually arrived. News broadcasts simply covered the happenings as a *bizarre* series of events. Violet's death was chalked up to a hunting accident and the discovery of Susan's dead body, along with Chance's unconscious one, had given them the impression that he was also a victim of whatever had occurred.

Luna was angry, to say the least, but she could understand how they'd reached that conclusion. With half of the events taking place in the Other Realm, the authorities would never be able to piece together the truth. Luna had considered going to the police, showing them the wound Chance had inflicted, and telling them that he was the cause of it all. But that would open up a can of worms in her new life. And she was ready to move on. Luna pushed all the bad thoughts out, focusing on the ceremony.

The valedictorian was giving the closing speech. "Never forget that there is a light burning in every one of us, leading us to greatness. This year has been hard on us all, but don't let it keep you down. Channel that inner fire and use it to become phoenixes, rising from the ashes."

Principal Wilson picked up the microphone and said,

"Congratulations, Class of 1989!"

Cheers rang around the field as everyone stood from their seats and threw their hats into the air. Luna did the same, smiling as she retrieved hers and made her way through her classmates, shaking hands and hugging people she'd never said two words to in the four years of her high school journey.

We've been going to the same schools for years and have barely said more than two words to one another, Susan had once said. *I feel like officially getting to meet everyone before the year ends. It can't hurt.*

And she was right. The world was beautiful when Luna believed it to be.

Her parents waited for her at the edge of the crowd, cheering louder than anyone else. The joy seemed especially foreign for her father.

"I knew you could do it," Rose said, scooping her daughter into a tight hug. They'd spent the morning together between the time her plane had gotten in and the ceremony, but Luna was uncharacteristically happy to see her. In this moment, her life felt complete.

They talked for a while before Luna slipped outside. Her social battery was running low, and a few minutes alone would be enough time for her to recharge. A bird tweeted overhead, and she let it resonate with the words of the closing speech. She *was* a phoenix. She had gone through hell and come out stronger than ever.

Then she saw something in the grass. At first, it was a glint of light and her curiosity drove her toward it. When she was close enough to see what it was, she froze. Chance's dagger had been driven into the soil as if someone had stabbed the ground. Her heart fell to her stomach, eyes volleying from side to side with the expectation that he would leap from the shadows and grab her.

That's impossible.

He was unconscious in a hospital room miles away.

She reached out, freeing the knife. Her hands trembled so hard that a scrap of paper wrapped around the blade came loose, fluttering to the ground. She caught a glimpse of the writing and that was enough to make her drop the knife. The wind made the paper spin in the air a few times before it landed face-up in the grass beside the knife.

It's only just begun.

Alive at Sunset

(Rituals of the Night Series Book Two)

Revenge is an obsession of its own.

Three years after her senior year horrors, Luna Ketz struggles to move on. Starting over in an apartment in Bowling Green with her new roommate hasn't made things easier. Nothing helps, including weekly check-ins to ensure her assailant, Chance Welfrey, is still in a coma.

When he disappears from the hospital, Luna's worst fears are realized. Chance remembers everything. The next time she sees him is on her doorstep. He's found a new way into her life, and this game of cat and mouse will take all her wits to survive.

About the Author

Raised in Michigan but moved to Texas and has experienced the best and worst of both, Kayla has interests in the dark and macabre. She enjoys '80s music and movies. A little neurotic and a huge lover of Halloween, creepy stories and cats are totally her jam.